USED FOR MURDER

A Used Bookstore Mystery

Heidi M Buck

LEGAL

Cover design and artwork by Heidi Buck

Heidi M. Buck
Visit my website at www.heidibuck.com

Printed in the United States of America

First Printing: January 2018

ISBN-13 978-1-9793474-4-0

CONTENTS

FOR THE LOVE OF WESTERNS

(October 6, late Thursday night)

Confrontation was something Stumpy worked hard to avoid.

Shuffling down the sidewalk, he paused momentarily to take in the sweet smell of French fries and grease wafting from the Burger Pit on the other side of the dead-end street. Although tempting, Stumpy knew better than to venture onto its property; they'd recently hired a new night manager with eagle eyes and a belligerent reputation. After one last deep inhalation of the tantalizing odors, he returned to the task at hand and made his way towards his goal.

The four dumpsters were located behind the paved employee lot of the strip mall adjacent to Rudy's, a large family owned grocery store. Of the retail shops whose backs faced these receptacles, four looked identical with a single window and puce colored steel door opening directly onto the asphalt. The unit at the west end was different, however, not only in size but in the fact it had no window and its door was four feet above the ground, accessed via a narrow concrete ramp. In a previous life it had been a pet store, but now operated as a used bookstore run by volunteers.

Around the glass-encased laundromat on the east end, Rudy's loading dock faced the pine woods where Stumpy spent his nights. Though it offered several monster-sized dumpsters, the glaring halogen lights equipped with motion sensors meant he avoided the area at all costs; his sensitive eyes much preferred the dim light surrounding these smaller bins to the north and the eclectic mix of goods they always seemed to offer. He wasn't the only person who checked their contents, by any means, but a silent understanding based on seniority meant tonight he had first dibs.

Stumpy was just closing the lid of the first bin when the sound of an approaching vehicle made him freeze. With a marked increase in the area's homeless population, he knew retailer complaints were causing police to crack down on trespassing after hours. As the car swung into the parking area, he instinctively crouched near the ground and held his breath, squinting in response to the sweep of bright headlights. When it parked behind the bookstore he realized it wasn't a patrol car; the beams momentarily created two spotlights on the brick wall before disappearing into darkness.

Cautiously moving to the side of the bin, Stumpy heard the driver exit the car. The trunk made a pleasant chirping sound as it popped open and, with the glow from the interior casting everything in silhouette, he watched the driver pull a large sack out onto the ground. After closing the trunk, the driver began to drag it across the asphalt and up the ramp.

Stumpy was curious; he was pretty sure the car belonged to one of the bookstore volunteers, as he had often seen it parked in this exact location, but why make a book delivery this hour of the night?

Maybe there were westerns in that sack — he loved westerns.

He moved closer to see if he could recognize the person, but it was too dark to make out any features before they disappeared into the store. Placing his gnarled hands on the hood of their car, he enjoyed the sensation of warmth while debating with himself whether or not to return to the dumpsters. After concluding it was probably best to go home, he thought he heard a child's scream coming from inside the store.

Was someone in trouble?

Stumpy liked the bookstore volunteers; they always treated him kindly and helped him out, especially when he didn't have exact change. If one of them was in trouble, he felt compelled to reciprocate. Creeping up the ramp, he tentatively knocked on the steel door, his bare knuckles making a soft echo sound. When no one answered, he pulled the handle and was surprised to discover it unlocked.

"Hello?" Stumpy called out as he poked his head into the doorway. Although it was dark inside, he could still see the entry area was empty.

"Hello?" Stumpy called out again, this time a little louder. He let the door shut behind him and slowly moved forward. Down at the end of the hallway, a light was coming from beneath a closed door; it's weak beam creating eerie shadows across the various bins and shopping carts piled high with books.

Something dry and dusty tickled his nose hairs. "Ah-Choo!" He sneezed loudly.

The light under the door suddenly went out, plunging everything into darkness.

Something isn't right.

He shuffled forward, inch-by-inch, down the crowded hall with its endless stacks of books. Reaching his arms out for guidance, he found a doorknob and twisted it, pushing inward while his left hand instinctively searched the wall for a light switch. When he flipped it on, his eyes were momentarily blinded by the sudden burst of brightness. Quickly diverting his gaze towards the floor, he focused on something reflecting the room's glaring light with a hypnotic sheen. A black plastic garbage bag lay on the linoleum tiles. Curious as to the contents, he reached down to see what was inside when he heard a scuffling noise from behind.

Then came a new sound, some sort of a "WUMP".

What was that?

Stumpy suddenly found his cheek resting on the cold floor, eye level with the bag he had just been leaning over.

How did I get here?

His brain throbbed and he felt quite sleepy. Although he tried to refocus his eyes, it was becoming nearly impossible to keep them open. Memories and images began to swirl and dance between his fluttering eyelids, and then they were gone, like wisps of camp smoke. A familiar scent, something soothing and sweet, reminded him of home and his mother... or was it his first wife? Opening his fading eyes one last time he focused in on the spine of a book.

Western.

He really loved westerns.

TEDDY IS HUNGRY

(October 7, early Friday morning)

The parking lot was uncharacteristically empty as I pulled into my usual spot behind the bookstore. Even though 7:45 AM was a bit early, I'd never known Pat and her burgundy colored sedan not to beat me to the punch. Letting the engine idle, I momentarily toyed with the notion of returning home and having a cup of coffee with my husband. The idea was tempting, but not practical; the drive was nearly twenty minutes in each direction and, besides, he was probably still asleep.

After turning off the ignition, for some reason, I hesitated. In front of me, the engine started making those weird clicking sounds it makes when it cools, and I wondered if it needed a tune-up. Outside, I could see the sun was dripping orange streaks down the upper edge of the strip mall's stone wall, teasing at a warm day. Somewhere in the distance, I could hear the cawing of crows.

Come on, Holly. Up and at 'em.

Hanging my volunteer lanyard around my neck, I grabbed my water bottle and opened the door.

It was a brisk October morning, even by northern California standards, and the blast of cold air that rushed past me caused the paper origami crane on my dashboard to take flight. Setting it back in place before locking up, I quickly scrambled up the concrete ramp towards the bookstore's back entrance. The wind picked up, with perfect timing, and whipped my name badge across my chest so one of the sharp plastic corners nicked the corner of my chin.

Ow.

Rubbing my wounded face, I paused on the landing long enough to survey the parking area from the higher vantage point. Other than my teal-green box, it was empty, so I turned and pushed the buzzer to the right of the door. After a few seconds of listening to the swishing of cars zooming along the nearby interstate and watching some crows jostle for position on the wall behind the dumpsters, I tried again. Unless someone was inside, since I didn't have a key, I would have to deal with extracting the spare from the lockbox - which was a major pain.

Darn. A coffee was beginning to sound really good right about now.

Removing my lanyard, I shoved it into the pocket of my sweatshirt and set my water bottle down on the cement before grudgingly stomping back down the ramp.

The bookstore's lockbox was attached to the water meter on the outer west wall of the building. Although it had been placed there without permission from the shopping center's owners, it blended well enough with the surroundings to have escaped both detection and vandalism. Its four letter combination was easy enough to remember: only a group who did cat rescues would think using the word 'MICE' was funny. But the mechanism was old and didn't always work, and oftentimes the key wasn't even there; volunteers sometimes forgot to return it after their shifts. I said a little prayer to the book gods before giving it a try and, on my third attempt, was relieved to discover the interior held its prize.

Snapping the box closed, I carefully repositioned it back behind the piping. My hands now cold from the chilled metal, I began to rub them together for warmth when a whiff of java hit my nostrils. Remembering that Rudy's had opened a new coffee bar, I made the executive decision to walk over and get myself a cup.

At the end of the narrow alley which ran between our building and the newly remodeled Mexican restaurant, I hopped up onto the sidewalk and caught sight of her car. It was parked on its own in one of the angled spots across from the bookstore, the distinctive 'Keep Tahoe Blue' bumper sticker facing me.

Why would Pat park here?

The only thing I could think of was maybe she, herself, had gone to get coffee and, for all I knew, had already returned to the bookstore through the front door which meant we had just missed each other.

Forgetting about my coffee, I retraced my steps to the back door. An eerie tingling sensation suddenly spread across the upper edge of my jaw; I turned and quickly scanned my surroundings. Satisfied I was alone, I turned back to push the buzzer when a sudden burst of cawing and flapping made me look back towards the dumpsters. The crows had scattered upwards, their black shapes silhouetted against the milky sky like that scene from the Alfred Hitchcock movie.

The reason for their disturbance became clear when I saw a heavily bundled figure on the sidewalk. As I watched, he came to a halt near the cardboard recycle bin and turned to stare directly at me. Although the details of his face were blurred at this distance, the intensity of his gaze felt palpable and I instantly froze in place.

A sharp clanking sound startled me out of my semi-petrified state; I must have kicked my insulated aluminum water bottle over as it was now rolling down the ramp. Diving for it, I fumbled and missed a couple of times, finally nabbing it just before it reached the bottom. With my heart beating wildly from the sudden exertion, I hustled back up the ramp and forced myself to look; the man hadn't moved and was still staring at me.

What does he want?

A vehicle revved its engine a couple of times in the Burger Pit's parking lot. I saw a flash of brilliant yellow as he turned to look, and then he began to shuffle in the opposite direction, down to where the sidewalk ended. Assuming he must be one of the homeless who camped out in the woods beyond the dead-end street, I inhaled deeply, the cool air stinging my lungs.

Human interference gone, the crows quickly resettled along the dumpster wall and I took this as my queue to turn my attention back to the door. After a couple of seconds of waiting for a response from the buzzer, I decided to forgo patience and use the key. Swinging the door outward, I was greeted with the familiar odor of musty books mingled with just a trace of cat litter dust. It was a strangely comforting smell, especially this morning, even though it always made me sneeze.

As the door latched closed behind me, I walked a few steps forward into the hall and paused, giving myself a few seconds to acclimate to the glare of overhead fluorescents. A piercing wail made my heart skip a beat.

"Pat?" I called out.

To my right the door leading to the small bathroom was ajar and I could see it was empty. To my left I noticed her familiar blue travel mug wasn't sitting in its usual spot atop the metal desk in the narrow storage alcove.

"Pat?" I called out again, setting my water bottle down amid the clutter before moving forward.

Halfway down the hall, on the right, the sorting room door was shut, which meant she wasn't in there; she hated having the door closed.

Walking further down the hall, I looked left into the cavernous sales area, but all was dark and now eerily quiet.

"Hello? Anyone here?"

Convinced I was alone, I returned to the back.

All the store lights were controlled by circuit breakers located in a junction box near the back door; one controlled the hallway and back room lights while three others activated various sections up front. Since Pat and I sorted books on Friday mornings, we usually didn't bother turning on the front lights until the cashiers showed up a little before ten. This morning, however, something didn't feel right so I decided to flip them all on.

As soon as the remaining fluorescents sputtered to life, a piercing scream filled the void. Moving back down the hall, I headed towards the source of the cry.

"Teddy!"

An extremely overweight white and gray tabby cat sat near the front of an eight-by-six-foot cage built from scrap lumber and wire meshing; his stomach and haunches spread around him like a furry inner tube.

"Yea-ow"

Pat told me customers complained his voice sounded like a child screaming, and I could fully understand why.

Glancing at the clipboard hanging from his cage door, I read the highlighted notes outlining his strict dietary requirements.

"Sorry Teddy, it says here I'm still not allowed to feed you. You'll just have to wait for Daphne to give you breakfast. OK?"

My words didn't seem to help as he continued to wail, all the while staring at me with vibrant green eyes the size of quarters. Tempting as it was to put my fingers in and pet him, I knew from experience he had a tendency to bite, especially when he was hungry.

Leaving him to his misery, I decided to check on the occupants of the other two cages. The one in the middle was empty, which was a good sign. That meant the orange cat with the missing eye had finally been adopted. The two older females in the end, however, were still there. Cali, the calico, was curled up into a tight ball on her bed while Princess, a tawny gray, sat in the litter box licking her paw.

"Good morning," I said, though she ignored me with typical feline aloofness.

Ignoring the still complaining Teddy, I walked back into the hall. Pat obviously wasn't in the bookstore; maybe she had run into someone she knew at Rudy's and, at this very moment, was enjoying one of their famous chocolate croissants. My mouth watered at the thought.

Turning the handle of the sorting room door, I glanced at the VOLUNTEERS ONLY sign Pat had put up after some issues with impatient customers trying to check out newly donated books. I hadn't paid it much attention since the door was usually open, but now noticed someone had embellished it with colorful stickers. Assuming they must be the handiwork of Daphne, who seemed to have an infinite supply on hand, I opened the door and promptly stumbled over some books laying just inside.

"What, the heck?"

I picked them up and stacked them onto one of the tables in the middle of the room, wondering who could have left them there. It was a good thing I'd found them instead of Pat; she would have been pissed, and rightly so — a volunteer could break a hip or something.

Turning, I noticed one of the large red FRC carts was sticking out at a weird angle. The Foothills Rehabilitation Center supplied these for us to fill with any unwanted donations and, although we usually had two or three on hand, always kept them shoved against the back wall to maximize our work space.

I tried to push it back where it belonged, but for some reason the thing wouldn't budge.

That's when I noticed the legs sticking out.

Chapter

3

NOW WHAT?

(October 7, Friday morning)

S hut up!" I yelled.

"Excuse me Ma'am?"

"No, not you, I'm so sorry! It's the damn cat! I need to report a death...I think it's an accident... I'm pretty sure it's an accident...no, I'm not sure!"

I had shut the door to the sorting room and was pacing back and forth in the hall, babbling a mile a minute into my cellphone while my heart pounded inside my chest.

"No... not breathing...no... nope... there's no pulse..."

Even though the 911 operator was treating my call like a trained professional, I don't know how she was able to decipher anything worthwhile from all my gibberish. Teddy howling at the top of his lungs in the background couldn't have helped either.

"OK... Yes, I'll be here when they arrive." I told her before hanging up.

Hands shaking, I looked at my phone and contemplated dialing home but decided against it. Nate would no doubt want to rush down the minute he heard the news, but what good would that do?

I continued to pace while debating what to do next; I had to unlock the front door for the emergency crews, but I also desperately needed to pee.

After taking care of business and washing my hands, I forced myself to look at my reflection amidst the swirl of black spots scattered across the mirror's surface.

"You look like crap," seemed an appropriate critique of the pale face staring back at me. Whoever said fifty was the new forty was full of it, or full of Botox. Since the paper towel dispenser was empty, I ran damp hands through my reddish-brown curls and inspected the ever-increasing number of creases congregating at the corners of my hazel eyes. At least in here Teddy's voice was muffled.

Pat was dead.

She was lying on a cold floor on the other side of this wall and I was in this dingy bathroom feeling sorry for myself; I needed to get a grip. Taking a moment, and a few deep breaths, I attempted to regain some of my composure.

I re-entered the hallway and was heading to unlock the front when the back door exploded outward.

"How-deeeee!"

A screeching twang of a voice penetrated the surroundings, followed closely by a small, dark-haired woman dressed entirely in khaki.

"Roxy?"

"Hayyyyy, how you doin'?!" She yelled in passing, without even so much as a glance in my direction.

Behind me the door slammed shut, making me jump for the second time that morning.

"Roxy!" I called out, following as she jogged past the bins and turned the corner, coming to a halt in front of Teddy's enclosure.

"Haaaay, why you howlin' ?!" She shouted at the cat.

Nate once said Roxy's voice reminded him of an old country western song - sung loud, off pitch, and meant to scare coyotes. It obviously didn't work on Teddy, however, as he was growling at her.

"Roxy!" I shouted, coming up from behind.

"Whaaaat? What's up?" She demanded, turning to finally look at me with eyes so close together, they made her look like a Siamese cat.

The founder of BARF, the unfortunately named Benevolent Animal Rescue Foundation which operated the bookstore, had her official-looking brass name tag gleaming on her uniform. It proudly advertised her as R. Rossen, 'Animal Rescue Officer' – a self-assigned role. Her choice of apparel for this position was a long-sleeved khaki shirt buttoned to the throat and stretched taut across a chest misshapen by some sort of heavy-duty sports bra. Cargo pants cinched tightly at the waist by a thick leather belt and a pair of black military style lace-up boots finished the ensemble.

"It's Pat," I told her, "she's in the sorting room."

Rolling her eyes, Roxy let out an exaggerated sigh.

"Now what?"

To be honest, at that moment I truly wished a different body was lying on the floor.

"She's dead," I said, taking a deep breath to steady myself before continuing, "I've already called 911."

"What?!"

She spun around and lunged for the sorting room door. My first reaction was surprise she actually knew where it was, but I quickly chastised myself; this was no time to get sarcastic.

While she knelt beside Pat, I hovered near the doorway. I had a clear view of the scene from here since I'd pushed the FRC bin out of the way after discovering the body, and decided to memorize every little detail just in case the police asked me any questions.

Pat was lying supine, with the top of her head facing the corner behind the opened door. Her left hand lay on her chest with palm facing down, while her right arm stretched out across the gray tiling with the hand partially hidden beneath the underbelly of a FRC bin. She was wearing straight-legged stonewashed jeans, an unbuttoned long-sleeved green and blue plaid shirt, and a cream colored t-shirt with a logo of some sort of bird. The toes of the dazzling pair of white tennis shoes she always wore pointed to the ceiling and seemed somewhat out of place against the drab flooring. Other than her glasses being slightly tilted to one side, she looked peaceful, as if she was taking a nap.

"You called 911?"

Roxy's uncharacteristically subdued voice yanked me away from my observations.

"Yes, they're on the way."

"Well, there ain't no rush. Looks like a heart attack."

Before I could ask how she could be so certain, I heard the sound of an approaching siren. It was coming from the direction of the fire station to the north of us on Front Street, and concentrating on it I realized Teddy had stopped his crying.

Roxy suddenly rose and began scanning the room, as if she was searching for something.

"Is the front door unlocked?" She barked, her voice returned to its normal decibel.

"No, I was on my way but you interrupted me." I snapped back, feeling my temper rise. All things considered, the last thing I needed was her yelling at me.

"Well, unlock it!"

She pushed past me and sprinted in the direction of her office. As I made my own way down the hall, I could hear the office door slam shut followed by the screeching of metal drawers.

What the heck was she doing?

Beams of sunlight were streaming through the tall picture windows as I approached the front of the store. Passing through intricate swirls of floating dust particles highlighted in the glow, I suddenly sneezed. My eyes watered, followed by tears spilling out and they began to run along the edges of my nose and I had to wipe them with the sleeve of my flannel shirt.

Get a grip, Holly.

I concentrated on my surroundings in an attempt to regain a sense of calm.

The bookstore was housed in a rectangular retail space built from tilt-up concrete walls. Exposed ducting and fluorescent lights hung just beneath the roof, matching the industrial feel of the polished cement floor. An assortment of hand-made signs were plastered waist high, along the lower portion of the front windows while, outside, the upper panes were streaked with dirty rain splatter and greasy handprints.

Unlocking the glass entry door, I swung it outward to step onto the sidewalk. I immediately spotted the flashing red lights of an emergency vehicle snaking its way through the maze of the shopping center's parking lot, and began to frantically wave my arms above my head in hopes of getting their attention. It must have worked as, within seconds, the fire department arrived in full force.

"She's in the room to the left!" I told them, motioning towards the rear of the store as I held the door open.

A rustling mass of synthetic-clad bodies carrying boxes of equipment hustled past me, and I watched as they jostled up the main aisle past shelves of VHS tapes and general fiction books.

A sheriff's deputy arrived and asked me to stay put so she could get my statement. She headed to the back with the others, and I took the opportunity to slip my phone out of my jeans to check the time. Amazingly, it was only a little under ten minutes since I'd made the 911 call. In the back, Teddy had started to howl again and it sounded like Roxy was shrieking instructions to the rescue group, both of which made my having to stay up front even more appealing.

Leaning against one of the glass display cases near the entry, I had just decided to call Nate when a voice dripping with drawl made me jump yet again.

"What's all the excitement about, hon?"

I looked over to see a large woman in a vivid tie-dyed shirt peeking inside the door. Below a frizzy mound of shocking yellow hair, her dark eyes were set deep within a pudgy face and her mouth was stretched wide into a grin of clownish proportions.

"Not now Kathy, we're closed!"

Lunging for the handle, I yanked hard which made her reel backwards. She threw her flabby arms above her head, causing her shirt to ride upwards to expose rolls of pale doughy flesh.

"Well, dang hon, you don't have to get all in a huff!" She cried out. "I was just curious."

"Come back later!" I told her, holding the door firmly shut.

She moved closer to the glass and began to talk to me in a creepy baby voice.

"Ah, sweetie, can't you just let me in to look at the cookbooks? I won't be any bother at all."

"No!" I snapped back.

She responded with a scowl, muttering something less than ladylike beneath her breath, before turning and waddling up the sidewalk in the direction of the laundromat. When I was sure she had gone, I returned to my spot against the counter and reached for my phone; I really needed to talk with Nate.

"Hello" A deep voice replied after the second ring.

"Is it too early for a cider?" I asked.

"They don't open until eleven." He chuckled, "Why, what's wrong?"

Chapter

4

WE'RE CLOSED

(October 7, Friday)

The shock of finding Pat's body was hitting me with the force of a charging rhino. After answering multiple questions from both the sheriff and the fire department, I was completely drained.

Daphne, one of the Friday morning cashiers, arrived a little before ten. After feeding Teddy, she made a sign letting customers know we would be closed for the day and hung it inside the front door. I thought it made perfect sense, all things considered, but when Roxy found out she'd abruptly vetoed the idea.

"Take that down!" I overheard her snap at Daphne, instructing her to reopen as soon as possible.

I wish I wasn't surprised. Since the bookstore was BARF's primary source of income, Roxy was adamant it remained open every hour possible. That meant other than Christmas, New Year's Day, and Thanksgiving our dedicated group of volunteers kept the place running from 10 am to 6 pm every day of the year.

"Holly, please, can't you persuade Roxy to keep the store closed today?" Daphne asked with a distraught expression as she cornered me near the cat enclosures.

With her thick silver braids, patchwork felted vest and oversized fur-lined boots, she looked like a sad homespun doll from years gone by. I couldn't help staring at the bright orange crochet flower attached to the green knit cap perched atop her head as its petals flopped from side to side whenever she moved.

A clanking sound made us both turn. The medics were maneuvering a gurney out of the sorting room, and we silently watched as they rolled Pat's covered body up the main aisle and out the front door.

As soon as they were gone, Daphne continued her plea while glancing nervously over at Roxy's closed office door.

"It doesn't seem right to open after, after..."

"I'm sorry Daphne." I interrupted, "I don't think there's anything I could say that will make her change her mind."

I felt bad for not supporting her but, in all honesty, just didn't want to deal with any more conflict; I wanted to hug my husband and drink some cider.

"Bummer."

"Where's Gerald?" I asked, changing the subject. As far as I could tell, the other scheduled Friday morning cashier was still missing in action.

"Oh, he left as soon as he heard what happened. We both thought Roxy was going to keep the store closed."

I glanced at my phone to check the time again. Eleven o'clock.

"I really need to get out of here. Will you be all right on your own? Marilyn and Cheryl won't be in for another couple of hours, but Roxy is still here."

"Sure, I'll be fine." Daphne replied, reaching into the multicolored quilted bag slung across her body. As she pulled out a package of tissues, sheets of colorful cat stickers followed and quickly scattered across the floor. After helping her pick them up, I watched her slowly shuffle towards the front while the orange flower bobbed a farewell.

I would have said goodbye to Teddy, but he was too busy washing his butt to care.

A SILLY QUESTION

(October 7, Friday)

H ey Holly!" the bartender called across the bar before the door had even swung shut behind me.

The Old Belgium Public House & Reading Room, or 'The Belgian' as the locals liked to call it, was located on the northern end of Main Street in Autumn's old town, across from the newly remodeled Chamber of Commerce. An eclectic mix of vintage California Gold Rush era buildings and modern stucco structures were found here, filled with restaurants and shops selling everything from high-end mountain bikes to mining supplies. The Belgian occupied one end of a single-story brick building that also included a Mexican restaurant, a sushi bar, and a shop at the far end that sold safes. Ironically, in all the years we'd lived here, I'd never seen that particular store open.

At this time of day, there were no customers along the pub's massive 'L' shaped bar, and the bartender was busy wiping the glossy surface with a rag. With a fluffy black beard, ears pierced with half inch stainless steel rings, and perpetual twinkle-eyed smile, he always reminded me of a happy pirate.

"Hey!" I responded, giving him a quick wave before joining Nate. He was sitting near the front window and there were two amber filled glasses gleaming on the counter in front of him.

"Hi Beautiful! I didn't think you'd mind if I already ordered." He said, turning to greet me as I approached.

"Hello Handsome."

I gave him a long hug and kiss before sitting down and reaching for the lighter colored drink.

"Mmmm, that's good, what is it?" I asked, finally coming up for air.

"They were out of the blood orange, so I got you a hibiscus."

I realized my hands were trembling as I set my glass down. Nate must have noticed too as he reached over and took them into his, squeezing gently for reassurance.

"How are you doing?" he asked.

"OK, still a bit shaky, obviously, but OK."

As the warmth of his skin began to calm my frayed nerves, I smiled up at him.

"Thanks for taking time off work."

As an off-site programmer for a small engineering firm, he worked primarily out of a home office located in our basement. When not traveling or working on a large project, his job offered the flexibility to take time when situations arose, and this was proving to be one of those instances.

"Of course." He answered, letting go and kissing me lightly before reaching for his drink.

I appreciated he was wearing the blue-white checked long-sleeved shirt I'd given him last Christmas, and the sunlight filtering through the window made the golden flecks in his dark brown eyes sparkle.

He rubbed at the stubbles on his chin when he noticed my gaze. "Sorry I didn't have time to shave. Australia called right after we hung up and by the time I got off the phone with them..."

"You look great, as always." I interrupted.

"Yeah, right." He said, laughing.

Taking another sip of cider, my mind began to wander back to the image of Pat's body lying on the cold sorting room floor. I must have shivered slightly as Nate asked if I was all right.

"Not really, it's a lot to take in."

"Were they able to figure out how she died?"

"If you mean the medics or the police, I don't know. They didn't tell me anything, though I did hear one of them say it must have happened sometime last night. Roxy sure seemed to think it was a heart attack."

"What do you mean?"

Before I could respond, Nate suddenly diverted his attention towards the front door.

"I thought I'd find you two here." A tall woman with brilliant white shoulder-length hair and matching cardigan wrapped her arms around me in a reassuring hug.

"Hey Sarra!" the bartender called out.

"Hello yourself." She said, disengaging from me to head in his direction.

Returning with a drink, she plopped her purse onto the counter where it's mass took up a large section of real estate. I couldn't help notice the baby-blue leather perfectly matched the color of her eyes.

"I feel bad... I never seem able to remember his name." She whispered before speaking in a normal voice, "They really need to put some sort of shade on these windows or something." Shrugging out of her fluffy sweater, she flung it onto an adjacent stool before sitting down next to me.

"You were looking for us?" I asked.

"Evelyn got a text about Pat this morning while we were working at the food bank." She said, as if that was a perfectly good enough explanation.

Nate chuckled. "Why does that not surprise me?"

Although Sarra didn't work at the used bookstore - Evelyn did, and the speed at which she learned about anything that happened in Autumn's volunteer circle was legendary.

"Once my shift ended, I took the chance you might end up over here."

"Guess you know us pretty well." I smiled.

Sarra had been our son's all-time favorite teacher. We had first met her during third grade orientation where she drily informed the parents that her students told her absolutely everything; Nate and I had both instantly liked her. After I volunteered as the classroom art docent, she'd been instrumental in helping me get a job as the school art teacher, and when she'd retired several years later to travel the world with her second husband, we had kept in touch. Last year, after hubby number two had taken off for Cuba and never returned, we had begun meeting up at the Belgian to indulge our passion for hard apple cider. Nate especially enjoyed the way she could handle his sarcastic sense of humor with aplomb.

Sarra swiveled slightly on her stool to give me a concerned look. "How are you handling everything?"

Shrugging, I pulled a paper napkin out of the dispenser and dabbed at some tears beginning to leak from my eyes.

"Did you know Pat?" Nate asked, coming to my rescue.

"Not really, I only met her once."

"She used to have her own used book store, the one off Miner's Street." Nate continued.

"I remember that place. Across from the Tibetan restaurant, right?"

"Yep, they mostly carried paperbacks."

As I listened to them talk about Pat, I pulled out more napkins and began to wipe up some of the liquid that had sweated off our drinks as it puddled dangerously close to Sarra's purse.

"You OK?" Nate asked me, no doubt concerned about my extended silence.

"I was thinking about the sorting room door." I said, explaining how it had been closed.

"That is odd." He agreed.

"And then there's Roxy. She actually asked me to take over for Pat - right in front of the sheriff. It was pretty unbelievable."

Even though the sun coming in through the front window felt warm against my skin, I shivered at the thought of her ill-timed request.

"That woman sounds like a piece of work." Sarra said.

"You're not considering it, are you?" Nate asked, but I shook my head.

"No, I gave her a 'you've got to be kidding' look and she dropped it."

"Good. Not that you wouldn't be great at it and all, but I'd worry about you taking on more than you already do."

While he returned his attention to what was left of his Belgian tripel, Sarra motioned out the window.

"Looks like we might get some rain."

Looking towards the sky, I noticed dark gray clouds gathering above the tall pines rimming the public parking lot across the street. As I watched, a few joined together to form one ominous shape, temporarily blocking the sun and plunging the entire scene into shadow.

"That it does." I agreed.

Reaching for my cider I realized there was nothing left but foam.

"I'm going to order us some lunch, would you two care for another round?" Nate asked, stepping off his stool and reaching for our empty glasses.

"Now that's a silly question." Sarra laughed.

Chapter
6

RING THE BELL

(October 15, Saturday morning – A week later)

E velyn disliked working as cashier almost as much as she disliked cooking. In fact, she often said the only reason she had a kitchen was it came with the house.

Sitting on the cold metal fold-up chair, she opened the top drawer of the desk and pulled out the well-worn notebook used as a sales ledger, adding extra paperclips to the edges to make sure even more loose pages wouldn't fall out. Next, she printed "RING BELL FOR SERVICE!" in black permanent marker on a yellow sticky note and stuck it onto the desk surface near the front edge, next to a small silver hand bell.

Standing back up, she glanced disapprovingly at the rest of the sales area. The glass display counters were covered with bags of donations and a fine layer of dust. Behind them, banquet tables shoved against the wall were nearly hidden beneath a chaotic mix of paper and plastic bags, stacks of books with hand written 'hold for' notes taped on top, and an assortment of empty food containers and plastic water bottles.

Having lived in London for many years, Evelyn spoke with a slight English accent, especially when she was annoyed.

"What a dump." She muttered before unlocking the front door.

Tall and slender, Evelyn's flawless features not only reflected her Jamaican and German heritage, but also gave her a timeless beauty. Customers were shocked to discover her age was closer to eighty than seventy. This seemed to please her somewhat, but mostly she was proud of the fact that, unlike the other volunteers, she never wore tennis shoes or, for that matter, flats of any kind.

Today she was wearing calf-high black nylon boots with four-inch heels that clicked sharply against the hard cement floor as she strode down the main aisle of the store towards the back.

"I don't want to hear a peep out of you." She warned Teddy, wagging an index finger in his direction. He stayed silent as even he knew better than to mess with Evelyn.

Entering the sorting room, she turned left and inspected a lidless banker's box placed on the floor against the wall beneath a handwritten sign which read "Coffee Table Books/Evelyn". Although it only contained two oversized books, both had been tossed haphazardly onto their ends with pages splayed, their mass warping the box's cardboard sides outward.

"My, my." Evelyn said out loud after surveying the rest of the room.

The genre boxes lining three of the four walls were in similar disarray with many having more books on the floor in front of them than within their confines, and both sorting tables were covered with stacks of hardcovers. So much for Pat's strict rules of placing books in boxes as neatly as possible and clearing the tables before leaving.

Peering into the FRC carts shoved against the back wall, Evelyn discovered both nearly empty of discards, while back out in the hallway, all the book bins and shopping carts looked to be filled to maximum capacity. This was not a good sign. Book sorting, it seemed, had come to a virtual standstill.

"Hmmm, someone is not going to be happy."

Finding her leopard print apron where it hung behind the sorting door, she tied it snuggly around her waist before carrying her two books over to a table. After making some space to work, she inspected the first book. It was a glossy photography travelogue of Yellowstone National Park, and looked almost new. Pulling a cotton rag and a sheet of pricing stickers out of her apron's front pocket, she wiped the jacket cover clean and applied a $3 sticker to the upper right hand corner.

The second book, an illustrated volume of western wildflowers, was in bad shape. Its spine was cracked with edges severely bent, and there was some sort of dried goo smeared across the back cover.

"Definitely 'icky." said, wrinkling her nose.

Holding the damaged book away from her body, she carried it to the galvanized garbage can near the back door and set it atop the jam-packed contents. She would have to wait for Marilyn to show up before hauling it out to the dumpster.

After a quick stop in the restroom to wash up, Evelyn retrieved the travelogue and carried it out to the 'boutique' section located in the opposite corner of the store. Here, several round tables were artistically laid out with knick-knacks, stationary, calendars and more coffee table books. While trying to figure out where to display her newest addition, she suddenly felt as if someone was watching her. Turning, she saw an elderly man cradling several books in his arms.

"May I please purchase these?" he asked.

"Why didn't you ring the bell?" she responded curtly.

"Oh, I didn't want to ring it in case I disturbed you."

"It's no bother... That's why it's there."

She wrinkled her forehead and gave him a stern look.

He froze, looking as if he was contemplating whether or not to ditch the books and flee the premises. After a few seconds of awkward silence, Evelyn let out a deep sigh.

"Well, come on then!" She set the coffee table book down on a table and clicked her way to the front while the customer dutifully followed.

After he left, a petite woman in a shimmering violet colored trench-coat entered the store. Approaching one of the glass display cases, she placed her fingertips on the edge for support while taking several deep breaths, wobbling slightly in the effort. When she noticed Evelyn sitting behind the desk she looked surprised.

"Where is Katrina?" She asked, speaking in a soft voice with just a hint of nasal.

"Well, good morning Marilyn. Nice of you to join us." Evelyn responded.

Marilyn pushed back from the counter and put one hand over the small diamond cross hanging at her throat.

"Will she be in later?"

"She asked me to take her shift. Now that you're here, I can put out the trash." Evelyn said, getting up from the desk.

Marilyn began to make a whimpering sound.

"But, I have to get to work on MY books."

"Well, be forewarned, there's not a lot of sorting going on at the moment." Evelyn told her before heading for the back.

After propping the door open with a brick, she pulled the plastic trash liner out of the can and dragged it down the ramp and across the parking lot to the dumpsters. Since both black poly lids were closed, she swung one open to inspect the interior. She'd heard enough stories about hidden creatures, both four-legged and two-legged, to make her want to check the contents before tossing anything inside. Thankfully, the container was empty save for a beach ball sized wad of what looked like black magnetic tape. When she heaved the trash bag on top, it made a swishing sound upon impact.

Back inside, Evelyn was surprised to see Marilyn standing by the door at the end of the hall with a panicked expression on her face.

"I need books!" She exclaimed, before disappearing into the room.

Evelyn followed, curious as to what the situation looked like.

The mystery paperback sorting room was the size of a small bedroom, barely big enough to accommodate the three tables lining the walls. Usually covered with paperbacks stacked alphabetically by author, the tables, along with the banker's boxes for the more prolific writers beneath, all looked uncharacteristically empty.

Marilyn emerged from a smaller adjoining room where a sign taped to the door read: "Mystery Hardcover - Marilyn Only".

She had her hands up in her perfect white curls and looked ready to burst into tears at any moment.

"I need more books to shelve, why can't you go and do some sorting now?"

"Because, Marilyn," Evelyn said calmly, "someone has to cashier and that someone would be me."

With that, she turned on her heels and returned to the front only to find a customer hovering near the desk.

"There you are." The woman said.

"Why didn't you ring the bell?" Evelyn asked her.

"I don't like ringing those things."

Evelyn sighed and sat down.

"How much are the books?" The woman asked.

"All regular books are a dollar." Evelyn responded, pointing to the large sign on the wall that displayed the bookstore's pricing information quite clearly.

"Hardcovers too?"

"All regular books are a dollar." Evelyn repeated.

"Well that makes it easy." The woman snarked.

"Yes," Evelyn said with a smile, "just like ringing a bell."

SORT OF LIKE THIS

(October 21, Friday morning)

My hand hesitated on the cold doorknob.

Even though Nate and I had come down to the bookstore a few evenings to work, this would be my first time alone in the place since Pat's death. I knew, with certainty, on the other side of the door an emotional tsunami was waiting to sweep me up and force me to deal with the loss of both a friend and a co-worker. In short, sorting without Pat was going to suck.

As the door clicked shut behind me, I switched on the lights.

It was a log jam.

Squeezing my body past a fleet of overloaded shopping carts and precariously stacked towers of boxes, I snaked my way down the hall.

The horrendous state of affairs gripping the back area didn't surprise me. Although most of the bookstore volunteers were happy enough to cashier or shelve during their required four hour shifts, only a handful were willing to sort. The task was demanding and required the ability to lift heavy items, something many of the senior aged volunteers were unwilling, or unable, to do. It also didn't help that the amount of donated books seemed to multiply on a daily basis.

Pausing in front of the closed sorting room door, I found myself reminiscing about my first day at the bookstore some eighteen months earlier. It had also been a day filled with trepidation.

I'd been volunteering at a local cat rescue center for three years when the lady in charge retired and Roxy took over. Since my job entailed cleaning all the cages early Friday mornings before the place opened, a job no one else wanted to do, I'd been mostly insulated from the subsequent fallout. Within weeks a large portion of the volunteers had quit, citing Roxy's rash management approach as reason, and within months the Feline House permanently closed its doors. Although Roxy had officially blamed the closure on the landlord raising the rent, I'd had my doubts.

A year later, while shopping for winter treads, I'd run into Roxy at the local tire store. Frankly, I was somewhat surprised she even remembered my name.

"Holly! Come on over and check out our used bookstore!" she had enthusiastically told me, rambling on about the location and a woman named Pat who was helping her get it started. She also made sure to let me know how desperate they were for volunteers. Although I love books and had always fantasized about working in a bookstore, I initially balked at the idea of working with her again.

When I lost my job at the school and our only child headed off to college, I needed something new to distract me and changed my mind. After a few introductory emails with Pat, I cautiously approached my first day of training not at all sure of what to expect. Thankfully, Pat and I instantly hit it off and, as the saying goes, the rest was history.

Focusing my attention on the here and now, I suddenly thought of Teddy. He hadn't made a sound since I'd entered and that was highly unusual.

"Teddy?"

He wasn't sitting in his usual spot and his food bowl was still full of dry kibble. Scanning the cage, I finally spotted some gray and white fur bulging out of one of the cubby holes near the top of the carpeted kitty tower. It must have taken a lot of effort for him to cram his hefty girth into that tiny space.

"Teddy? Are you OK?"

I briefly contemplated opening the door and checking on him, but decided against it. Daphne would be in soon enough and, as far as I knew, he had never bitten her.

Looking over towards the girl's enclosure, I noticed the door was clear of paperwork. That could only mean one thing.

Way to go ladies. I thought, feeling gratitude towards whoever had given them their much deserved forever home.

"Well, looks like it's just you and me now." I said to Teddy's backside. His tail twitched and I realized he was ok, just being a cat and ignoring me.

Grabbing the handles of the shopping cart nearest the sorting room door, I carefully maneuvered its bulk into the room and parked near the center.

The first hardcover I lifted out of the cart was a biography. After placing it into the appropriate genre box, I chose another. At first it looked like general fiction, but upon further inspection, I realized the story was set in the 1920's so it ended up going into historical fiction. Working my way through the cart, I stacked any general fiction, romance and mystery books on the table and tossed a couple of volumes with torn covers into an FRC cart.

When the shopping cart was empty, I pushed it back out into the hall and began to load it with books out of one of the bins. These came from another non-profit who held a gigantic monthly sale in a barn, and Pat had negotiated with them to collect all their unsold books for free. The deal, however, specified we had to remove them in one single 'drop' on the second Sunday of each month.

Pausing, I surveyed the six large steel bins full of the barn books. Could they be partially responsible for Pat's heart attack? I knew that trying to get them emptied by month's end was one of her biggest stressors, especially since we got a lot of 'walk-in' donations as well. These walk-ins were accepted pretty much without question and it wasn't uncommon to get boxes of damaged books that were torn or moldy or even covered in rodent droppings, another reason sorting was such an undesirable job.

Regardless of all of this, I had to admit I enjoyed it. Every time I reached into a bag and pulled out a book, it was like a wonderful combination of sleuthing and Christmas all wrapped up into one.

"This place has magic." Pat had told me, and she was right.

The first time I discovered it was during my training. We'd been talking about places we'd lived and had realized we'd both spent time in the same small town in Colorado. Minutes later, I found myself holding a travel booklet, featuring the exact same place, in my hands.

"Those connections happen to me all the time." Pat had laughed.

Soon I was experiencing this phenomenon on a regular basis; finding books about the most random of topics that I had either recently been thinking about or discussing with someone. Nate was convinced it was merely coincidence - by thinking about something I was more aware of it in my surroundings. But I believed there was something magical going on inside the bookstore.

"Either that or I'm just crazy." I said out loud.

After sorting two loads of barn books, I carried all the books I'd stacked out to their appropriate places. Romance and general fiction were easy enough to deal with and were simply placed on tables set up near the back of the store. Sometime during the week, various volunteers would shelve them out on the main floor. Mystery books went into the room at the end of the hall. While the paperbacks took a little bit more time to separate alphabetically by author, the hardcovers only had to be stacked in the corner by the closed 'closet' door. Pat said Marilyn had a special storage system in there and didn't want it messed with, and that was fine by me. I had enough to do.

I was carrying an armful of romance out of the sorting room when the back door exploded outwards, startling me into dropping most of them onto the floor.

"How-deeeee!"

Roxy's usual quick jog through the hall was cut short by all the obstruction.

"Daaaang! It IS bad!" she exclaimed.

"Yep, it's bad." I said, bending down to pick up the strays while my heart thumped hard against my chest. Roxy's dramatic entrances were as jarring as they were annoying.

She snaked past me and popped out into an open area beyond.

"We've got a problem here, Holly!"

I ignored her and continued to work.

"Some of the volunteers are complainin' about not enough books bein' sorted!"

"Oh?" I said, straightening to my full height.

She was pacing back and forth and her cheeks looked flushed. I noticed that her usually pressed khaki shirt was heavily wrinkled, as if she had slept in it, and there were bits of hay sticking out of her frizzy dark brown hair.

"Neigh... neigh... neigh."

The muffled sound of a horse whinnying caused her to dig into her pant pockets. Briefly looking at her phone's screen, she began to stomp her feet on the ground like an angry toddler, causing strands of straw to flurry around her like snowflakes.

"It's Marilyn! AGAIN! This is the fourth time she's called me this mornin', she's COMPLETELY freaked out!"

She shoved the phone away without answering.

"Katrina says we're gettin' complaints from customers too!"

Her voice had risen in amplitude and there were beads of sweat running down the sides of her face.

What is wrong with her? I wondered.

"I NEED you to take over for Pat. I can't trust anyone else."

Her plea caught me by surprise.

"But I don't want to end up like her." I snapped back.

Roxy flinched as if she'd been struck, and I instantly regretted opening my mouth.

"I'm goin' to Rudy's and get some coffee" she said, quickly recovering, "when I get back we can talk 'bout this some more."

Spinning on her heels, she headed towards the front of the store.

After she'd gone, Teddy began to howl again.

What have I gotten myself into?

Chapter

8

TOUGH GUY

(October 21, Friday)

K eeping concise records of all observations was an essential and necessary element of good detective work. This bit of sage advice had been the modus operandi of a fictional character he admired, and though the concept in general wasn't at all appealing, he was determined to give it a go.

With a small notepad balanced precariously on the top of one of his bent knees, he methodically printed the date in the upper right hand corner of the first page with a mechanical pencil - since pens couldn't be trusted, especially in the cold.

October 21: Morning

The inside of the enclosure partially surrounding the dumpsters was the perfect vantage spot. Crouched low against it with his back against the cold brick, he was hidden from sight yet still had a clear view of the rear entry of the building under observation. Shifting his weight slightly, shards of broken glass beneath him made a satisfying crunching sound as they ground against the asphalt; sitting on a piece of cardboard had been a prudent decision.

Ignoring the stench of old garbage that permeated the fibers of his clothing and pores of his exposed skin, he patiently waited as a cloud of condensed breath gathered around his face. All was silent as there were no crows hanging around the dumpsters this morning, and for that he was glad. Suddenly, the sound of an approaching vehicle made him snap to attention. Bingo. Watching it park behind the store, he checked his phone.

Damn.

It was dead. Scrambling to his feet, he ducked around the wall and made a mad dash across the dead-end street to check the electronic menu board of the Burger Pit's drive-through. Along with colorful photographs advertising their tasty offerings, it also indicated the exact time.

8:16 am

The move had meant exposing himself to possible detection, but the detail was important enough to make the risk necessary and he was certain the driver of the vehicle hadn't seen him.

Once back in position, he quickly scribbled down the information along with other descriptive details of the individual now making their way up the ramp toward the bookstore's back door.

Female. Taller than average. Flannel jacket.

Even though at this stage he should be keeping his mind open before forming a hypothesis, as per his fictional hero, this was the person he favored most as his primary suspect and he planned on keeping a close tab on her movements.

The sound of an approaching diesel drew his attention and he watched as a large pick-up truck rumbled into view. When it ended up parking near the first vehicle, he jotted down the license plate number; this was turning out to be a good morning. If he could detail all this to review later, perhaps he could paint a depiction of what was known and discover things that really mattered.

Above all else, he really needed to find his missing partner.

Chapter

9

CIDER AND A DIP

(October 21, Friday afternoon)

"What?" I yelled.

It was standing room only in the Belgian's front room, and even though the bartender was waving and calling out something to me, I had no idea what he was saying.

Slowly maneuvering my way to the bar, I caught sight of Sarra sitting at the corner table in the back room.

"Blood orange?"

This time I heard him. He looked flushed but still gave me a smile as he poured a bottle of an orangey-gold liquid into a glass.

"Thank you." I said, squeezing in between a couple of broad shoulders to hand him my credit card.

"The usual with Swiss cheese?" he called out before moving towards the cash register in the corner.

"Yes, thanks."

"What's that?" The man to my right asked as I carefully lifted the nearly overflowing drink off the counter.

"Cider."

The customer shuddered slightly and turned his attention back to his beer, which was fine by me. Elaborating on the virtues of hard apple cider to someone obviously not interested would have been a total waste of time.

Leaving the bar, I passed through the rough-hewn lumber framed entrance of the Belgian's back room. Making my way down the short ramp, necessitated by a sinking floor, I took in the kitschy old-world ambiance of the narrow space. On the left, five sturdy tables with straight back chairs sat perpendicular to a row of windows covered in wooden louvers. To the right, a small food order window had been cut into the white stucco wall and in the rear a short hallway led to both the kitchen and a unisex bathroom, cleverly converted from an old walk-in freezer. Almost every inch of wall space was covered by European brewery advertisements while, overhead, two antique ceiling fans twirled beneath dark stained beams.

Other than a middle-aged couple seated near the front, Sarra and I had the place to ourselves.

"How are you?" She asked as I sat down opposite her.

"Better now." I said, after taking a sip of my cider.

"Blood orange?"

"Yep."

Moments later a lanky young man swung around the corner from the kitchen carrying two plates. The pub's newest sandwich maker was dressed in clothes reminiscent of the Seattle Grunge scene: torn jeans, faded flannel shirt and a knit beanie rolled up to enough to expose long strands of ash blonde hair.

"A Rueben and a dip?" he asked hovering near the edge of our table, a somber expression on his face.

"That was fast." I said. "I'm the Rueben."

"I guess that makes me the dip." Sarra chuckled.

His total lack of reaction indicated he hadn't picked up on her cliché of a joke.

"Mmm, looks good, thanks!" I commented as he set the plates down in front of us, but even that didn't get a response.

"Kids these days, so serious." Sarra said after he'd left.

While we ate, I filled her in on my conversation with Roxy.

"Are you sure that's something you want to do?" She asked between bites.

I shook my head. "Not really, Pat was there almost every day."

"That's a lot to ask of a volunteer. Besides, I thought you were going to focus on your art. How's that going, anyway?"

Looking out the window, I thought about the empty canvas set up on my easel back home.

"It's going." I said, not wanting to admit my frustration. Rekindling an art career had been proving painfully slow in both motivation and sales.

The noise level in the pub had diminished somewhat and I could hear the bartender laughing with someone in the kitchen, and I wondered if it was the reticent sandwich boy.

"Was there a service for Pat?" Sarra asked.

"Not here, her family lives in SoCal so I'm assuming they did something down there."

"How sad to lose a loved one so suddenly."

An image of Pat laying on the floor with her dazzling white tennis shoes pointing towards the ceiling played across my mind.

"It was sudden for sure, and strange." I said.

"What do you mean, the heart attack?"

"Even though the autopsy confirmed it, I still can't believe it's true. She played tennis a couple of times a week."

Sarra shrugged. "Even people in good shape have heart attacks."

"I know, but I can't help feeling there's something off about the whole thing."

"Like what?"

"Like her car being parked up front. She always parked in back."

"Maybe she wasn't feeling well." Sarra countered. "People do strange things sometimes, especially if they're in pain."

"True, but why did she close the sorting room door?"

Sandwich boy interrupted our conversation by suddenly swinging out from the kitchen with another plate of food. Plopping down at a table across from us, he began to attack his own creation with gusto.

"I guess that's a good sign." Sarra commented and we both shared a smile.

After our own lunches were finished, I gathered up our plates and carried them over to the pass-through. Returning to the table, the young man nodded his head at me in what I took to be a silent "thank you."

"I was in your bookstore the other day and Evelyn was right, it's a mess." Sarra said when I sat back down.

I had to agree with her assessment. Most of the bookstore was an organizational nightmare, to put it mildly, in large part due to Pat's organic approach to management. After initially setting up the store's sections when it opened, she had trusted the volunteers to keep things going on their own, with little or no monitoring, and had only ever got upset if their books piled up in the sorting room.

"Pat didn't push anyone to do anything they didn't want to do." I explained. "That's one of the reasons we don't have a lot of sorters."

"I wouldn't mind sorting, but only if you were in charge. From what you and Evelyn have told me, working for Roxy would make my blood boil."

"She is definitely an acquired taste, to put it mildly."

"If she's so upset about the backlog, why doesn't she pitch in?"

That made me laugh. Roxy's only contribution to sorting had been to occasionally order pizza the Friday night before a drop at Pat's request. The hope was food would entice volunteers to come in and help, but few, if any, had ever taken the bait.

"She doesn't seem to have a clue as to what we do there, and I think Pat liked it that way." I said.

"Oh?"

"I don't know, just a feeling I got. I don't think she really trusted Roxy. They argued about things, and I overheard a couple of phone conversations where it got pretty heated. For the most part Roxy stayed away and focused on her animal rescue. With Pat gone, I'm not sure what's going to happen."

"Well, if you do decide to take on more responsibility, make sure the terms are very clear. Don't let her push you around."

Or throw me under an FRC cart, I thought to myself.

Chapter

10

TRAIL OF DIRT

(October 26, Wednesday morning)

B ecause, we need more help in the back." I said, this time with definite irritation in my voice.

Marilyn sighed dramatically.

"I don't see why."

She was seated alone at the bookstore's front desk sans her usual sidekick, Cheryl, who was home sick with the flu. Somehow, not only had she found out I was taking over for Pat, even though the decision had only been confirmed the day before, she also seemed to know the reason for my scheduled meeting with Katrina.

"You just said you weren't getting enough hardcovers." I responded, confused as to why she was balking at the idea of us getting more sorters.

Evelyn had come in to substitute and was silently listening to our exchange while dusting the glass display cases near the front door. I couldn't help think her canary yellow pantsuit looked simply dazzling against the gray sky backdrop outside.

"Well, maybe the ones we have need to work harder." Marilyn said, smugly.

Evelyn, I noticed, had stopped swishing the pink duster.

"What are you talking about?" She called out from across the counter top.

"Why, the sorters, of course." Marilyn responded.

It was obvious she still thought sorters were some mysterious group of volunteers who only came in at night, like a cleaning crew, even though Pat had explained ad nauseam that no one only sorted and of those who regularly did (now only Evelyn, Gerald, Nate and myself) also managed their own sections.

Evelyn, however, was not going to let this misconception continue.

"Exactly which sorters are you referring to?" She asked, her sideways glance in my direction making it quite clear she was enjoying this confrontation.

Marilyn focused all her attention on an invisible object attached to the sleeve of her baby blue cashmere sweater.

"You know, you people who sort." She mumbled.

"You people?"

Evelyn smacked the duster down onto the glass with a loud thwack.

Looking over at Marilyn, I saw thin streaks of pink flushing across her cheeks as she bent over the desk, busying herself with straightening loose pages in the sales ledger.

"I hope Cheryl feels better soon." She muttered, keeping her head down.

Evelyn flashed me a satisfied smile before going back to her dusting.

I considered Marilyn with mixed emotions. Although a part of me felt sorry for this frail and misguided volunteer, I was proud of Evelyn for not backing down. In the world of this particular used bookstore, certain prejudices were alive and well, especially when it came to sorters. We were often used as scapegoats, especially by those like Marilyn who didn't sort, and blamed for everything from throwing away books to messing up shelves.

Checking my phone for the time, I meandered across the main aisle to the children's section which took up the front corner of the store. Here, old banquet tables had been arranged into an 'L' shape along the windows and east wall, while two more were set up side by side near the center. These weren't the new plastic ones either, but old sagging wooden beasts that were splitting along the edges of their heavy metal frames. The children's books were stored on these in a mishmash of cardboard boxes, trimmed down to about a six-inch height, with spines up and covers forward. Glancing at them I noticed a haphazard approach to their organization, with only a few of the boxes labeled with any indication of subject matter or reading level.

"I don't know how anyone finds anything over here." Evelyn commented from behind me.

She'd followed me with her duster, still attacking every surface.

"Didn't the twins take this over?" I asked, remembering the name change on the genre sign in the sorting room.

"Yes, they're trying, but I think they're overwhelmed. Oh, I should buy this."

She'd pulled a small hardcover with a distinctive blue cover out of one of the boxes, and I instantly recognized it as a classic Hardy Boy Mystery.

"I loved reading those as a kid, much more than Nancy Drew."

"Speaking of kids, how is that handsome son of yours doing?" Evelyn asked, flashing me a smile.

"He's good, I think, even though I haven't heard from him in a couple of weeks."

A sudden pang of maternal abandonment shot through me as I thought of my son, Philip. Although the campus he attended was only a few hours' drive away, over the past couple months his visits and communications had been rapidly diminishing.

"Don't worry, they always come back. All five of mine did."

"I'd be happy with a text message."

Evelyn poked my shoulder with a finger, her eyes twinkling with amusement.

"Just enjoy the time you have with Mr. Vampire."

Her use of the nickname she'd given Nate, since he usually only came in at night, finally got me to smile.

Pulling out my phone, I realized Katrina was over half an hour late and I wondered what could be keeping her.

"Ugh, this is filthy, I better clean it."

Evelyn had moved towards the entrance, and when I looked up to see what she was referring to, something caught my attention. A dark shape was looming on the other side of the door, details distorted by the smudges and streaks that covered the glass.

Before I could say anything, Evelyn swung the door outward to reveal a man standing just outside.

"Are you coming in or not?" she snapped at him.

The man recoiled a few steps, almost to the edge of the sidewalk. He was wearing a bulky camouflage jacket that hung well below his knees and a baseball cap emblazoned with a bright yellow smiley face.

"Well, come on, I'm not going to hold this open all day." Evelyn said, pushing the door out further and standing to one side to give him room to enter.

The man cautiously slipped past her and walked a few feet into the store before removing his cap.

"Can we help you find something?" I asked.

He turned to look at me and his eyes widened, their paleness contrasting dramatically against the darkness of his weathered skin.

"I, um... I was looking for Stumpy." He said.

"Stumpy? Is that your dog?" Evelyn asked with concern in her voice.

I knew she was thinking of a recent experience involving the escape of her own precious Boo-Boo inside Target. By her account, it had taken nearly half of the store's employees to finally capture the little Maltipoo.

"No, Ma'am, he's a friend." The man responded. "Been missing for a while and I was wondering if you've seen him since he comes in here to buy books."

He was still looking at me as if he recognized me, though I was sure we'd never met.

Evelyn, on the other hand, looked relieved to hear Stumpy was only a misplaced person.

"What does he look like?" She asked.

"He's about my height and wears a brown jacket."

"OK." I said, glancing over at Evelyn. She was frowning down at his muddy boots.

The man noticed too and shifted slightly, the strong scent of campfire smoke drifting off his clothing in the process.

"Stumpy likes those old paperbacks. You know, the ones with the cowboys on the covers. He says they have them in the back sometimes." He said.

"Oh, I think I know who you mean now." Evelyn responded, "Sorry, I haven't seen him recently."

Turning, she called over in the direction of the desk.

"How about you, Marilyn, have you see this gentleman's friend?"

Marilyn mumbled something unintelligible before shrinking down into the chair.

"What was that?" Evelyn asked, moving closer.

Marilyn abruptly scooted her chair back, the metal legs screeching across the hard cement floor, and bent forward to inspect the ground as if she was looking for a lost pen. Although I knew there were volunteers who did everything possible to avoid certain customers, this was one of the most blatant examples of evasion I'd ever witnessed.

"If we see him we'll be sure to let him know you're looking for him." I told the man, feeling embarrassed over Marilyn's display of rudeness.

This seemed to satisfy him and he put his cap back on. Moving towards the door he suddenly stopped and pointed a finger at Evelyn.

"Is that a Hardy Boys Mystery?"

She was momentarily surprised but quickly recovered and handed him the book.

"Would you like to buy it? It's only twenty-five cents."

"Oh, I didn't bring any money."

He tried to give the book back but she waved him off, digging into the pocket of her apron and handing him a quarter.

"Here, take this to the nice lady over there." She said, motioning towards the desk.

The man thanked her and walked over to Marilyn, who had frozen in place like a deer caught in the headlights of an on-coming semi.

"We never had to deal with anyone like that back in my shop in Marin." She complained after he'd left, suddenly reanimated and fanning the air with her hands.

I could tell Evelyn wanted to say something choice, but opted instead to only give me one of her quiet raised eyebrow looks.

"I better sweep up Mr. Smiley's mess." She pointed to the trail of ashen dirt the man's boots had left on the ground.

"I'll go get the broom." I said, thankful for something to do.

Returning up the main aisle, I could hear Marilyn talking to someone.

"I haven't gotten any books in ALL week and I'm completely out of Evanoski hardbacks."

A woman dressed entirely in black was standing in front of the desk facing her and when Marilyn acknowledged my approach, she turned to look at me.

"Hey, I know I'm late."

"No worries, Katrina, let me sweep the floor first and then we can talk."

Marilyn pouted and crossed her arms, looking like a petulant child annoyed at not having the full attention they were sure they deserved.

"Here, give me that." Evelyn said, taking the broom from my hands.

Katrina strolled over to the VHS section, which ran along the right side of the main aisle, and I followed. Although she was a small-statured woman with narrow hips, her upper body was thick from what I assumed was weightlifting and it gave her the appearance of an inverted triangle. With her dark eyes, long straight ebony hair, and a resting expression that resembled a scowl, she let off a stern persona.

Although we had both started volunteering at the store around the same time, up until now we had never crossed paths. Katrina didn't sort and, as far as I knew, only came in once a week to help cashier and shelve the VHS tapes. About a year ago she had convinced Roxy to let her be in charge of scheduling cashiers and Pat hadn't seen any reason to object, especially since it was a job she hated doing. She'd also taken over picking up the barn books since the volunteer formally responsible had left following a car accident.

"So, I hear you're now in charge of the sorting and need some help." Katrina said. The way she said it made it sound as if asking for more volunteers was a sign of weakness.

"Yes, I'm going to be managing both the sorting and shelving." I responded, deciding to ignore the possible jab. "I thought maybe we could put a flyer in the window or put a notice in the paper to try and get some more applicants."

Glancing over at the desk I could see Marilyn watching us with an anticipatory expression on her face, and although Evelyn was sweeping the floor, she hadn't moved far away.

"I'll have to think about that." Katrina said, sounding annoyed.

"What do you mean?"

I was starting to get irritated myself. She had made me wait for nearly half an hour and was now acting as if I was wasting her time.

"Someone filled out an application the other day and I put it in the file." Evelyn said. She set the broom against the edge of the desk and quickly slid open one of the drawers to pull out a manila folder before Marilyn could even react.

"It's in here." She said, striding across the aisle to hand it to me.

"We get lots of applications." Katrina said. "Most of them are junk."

"Junk?" I asked, confused.

Leafing through a pile of BARF Volunteer application forms, I pulled one out that had an extra page stapled to the back.

"What about this one? It even has a resume attached and..."

"If they can't work the shifts I need, interviewing them is a waste of time." Katrina said, abruptly cutting me off.

"I don't understand, what shifts?"

"All new volunteers need to commit to a cashiering shift." She said, putting a hand out for the folder.

"But Roxy agreed the priority is getting people who can sort."

I straightened my spine to take full advantage of my height, something that sometimes works, and she hesitated slightly before answering.

"Well, Roxy also wants all new volunteers to be properly vetted and trained by me first."

"What do you mean properly vetted?"

This was new. Pat had only ever required volunteers to fill out a simple application form and spend a couple of hours with her in training. In fact, she used to joke how as long as we didn't show up drunk or on drugs, anyone willing to work was welcome.

Glancing over at Evelyn I saw a puzzled expression on her face that no doubt mimicked my own.

"We have to be careful," Katrina explained, "we don't want just anyone working here. I'm also looking into doing background checks and drug testing."

She seemed rather pleased at the prospect of making people jump through hoops.

"Oh good grief!" Evelyn snapped and twirled on her heels, heading towards the back with broom in tow.

I wished I could have joined her. Katrina was obviously on some sort of power trip and working with her was not going to be easy. Feeling my stomach begin to knot up with tension, I decided to switch gears and attempt a more reasonable approach.

"Look, I don't want to interfere with your cashier schedule or anything, but I need at least two or three more volunteers who can sort. OK?" I asked, trying to keep my voice as neutral as possible.

Katrina turned away from me and ran a finger across some of the VHS spines, her long painted nail making a clicking sound as it hit the hard plastic edges.

"If that is what Roxy wants, then I suppose it's OK."

She didn't sound thrilled, but at least it was a move in the right direction.

"Great, let me know when you get some in and I'll coordinate times to train them in back."

Her tight leather pants squeaked as she crouched down to inspect some of the tapes on the bottom row. They were jammed vertically into wooden bookcases with no discernible organization and although Pat wanted to get rid of them, Katrina had been adamant sales were constant.

"Good, looks like I don't need to bring any more out" she mumbled to herself, slowly rising up and rebalancing on her heels.

Although I happened to know there were at least five boxes of VHS in the sorting room that needed shelving, I decided to keep that piece of information to myself. Instinct told me I was going to have to pick my battles very carefully when it came to Katrina. Besides, I was more than ready to end this conversation.

Evelyn didn't look at all happy when I passed her on my way out the back door.

"I can tell you right now," she told me, "nobody's going to force me to pee in a cup to volunteer here."

Chapter

11

KEVIN

(November 10, Thursday afternoon – Two weeks later)

Warm water poured across the palms of my hands and trickled through my fingers. Even though the soap suds were all rinsed, I let the faucet run a little bit longer to prolong the comforting sensation. Turning off the faucet, I reached for a paper towel from the dispenser and dried my hands before pushing the bathroom door open and heading to the front of the pub.

"Did you already order?" I asked Sarra and Lynn Mason, our newest bookstore volunteer, who were both standing next to the bar studying the menu.

"Not yet, our friend is checking to see if there's any more blood orange in the back." Sarra said.

"You mean Kevin?" Lynn asked.

"You know his name?" I said, looking at her with amazement. As far as I knew, this was the first time she'd ever been to the Belgian.

"I heard someone else calling him that."

She seemed confident and leaned her petite frame against the counter.

The bartender returned from the kitchen shaking his head.

"Sorry ladies, we only have hibiscus and extra dry."

"Try the hibiscus, it's really good." Sarra told Lynn.

After ordering our sandwiches, Sarra left for her turn in the bathroom while Lynn and I carried our ciders over to the corner near the front window and situated ourselves onto some stools. Since it was past one o'clock, the normal lunch crowd had long since cleared and we had the counter all to ourselves.

"Why does the bookstore only have cold water?" Lynn asked.

"Because the hot water heater is turned off." I said, explaining Roxy had done it in order to save money. Although she claimed the water temperature didn't affect it's cleaning abilities, none of us were convinced.

"Well, that's just plain dumb." She responded, rolling up the sleeves of her beige fleece sweatshirt. It had an embroidered wolf head on the front and had looked brand new this morning, though now it was streaked with splotches of dust and grime.

During the course of working together, I'd learned Lynn was a widow and had recently moved to the area from Seattle. At barely five feet tall and somewhat pear shaped, she had legs that never seemed to stop moving and, below a tightly cropped helmet of dark gray curls, her generous smile and brown eyes were outlined with deep laugh lines.

"This is good!" She said, after taking a sip of her cider.

"I knew you'd like it." Sarra responded, having returned from the back and pulling out the stool next to mine. Once she had settled, I lifted my glass into the air to make a toast.

"Here's to our newest bookstore volunteers and their successful day of sorting."

"We all sorted." Lynn said, raising her glass to match mine.

"Well, here's to all of us then." I laughed and we all clinked and drank.

Outside, though the afternoon sun was blazing down at us through a clear sky, the temperature must have dropped as a thin layer of condensation was beginning to creep its way up along the lower portion of the pub's windows. It was good to be inside at a time like this, I thought, enjoying the sweet taste of cider and comforting surroundings.

"That must have been an entire storage unit." Sarra said, setting her glass down to inspect her fingernails. "My manicure is shot."

"It definitely was big." I agreed.

The man who donated the boxes had warned us his recently deceased father was somewhat of bibliophile. Unfortunately, he hadn't stored the books in a dry location and moisture had deteriorated many of them, especially those stacked near the bottom. The three of us had worked the better part of the morning digging through thick layers of mold and dust trying to salvage what we could.

"How often do you get big donations like that?" Lynn asked.

"Not often," I said, "maybe every other month or so."

"Well, I sure won't have to hit the gym later."

I wasn't surprised to hear she worked out. Her stamina had nearly matched my own, despite our age difference.

"Some of the books looked pretty valuable, they should sell." Sarra said before twisting around on her stool to survey the bar area. "Wonder what's taking so long with those sandwiches, I'm starving."

The bartender must have heard her as he quickly vanished into the kitchen. Within minutes, he reappeared holding a plate of food followed closely by the sandwich boy carrying the other two.

"Thank you Kevin." Sarra told him, winking at me behind his back as he set her lunch down on the counter.

Lynn was rubbing her palms together in obvious delight.

"This looks fantastic."

From the looks of it she had ordered one of Nate's favorite called the Fireman's Special; a monster of a sandwich piled thick with layers of roast beef, cream cheese and jalapeños.

Watching her dig into her lunch, I couldn't help but feel grateful that both these spunky ladies were now volunteering at the bookstore. Lynn, as it turned out, was the applicant who had stapled her resume to the back of the application form I'd pointed out to Katrina. She and Sarra had already completed their required cashier training up front, and this week were learning how to sort. We'd had so much fun together that we had decided to celebrate by coming to the Belgian.

As we ate, our conversation quickly turned to bookstore gossip.

"What was up with that old fart who was stacking books everywhere?" Lynn asked between bites.

"You mean Gerald?" I said, "I know, he has a weird sorting method."

"His piles were annoying," Sarra added, "I couldn't tell which ones he was still working on or which ones he'd abandoned."

"They used to drive Pat crazy too. Eventually he'll get rid of them, but sometimes it takes a while. Pat told me he rents a space over at the big used bookstore in Grant City so I think he's searching for books he can sell."

"Is that allowed?" Sarra asked.

"Technically its fine as long as he pays for them. It's one of the perks of being a volunteer; first dibs to buy any books that come in."

"He kept trying to talk to me about religion, but when I told him I'd been excommunicated he avoided me like the plague." Lynn said, giggling.

"Trouble maker." Sarra said.

Lynn nodded her head. "I seem to have that reputation wherever I go."

"Well, you're not the only one. I guess I shook up the resident ghost yesterday."

"The bookstore has a ghost?" Lynn asked, eyes widening.

"She means Peg, another of our volunteers with a unique sorting method." I said, going on to explain in more detail.

Peg was the bookstore's oldest volunteer, with a frizzy halo of white hair, pale skin, and habit of wearing white clothing that had earned her the nickname 'Casper, the friendly ghost' from Evelyn.

Two days earlier, while Sarra and I had been working on emptying one of the bins in the back hall, Peg had interrupted us by slowly perusing the top layer, mumbling random comments about the various titles and authors. Finally, after an agonizing amount of time, she had chosen a single book and drifted back to the front of the store to shelve it.

On Peg's fourth trip to the bin, Sarra had decided enough was enough.

"Here, take this one." she had said, grabbing a random book and thrusting it into her hands. Peg had frozen in place; eyes wide and mouth agape, and after a few awkward seconds I had intervened. Since, technically, the animal books were hers to shelve, I suggested she take some of them up front since they were stacked precariously high in the sorting room.

"Sarra felt bad afterwards and ended up carrying an entire box up front for her." I concluded.

"She's a ditz, but means well." Sarra said, chuckling before turning to look at Lynn. "Speaking of ditzes, I heard Katrina abandoned you during training."

"I wasn't going to say anything but, since you brought it up..." Lynn said, rolling her eyes.

She had finished her sandwich and was helping herself to the uneaten chips on my plate.

"What happened?" I asked, more than a little curious to hear this bit of gossip.

"Well, when she first called me about my application, I'd forgotten about turning it in, it had been so long. Then, when she interviewed me at the store, she asked all these weird questions."

"Like what?"

"Oh, you know, like if you were a car what kind would it be."

"Oh my gosh, she tried to ask me those too." Sarra interjected. "But when I told her I was friends with Holly and Evelyn, she ended the interview just like that." She snapped her fingers for effect.

"Believe me, I wanted to tell her to stuff it." Lynn said, shaking her head. "But I heard Lenny's voice in the back of my head telling me not to put my foot into it, so I let it go. Guess I was meant to volunteer here."

I sent a mental 'thank you' to her late husband. He'd told her to always keep busy, and volunteering had seemed like a good way to connect with her new community.

"So, what happened at the training?" Sarra asked, prodding for more information.

"That was a complete joke. First of all, we were supposed to meet Saturday morning at 9:30 but she didn't show up until ten. Then she only spent a couple of minutes going over the ledger and tax sheets before I was on my own to help customers. Good thing I was a bookkeeper and could figure it out fast."

"You mean she didn't stay with you?" I asked, shocked.

"No, she said she had some family thing to deal with and left. Luckily, Evelyn showed up a little while later. She's a real hoot to work with, so it worked out OK."

"I wish I could have trained with Evelyn." Sarra said. "Katrina farmed me off onto Daphne and believe me, after four hours of her nattering, I felt like I had relived the sixties all over again."

Listening to their experiences, I couldn't help but feel annoyed at Katrina, especially since she had been so adamant about personally dealing with all new volunteers. From the sound of it, vetting was nothing more than a series of random questions and training was left for someone else to handle.

"Did she try and get you to work Sundays?" Lynn asked Sarra.

"Yes, but that's the day I visit my Aunt up in Trenton so I told her I couldn't. She got pissy about it, but oh well." Sarra laughed.

"Sundays are my walking days so I told her no too. Your Aunt's in Trenton? They were talking about the drug problem they're having on the news last night. Sounds terrible."

Sarra gazed down at her drink and slowly shook her head.

"I saw that too. It's definitely a sad situation."

I was about to take another sip of my own cider when I realized, once again, my glass only contained foam.

"It's empty, dear." Lynn giggled.

"So is mine." Sarra said, standing up and reaching for her purse. "Let me get another bottle and we can share."

Returning in a few minutes, she skillfully began to distribute the cider equally among our glasses.

"So what day ARE you working up front?" Lynn asked her.

"Katrina texted me my schedule yesterday. Looks like I'm down for Monday mornings."

"Fantastic! So am I." Lynn looked pleased.

"By the way," Sarra continued, "the bartender wants to know why we keep calling him Kevin."

Chapter

12

TINY BUBBLES

(November 11, Friday morning)

H oly carp!" Sarra exclaimed.

"Huh?"

"Well, you did say it's called the 'fish' room."

"Right..."

I parked the empty shopping cart outside the entrance and surveyed the cavernous space. Somewhere towards the end of our second round of ciders yesterday, we had decided tackling the massive amounts of donations piled within would be a good idea. Looking at it now, I wasn't so sure.

The majority of floor space within the rectangular shaped room was filled with pillars of cardboard boxes stacked as high as any volunteer could reach, their conjoined structures leaning like Towers of Pisa. Every visible nook and cranny between was stuffed with plastic and paper bags burgeoning with donations, many of these ripped and torn so contents avalanched onto the floor.

Four tiers of two-foot cube shaped cubbyholes, built out of painted plywood, lined the back half of the room's walls. These had been used by the previous occupants to accommodate their fresh water aquariums, (hence the name 'fish' room), but now were used as depositories for miscellaneous donations.

"Where should we start?" Sarra asked.

"Might as well start at the top." I said, stepping around a plastic milk crate filled with encyclopedias and reaching for the box at the top of the nearest tower.

"Good thing you're so tall." She laughed.

As I lifted each box down and over to her, she swung it into the cart with a satisfying thud. When the cart was full, I wiped at my brow with a sleeve while Sarra massaged her lower back.

"You OK?" I asked, concerned for my older friend.

"I'm fine, just a bit stiff." She said. "Too bad Lynn had a dentist appointment and is missing out on all this fun."

"Yeah, right." I laughed.

It took our combined efforts to turn the loaded cart around and maneuver it out of the fish room. Momentarily pausing near the cat enclosures to catch our breath, Teddy must have seen us as he began to cry.

"Poor baby, he's lonely." Sarra said, bending down near his cage with an outstretched hand.

"Careful, he bites." I warned.

"Is that why he's still here?"

"Partially, he's got health issues too." I told her, explaining how he'd been brought to the Feline House three years earlier after his elderly owner had died and no family members or friends had wanted to keep him.

Sarra glanced over at the other two empty enclosures.

"Will more cats be coming in soon?"

"I don't know; Roxy is in charge of that."

"I hope so, I love cats."

"So do I, but I also hate seeing them stuck in these cages all alone."

On our third trip to the fish room, while I worked at detaching a cardboard box glued to the concrete floor with some kind of dried goo, Sarra decided to explore.

"Hey, I found something I'm sure Evelyn would love."

Looking up from my struggles I saw her holding the tackiest ceramic cookie jar I'd ever seen. It was shaped like a droopy faced yellow dog with a red bow tie around its neck.

"Great, I'm sure she'll be thrilled." I said, sarcastically, before yanking at the box again. The cardboard suddenly ripped apart in my hands, causing the contents to scatter across the floor in every direction.

"Darn it!"

Frustrated, I plopped down beside it to take a break.

"What is this for?" Sarra asked, holding up another object.

With over half of the overhead fluorescent bulbs missing, there wasn't much light to work with and I had to squint to figure it out.

"It looks like an aeration stone from an aquarium." I said, focusing on the black plastic disk with a light gray stone center and clear tubing attached to one end.

"Oh, you mean to make tiny bubbles, like in the wine?" she laughed.

"A glass of that sounds good right about now."

I struggled back to my feet and gathered up the books, tossing them into the cart. One of them had slid far beneath a sagging banquet table and reaching for it, I predictably hit the top of my head. Noticing the title, I began to laugh.

Don Ho: My Music, My Life

The bookstore obviously hadn't lost its magic touch.

At a quarter to ten, Daphne showed up and, after feeding Teddy, poked her head into the sorting room as I happened to toss a copy of *Walden* into her classic literature genre box.

"Is that for me?" she squealed, clapping her hands together and causing the bells hanging around her neck to jingle. "Groovy!"

In the corner I noticed Sarra cringing at the choice of vocabulary.

"It sure is." I responded, smiling at Daphne's childlike enthusiasm. She sure loved her classics.

Retrieving the book, she wrapped it in her arms and held it tightly against the front of her fuzzy lime green sweater. As usual, her entire outfit was unique and included batik cotton wrap pants and a pair of neon orange Birkenstock sandals.

"You guys sure are booking through the sort and it looks awesome in here" she said, glancing around the room.

Stopping my work to follow her gaze, I had to agree with her assessment. Even with the volume of books we'd been pushing through, the sorting room did look pretty good. Old torn banker boxes had been replaced with new ones and all contents were neatly packed for maximum efficiency. There were new laminated signs printed in an easy-to-read font, thanks to Nate, and Lynn had even swept and mopped the floor.

"Hey, did you want to do any more training up front?" Daphne asked Sarra.

"No, thanks, I'm good." Sarra said.

"Groovy! Well, I guess I better go shelve this and open up."

Daphne turned and left for the front, bells jingling.

"If I hear the word 'groovy' one more time, I think I'm going to scream." Sarra said after she'd left.

That made me chuckle. Daphne did act scatterbrained at times, but I knew from experience beneath the flower child exterior lay an individual with a vast knowledge of poetry and literature. No matter how obscure an author landed in her box, she always seemed familiar with their work.

"It's after ten, should we finish up?" I asked.

"Works for me. I have to take these romances out." Sarra said, tossing the paperbacks she'd sorted into an empty box.

"Lordy, check this out."

She handed me one with cover artwork depicting a dark haired woman with gigantic breasts spilling out of a low cut frilly blouse. Her torso was twisted at an odd angle and her half closed eyes were gazing up at a shirtless man with glistening muscles.

"Pat used to call these bodice rippers." I laughed, tossing the book back to her.

"I can't believe anybody reads this junk."

While Sarra left for the front, I took the opportunity to use the bathroom.

Opening the door a few minutes later, I heard a woman's shrill voice coming from the end of the hall.

"Hey now, watchya think you're doin' there?!"

My heart skipped a beat when I realized it was Roxy.

Bolting around the corner, I saw Sarra standing by the romance sort table holding the box of books. She was staring down at Roxy who had both hands hovering near her hips, as if she was preparing for a western style shootout.

"Roxy, this is Sarra, one of our new volunteers!" I called out, quickly moving over to stand next to my friend.

"New? Why wasn't I told?" Roxy snapped, twirling around to glare up at me. Her face looked puffy and there were dark pink blotches scattered across both her cheeks.

"We agreed we needed more sorters, remember?" I said, trying to keep my voice as calm as possible. Sarra, who hadn't said a word, was sporting an incredulous expression.

"Does Katrina know? We can't have just anyone working here!" Roxy shrieked.

"Of course, she trained them last week."

I was beginning to feel my own cheeks flare hot with a simmering mix of anger and embarrassment.

"Harumphf."

Roxy exhaled and turned to stride toward her office, slamming the door after she'd entered.

"What drugs is she on?" Sarra asked, slapping the paperbacks onto the table in a way that told me she was pissed.

Glancing over at the office door, I contemplated going over there and banging on it with demands for an apology.

"Let's get out of here." Sarra said, interrupting my daydream.

A sound of onrushing bells stopped us in our tracks.

"The man's here! The man is here!" Daphne gasped as she jogged up the main aisle, still clutching *Walden* against her chest.

"What man?" I asked.

Looking past her I could see someone tall standing near the entrance.

"It's the fuzz!" She replied, eyes wide with excitement. "He wanted to talk to management but I told him we're all volunteers."

"It's OK Daphne, Roxy's here. I'll let her know."

"This should be entertaining." Sarra said. "Should I go make some popcorn?"

Sighing, I trudged towards Roxy's office and knocked. Although I didn't want to deal with her again, technically she was the boss.

"What?!" She screamed at me from behind the closed door.

"There's a sheriff up front who needs to talk with the manager!" I yelled back, surprised at how good it felt to raise my voice at her.

The door burst open and she pushed me aside, dashing over to the end of the aisle to look up front. Daphne had rejoined the officer and both were waving at us.

Roxy inhaled sharply and made a sudden sharp U-turn, breaking into a sprint towards the hall.

"You handle it!" She yelled back at me before disappearing around the corner.

"What the heck just happened?" Sarra asked, when we heard the back door slam shut.

"I don't know, but I guess I better go see what the cops want."

* * *

The young sheriff didn't look much older than my own nineteen-year-old son, and their physical similarities were striking; tall with dark brown hair and eyes beneath thick expressive eyebrows and a closed mouth smile with a slight crease to one side and a hint of a dimple.

"Can I help you?" I asked, shaking his outstretched hand.

"Yes, Ma'am, I'm Scan Stratton from the County's Sheriff's department. We're asking all the store owners in the area some questions concerning a recent death."

As he spoke, he pulled a streamlined computer tablet out of the inside pocket of his County issued bomber jacket.

"Death?" I asked, confused. The only recent death I knew about had been Pat's.

53

"You may have heard about the body found in the woods behind Rudy's? We've deemed it suspicious and are asking if any of your employees have noticed anything out of the ordinary."

He had raised his thick eyebrows slightly, as if in anticipation.

"We're not employees, we're volunteers!" Daphne called out from behind the desk, obviously eavesdropping.

Ignoring the peanut gallery, I responded to his inquiry. "No, I hadn't heard about that."

Sean hesitated for a moment, glancing briefly over at Daphne before continuing.

"The deceased was a known resident of one of the homeless camps and apparently frequented this shopping center."

Although he spoke in a hushed voice, Daphne had extremely good hearing.

"Whoa, heavy. Two deaths in one month. You know, this shopping center was built on a Native American burial site."

She was wiggling in her chair which made her bells jingle.

"Excuse me?"

Sean obviously hadn't heard about our recent tragedy and his eyebrows raised even higher at the news. Indian burial grounds withstanding, even though I didn't see how Pat's death could be connected with the body in the woods, I did my best to tactfully fill him in on her tragic demise. As I talked, he swiftly tapped the information into his tablet.

"When exactly did this occur?" he asked, fingers moving at light speed as I told him the date.

"You must text really fast." I commented.

He blushed slightly and put his tablet away before handing me his business card, its glossy white surface stamped with the County's gold logo.

"If you think of anything else, give me a call. You, or any of the other... volunteers... that work here." He flashed Daphne a grin and she waved back with enthusiasm.

After he'd exited the store, I rejoined Sarra in the back.

"What was that all about?" She asked.

"Another person died - seems a homeless person was killed in the woods behind Rudy's."

"Oh my gosh, that's awful."

After grabbing our purses from behind the sorting room door, I pushed open the back door to the sudden appearance of a grinning face which made us both gasp. It was Lynn, her arm outstretched with an index finger about to push the buzzer.

"Hi girlfriends! Did I miss anything?"

Chapter

13

AN EARLY CHRISTMAS PRESENT

(November 18, Friday afternoon)

There was a posterior sticking out of one of the FRC delivery carts.

Although the upper half of the person was submerged inside the container, I had a pretty good idea of who it was based on the crisply creased navy blue slacks and pristine penny loafers.

Emerging from the depths, Marilyn shrieked when she saw me.

"Why was one of my mystery books being discarded?" She demanded, face flushed pink from the elevation change. Her usually controlled snow-white curls were disheveled and her eyeglasses were skewered to one side, giving her face a somewhat less than dignified expression.

Glancing at the hardcover she was holding, I made a quick assessment.

"Because, Marilyn, it doesn't have a jacket."

"But there's nothing WRONG with it." She said, her voice taking on its distinctive whininess.

"No, but it doesn't have a jacket either and you know we don't keep hardcovers without jackets." I responded in a firm tone.

Although I have pretty good patience with most people, whiners really push my buttons.

"But this author sells!" She said, waving the book in the air like an excited preacher at the pulpit.

"Yes, and we get loads of that exact book in every month, with jackets."

Marilyn widened her eyes and clutched the book against her chest with trembling hands.

"It doesn't matter; people will buy this."

I was all too aware of her habit of checking the contents of the bins. In fact, it had been an area of ongoing frustration for Pat, especially since it hadn't gone unnoticed. Evelyn in particular had complained it made her feel as if her work was being undermined, and much to my amusement had dubbed the practice 'dumpster diving'.

"We're not changing Pat's rules." I told Marilyn, in defense of my late friend.

"But you're in charge now, aren't you?" She responded in a sweeter tenor, while a disingenuous smile spread across her face.

Her attempt at theatrics fell on deaf ears.

The jacket rule for hardcover fictions had been one of the few rules Pat had been adamant about, mostly in an attempt to keep the store from becoming completely overrun by certain books. There was no way I was going to change it for anyone, especially Marilyn.

"Doesn't matter, those are the rules."

Thanks to Lynn, I also happened to know there were at least a dozen of this exact title, with jackets, stacked inside her closet. Lynn had snuck a peak into the forbidden enclave last week and had promptly reported the findings to me, but I was smart enough not to let that bit of information slip.

"Well, I don't think we should be throwing good books away." Marilyn said, pouting.

"We're not throwing them away; we're donating them to FRC."

Letting out an exasperated sigh, she turned briefly towards the cart.

"Fine. Just make sure your new sorters don't throw any of my GOOD books away."

After she'd left the room, I peeked into the bin to see if she had actually tossed the book back when a much happier voice greeted me from the doorway.

"Hello Holly!"

Looking up I saw the smiling face of a woman dressed in an oversized plaid flannel work shirt and baggy stonewashed jeans, her graying ash blonde hair pulled back into a ponytail.

"Hello Cheryl."

"I have to tell you the sorters are doing a heck of a job!"

The creases near the corners of her gray eyes deepened further, and as always I was amazed at how she could maintain such an upbeat attitude while working in such close proximity to Marilyn.

"Thanks. How are you feeling?" I asked.

"Much better. You know, love my grand-babies to pieces, but every time they visit I end up getting sicker than a dog."

I tried to remember how many grandchildren she had but couldn't come up with an accurate number.

"How long were they here for?"

"Only three days. Hubby wants to drive up to Oregon for Christmas, but I don't know."

"You don't want to travel over the holidays?"

"No, I don't think I want to take the time away from here. Ted says my attachment to this place is a sickness."

Although she laughed heartily, I knew she was serious. Cheryl was one of those overly dedicated volunteers who seemed to need the place as much, if not more, than it needed her. I'd even heard Marilyn trying to convince her to take a couple days off once in a while to no avail.

"Well, hopefully you can get away and see them soon." I said.

Cheryl looked briefly in both directions before turning back to me, her smile replaced with a more serious expression.

"There's something I need to tell you." She said, her voice lowered to a near whisper.

Before I could respond, the back door slammed open and an all-too-familiar voice pierced the air.

"How-deeee!"

"Darn, I better get back to work." Cheryl said, quickly scooting in the direction of the mystery room.

"There you are!"

Roxy stood in the doorway and peered inside while Katrina, dressed in her usual black leather ensemble, hovered close behind.

"Let's go to my office" Roxy said, and I took a moment to retrieve my folder from the sorting table before following them with mixed emotions.

Although the meeting had been scheduled at my request to go over ideas on how to improve the bookstore, something I was looking forward to discussing, the butterflies flitting around in my stomach indicated I had other concerns. For one thing, Roxy had been adamant Katrina join us and, after our less-than-positive interchange from before, I was more than a little uncertain as to how this was all going to play out.

Down at the end of the hall, I could see Cheryl and Marilyn watching from the mystery room doorway with curious expressions. I had no doubt it wouldn't be long before the entire store heard the news about this meeting.

As I entered the drab ten-by-ten-foot windowless room, Roxy was already seated in a rolling chair in front of her pale-green metal desk with one foot resting over the thigh of the other leg and both hands locking everything in place. I remember reading this "power position" indicated a tough-minded and stubborn individual; no big surprise there.

In contrast, Katrina had perched herself up onto the edge of the desk and looked like she was trying to be one of those cool kids stuck in detention straight out of a nineteen-eighties movie.

"Better shut that." Roxy said, indicating for me to close the door.

After following orders, I spotted a folding chair leaned up against one of the battered filing cabinets and pulled it open to join them.

"BURP"

Roxy belched loudly, causing Katrina to laugh.

"That's what you get for eating an entire stack of pancakes."

"But they were DANG good." Roxy said, rubbing her stomach with a sheepish grin on her face.

I must have looked confused, so Katrina explained.

"We just ate over at the Big Buck Diner."

"OK," I said, nodding my head and opening my notebook, "so, I've put together some ideas..."

"That bacon WAS darn tasty." Roxy interrupted.

"It was extra crispy too, just the way I like it." Katrina said, giving Roxy a sly smile. "We should meet there more often."

"Sure we can, as long as the store is footin' the bill." Roxy snapped back.

Listening to their strange interchange I suddenly felt out of sorts, like I was missing some integral thread of this conversation.

"I've made a list of some changes we can make to improve the bookstore." I said, deciding to push my talking points regardless of my discomfort.

The two suddenly gave me their undivided attention.

"What's wrong with the way things are now?" Katrina asked, her eyes narrowing slightly.

58

"Well, for one thing customers are having a hard time finding books, especially in the non-fiction sections. Many of them don't have any rhyme or reason as to how they're organized" I explained.

"Volunteers won't like having to make changes." She said before looking over at Roxy.

"She's right, volunteers won't like changes." Roxy agreed, nodding her head up and down.

I had no idea which balking volunteers they might be referring to, so ignored the comment.

"These aren't big changes I'm talking about, mostly putting up some uniform signage and cleaning up a few of the shelves," I said, pausing slightly for effect. "I think it would help us sell more books."

"I like the idea of selling more books." Roxy said almost cheerfully as she began to pick at something stuck to the bottom of her boot.

Her positive response bolstered my confidence so I continued.

"I also think we should have a meeting with all the volunteers, especially in light of everything that's happened recently, and we can discuss these ideas with them."

Sometimes you have to go for broke.

"A meeting? Why do we need a meeting?" Katrina responded with voice raised.

"Woo-eee!" Roxy suddenly exclaimed, pulling a piece of an embedded nail out of the sole of her shoe and holding it up for us to see. "Looks like we better hurry up and make some money fast, I need a new pair of boots."

She jumped out of the chair and stomped her feet on the floor before plopping back down and swiveling it in my direction.

"What's going on with Gerald?"

"Gerald?" I asked, taken aback at the abrupt change of topic.

"People have been complainin'." Roxy continued after a quick glance over at Katrina, "What's your take on him Holly?"

"You mean his stacking?"

Although the habit was annoying, most of the volunteers seemed to ignore his eccentricities and I wondered who had possibly been complaining.

"He has his own agenda." Katrina piped in with palpable hostility in her voice.

"Yeah, I know." Roxy said.

"We should have gotten rid of him months ago."

Looking at Katrina, I couldn't for the life of me figure out why she would care whether or not Gerald bought books to resell.

Roxy nodded her head. "Maybe it is time to get rid of him."

They were apparently referring to something other than Gerald's stacking and book buying, though I had no idea what it could be, and I felt as if I was being forced to participate in their ongoing discussion.

"So are you going to deal with it? Katrina asked.

"He is really annoying..." Roxy muttered, looking back down at her shoes.

"That would be the best early Christmas present ever." Katrina snickered in return.

"Fine, I'll take care of it when I get back to the ranch."

Roxy suddenly stood and looked ready to leave, and Katrina hopped off the desk to open the door.

The meeting obviously concluded, I was torn as to what to do next. Although a part of me had wanted to defend Gerald, especially since we needed all the sorters we could get, Roxy and Katrina's attitude towards him had me feeling it was best to hold my tongue. There was something strange going on within that particular triangle and I wasn't sure if I wanted to learn all the details.

Folding my chair, I was about to ask when we could schedule the storewide meeting when Cheryl appeared in the doorway.

"They've escaped!" She exclaimed.

"What?" Roxy responded, sounding more annoyed than worried.

"The kittens! They've escaped and I can't find them!"

"Whaaaat kittens?!?"

"I know you said we couldn't take in animals anymore," Cheryl said, gasping for air and looking as if she was about to cry "but a man dropped them off and ..."

"No, No, NOOO!!" Roxy shrieked, her face beginning to turn a vivid red.

She abruptly pushed Cheryl aside and stomped away in the direction of the back hall.

"Have fun." Katrina said, giving me a smirk before following.

Turning back towards Cheryl, I patted her on the shoulder.

"Don't worry, I'll help you find them."

Chapter
14

HERE KITTY, KITTY

(November 18, Friday late afternoon)

H ere's number five!"

I cradled the squiggling orange tabby in my arms, feeling it's little heart pounding fast through its fragile ribcage.

"I think there were five... but I'm not a hundred per cent sure." Cheryl fretted as I handed her the tiny kitten.

Fortunately, the first three hadn't wandered far from the front desk and had been easily captured. Numbers four and five, however, had decided to chase each other down the entire length of the store, scooting under book racks into parallel aisles as soon as we got close to them. I didn't know kittens could move so fast and it had taken some major coordinated maneuvering on our part, with Cheryl clapping her hands in one aisle while I dashed around the other, to finally nab them.

During the chase, Teddy howled support from the back for his feline compatriots.

"Yeowh!!"

"Traitor!" I yelled back at him.

Searching for a possible number six, I decided to make another sweep of the store's side aisles just to be safe and my decision proved fortunate. Escapee number six had squeezed between two cardboard boxes set on the floor beneath the biographies and, if not for the end of a flicking tail, I would never have noticed.

Gently pulling the little body out I saw its sharp claws were still attached to a discarded candy wrapper.

"Hello kitty," I said, holding the gray tabby up to the light, "you are a feisty girl, aren't you?"

She was as thin and dirty as the others and as I carried her up to the front, I realized how much she looked like my own cat, Martha, at that age. For a second I played with the thought of taking her home, but quickly nixed that idea.

Up front, Cheryl had prepared a much larger cardboard box for the kittens in hopes of preventing any more escapes.

"I would have put them into the kitten cage but it's gone." She said as she carefully extracted number six's tiny claws from the sleeve of my denim shirt.

Glancing over at the wall behind the desk, I saw an obvious empty spot.

"Maybe Roxy took it." I guessed.

"I know she said not to accept animals here at the store but I couldn't say no to the guy. He found them at his shop this morning and figured we would know what to do with them."

Cheryl sighed before bending over and placing the tabby into the box next to her siblings.

Watching the six little heads bobbling around I wondered what had happened to their mother; all of them looked to be in desperate need of some nourishment and TLC.

"Can I get some help please?" Marilyn said. She was trying to push a shopping cart loaded with hardcover mysteries down the main aisle and looked to be running out of steam. Cheryl rushed over to help her and, as they approached the desk, Marilyn spotted the kittens.

"What are they doing here?" She asked.

After Cheryl explained, Marilyn gave her a scolding look.

"Really, you should know better than that. Was Roxy mad?"

"She definitely wasn't happy." I said.

"Why didn't she take them with her?" She asked, her brow furrowing into a sharp vertical line.

"I'm not sure."

It was a good question. Roxy's abrupt departure hadn't made any sense. After all, she was the animal control specialist.

"Well, we don't have time to fuss with them, we have books to shelve." Marilyn said before pulling a few books out of the cart and tottering over to the mystery section.

Cheryl, shoulders visibly slumped, gave me a pleading look.

"Can you get them something to drink?"

"Of course."

After finding a shallow plastic container in the back alcove, I filled it with water from the bathroom sink. Setting it down in the bottom of the box, I watched as the kittens cautiously approached, sniffing at the surface and sneezing as they inadvertently inhaled liquid into their nostrils. They were too young to be on their own and definitely needed some expert care.

Reaching for my phone I dialed Roxy's number.

"What should I do with the kittens?" I asked when she answered, not even trying to hide the agitation in my voice.

"Holly! Dang it! I told everyone NOT to take in animals at the store!"

"Yes, I know, but what should I do with them NOW?"

There was a moment of silence before she responded.

"Can't take 'em here at the ranch."

I couldn't comprehend what I was hearing. When did BARF stop rescuing cats?

Before I could ask any questions, Roxy rattled off the name and number of a kitten rescue group down in the valley. Searching on the desk for a piece of paper and something to write with, I noticed Cheryl and Marilyn intently watching me from the mystery section.

"Tell them I'll pay for any vet fees, but make it DANG clear to Cheryl this WAS NOT OK!!"

Roxy's voice echoed out of my phone's speaker and I was pretty sure everyone in the vicinity could hear, especially since Cheryl looked like she was ready to cry again. Marilyn merely shook her head and turned back to shelving books.

After I hung up, I texted Sarra. We'd planned on catching an afternoon movie with Lynn but I was pretty sure I'd miss it now that I had to deliver kittens. She responded within minutes, suggesting we meet at the Belgian instead and for me to text her when I was heading back up the hill. That's what I call a good friend.

"Holly?" A tentative voice asked.

Turning, I saw Cheryl kneeling next to the kitten's box.

"Do you know why we aren't getting cats here at the store anymore? Is Roxy keeping them at the Secret Ranch?"

"I don't know." I said.

Up until now, I hadn't paid much attention to the property recently purchased by BARF that everyone was calling the 'Secret Ranch'. Roxy had apparently moved onto the property to take care of any rescued animals and had said they needed to be kept hidden, even from the volunteers, until their court cases were resolved. There was a poster with photos of all those ready for adoption propped up on an easel near the sales area but, after examining it more closely, I couldn't see any felines listed.

"At least we still have Teddy." Cheryl said, slowly getting to her feet.

"That's true. Well, I better get these little guys going."

I removed the water dish and handed it to her before lifting the box, balancing it in my arms as the kitten's weight shifted.

"Goodbye kitties," she called out as I carried them towards the back, "goodbye!"

SECRET RANCH

(November 18, Friday evening)

L ynn waved as I made my way down the ramp.

"There you are!"

She was seated opposite Sarra at the corner table and both were already working on their respective glasses of cider. Although the front of the Belgian was filled with patrons enthusiastically watching some game or other up on the flat screen above the bar, the back room was relatively empty.

"I better go wash up first."

I shrugged out of my coat and slung it over the chair next to Sarra's.

"Did you order something to eat?" she asked.

"Not yet, you?"

Sarra nodded her head while Lynn grinned and wiggled in her chair with obvious delight.

"Firehouse Special, on its way!"

Laughing, I headed towards the bathroom. After cleaning up, I ordered a chicken pesto panini at the bar and returned to the table with my own glass of liquid gold.

"What a day," I said, plopping down into my seat. "thanks for changing plans at the last minute."

Sarra smiled. "Of course."

"The movie can wait for another time." Lynn said.

As I took a sip of my cider, the entire pub seemed to hush as if on cue, with the only sound the metronomic squeaking of the overhead fans. Beyond the louvered windows the sky had begun to darken and a fine haze of cooling air was beginning to settle around the cars parked in the side lot. The warmth inside the pub combined with the cool drink was sedative and, taking a deep breath, I could feel myself approach a much calmer state.

"CLANG"

A dish suddenly clattered against the kitchen floor, followed by pots and pans rattling as if in response. Up front, someone whooped loudly which was immediately echoed by more intense yelling and cheering.

The pub had come back to life.

"Is Nate still in Connecticut?" Sarra asked, breaking the silence at our own table.

"Yes, but he's flying home tomorrow." I said.

For some reason I had been missing him more than usual during this particular work trip, and her inquiry made me double check my phone for any possible messages.

"So what was up with the kittens?" Lynn asked.

"Yes, and how did it go with Roxy?" Sarra added.

The two listened intently as I filled them in on the details of both the meeting and the kitten adventure, swearing them to secrecy concerning the expected news of Gerald's soon-to-be firing.

Halfway through my storytelling our food arrived via a young woman with violet hair and extremely short cut-offs. As she walked away, I noticed a Hello Kitty tattoo on the back of one of her calves which made me think of the little gray tabby.

"If Gerald is getting the axe, I'd better watch my step." Lynn said with a giggle. "I've already been labeled a trouble maker by Katrina."

"Oh?" I asked, cringing slightly as she extracted a jalapeño from her sandwich and took a bite.

"This one here decided to clean up the cashier area during our shift on Monday." Sarra explained, nodding at Lynn.

"What's wrong with that?"

"Evelyn told me Katrina threw a hissy fit when she saw it."

"I just organized a little." Lynn continued to smile.

"That's ridiculous," I said, "she should have been grateful, the place was a total mess."

"That's what I thought, but now I'm a trouble maker."

Lynn began to reach across the table for our uneaten tortilla chips and Sarra pushed her own plate towards the center for easier access. The sincerity of the gesture made me think of the strange way Katrina and Roxy had interacted; their relationship seemed forced and more 'fake' than 'friendly'.

Picking up my own sandwich, I glanced out the side window again and noticed the street lamps had turned on, their bulbs burning an eerie glow through the gathering mist. Across the street I could barely make out the white rocking horse prominently featured in the display window of the antique shop. For some reason it made me think of the ringtone I had heard on Roxy's phone.

"Why didn't Roxy take the kittens?" Sarra asked, surprising me with her well timed question.

"I don't know. The woman who runs the rescue facility where I dropped them off told me BARF hasn't been taking cats in for some time now and their place is swamped because of it. She only agreed to take in the ones today because Roxy promised to pay the vet fees."

Sarra didn't look happy at this bit of news.

"Along with a dog and a horse, the BARF logo has a cat on it which implies we help them too. If that's not the case anymore, people should be told." She said.

"On Monday a couple of customers put money into the donation box and said it was for the kitties. Now I feel bad." Lynn added, looking equally disturbed.

I knew the clear plastic container she was referring to; it was shaped like a dog house and sat on the edge of the desk, and it wasn't uncommon to see it filled to the peak of the roof with bills. Sarra was right in that if BARF was no longer rescuing cats, the volunteers and customers needed to be informed.

Lynn grabbed the last chip from Sarra's plate and leaned back in her chair.

"Speaking of money, I have to say the way the bookstore handles it is definitely iffy."

"You mean stuffing money into baggies isn't professional enough for you?" Sarra said with a chuckle while Lynn dramatically rolled her eyes.

Since I'd never cashiered at the store, I asked them about the procedure and Sarra explained;

"The closing cashiers add up the total sales of the day and just write the amount on a yellow sticky note. Fifty dollars stays in the cash box for the next day and the rest goes into a zip lock bag we put into the safe in Roxy's office..."

"And hopefully the cash in the bag equals the total ledger sales of the day." Lynn interrupted.

"I didn't know there was a safe in Roxy's office. Does everyone know the combination?" I asked.

"No, it has a drop slot," Lynn said, "Supposedly, a bookkeeper picks up the baggies once a week and makes photo copies of the ledger to check if everything balances before depositing the cash into the bank."

"Supposedly is right." Sarra interjected, emphasizing the word. "Evelyn told me she's seen Roxy leaving the store with baggies of cash, so not sure what that's all about."

Her eyebrows raised to indicate she thought this was a questionable activity.

Lynn frowned at this bit of news. "If we have a bookkeeper, the president of this non-profit really shouldn't be handling the money."

"Well, it sure didn't seem Kosher to me. Maybe we should ask her about that at the meeting, along with why she isn't taking cats anymore." Sarra said, turning to give me an expectant look.

"I don't know..." I said.

Although Sarra's questions were reasonable, for some reason I had this growing sense of trepidation that tackling everything head-on at the first ever volunteer meeting wasn't the best approach.

Sarra suddenly gasped.

"I wonder if Evelyn knows the address for the ranch." She reached for her bag and pulled out her phone.

"Oh, if she does, we could drive down there and check it out tonight." Lynn responded eagerly.

"I don't know," I repeated, glancing out the window into the looming darkness, "it's already dark and looks pretty foggy."

Sarra ignored me and kept tapping on her phone.

"She thinks it's somewhere on Gold Road."

"I can drive!"

Lynn stood up and reached for her jacket, car keys jingling somewhere in the depths of her pockets.

"There's no way we'll be able to see anything." I argued without success.

"I'm game." Sarra said, standing as well.

Succumbing to the physical momentum of getting vertical, I followed suit. From experience I knew there was no use arguing with Sarra once she made her mind up about something, and Lynn seemed just as stubborn if not more so. Besides, I had to admit I was more than a little curious to sneak a peek at the infamous ranch.

"You OK to drive?" I asked Lynn.

"Hundred percent" she responded with her signature giggle.

Waving farewell to the bartender, we approached the front door just as a man in a black leather jacket pulled it open. A blast of cold air ruffled my hair as he quickly stepped to one side to let us pass and I suddenly realized it was Sean, the young sheriff who had questioned me at the bookstore. He smiled in recognition but before either of us could respond in greeting, the distinctive shrill of a car alarm suddenly pierced the air. It was coming from the pub's side lot where all three of us had parked.

Bolting out the door, Sean headed in that direction while the three of us followed, though not as swiftly.

"Hey, you there!"

Sean shouted at a blurry form dashing out of the parking lot. The lack of light and mist had washed the color from everything, and it wasn't until I got closer to the car making all the noise that I realized it was green.

Teal green, to be exact.

"Everything OK?" I cried out, tearing into my purse in search of keys while my car's emergency lights pulsated bright orange flashes across the blacktop.

"Stay put." Sean told us before sprinting across the street.

Keys found, I pushed the alarm button and my car chirped happily silent. As the three of us huddled by the back bumper, we watched Sean inspect the entry to the alleyway directly behind the antique store. After a few minutes, he returned and checked my car windows. Thankfully, everything looked in order.

"Must have been someone looking for something easy to steal." He said, his breath vaporizing in what was now turning out to be a very chilly evening. Glancing over at Sarra and Lynn, I noticed both were shivering.

"We better call it a night." I told them.

All things considered, our reconnaissance mission no longer seemed such a good idea and my cohorts readily agreed to abort without hesitation. After thanking Sean for his help, we quickly dispersed into our respective vehicles and I saw his tall form disappear into the brightly lit pub through my rear view mirror.

*   *   *

On the drive home, I debated whether or not to tell Nate what had happened. He'd been worried enough about the stranger watching me the morning I'd found Pat's body, and as far as I could tell, this was even more of a trivial incident. Cruising up the interstate, I turned the heat to maximum and patted the dashboard of my little car, thankful for happy endings.

Barrcling along in the darkness, a faster moving semi-truck overtook me and passed on the right. As the blur of its running lights streaked past, I glanced over to see something silhouetted on the passenger side window that made me gasp; it was a large handprint.

Securely parked behind a closed garage door, I grabbed the flashlight hanging near the workbench and inspected the print. It looked to have been created by force; fingers splayed and planted directly in the middle of the window, as if the person had intended to shatter the glass.

Hopefully Sean was right and this was merely the handiwork of some would-be thief, but even after I was safely tucked behind a locked door, a persistent tingling at the nape of my neck continued. There had been something familiar about that running shape and I couldn't shake the feeling that the handprint was more malicious than random.

In an attempt to defuse my tension, I changed into PJ's and made myself a strong cup of chamomile tea. Sitting down on the family room couch, I was quickly joined by Martha, my brown tabby cat. She tucked herself into a warm purring ball at my side and was the perfect accomplice as I phoned Nate and fibbed that everything was just 'fine' at home.

"Love you, see you tomorrow." I told him before hanging up.

Opening my laptop to peruse the news, the distinctive sound of an incoming email chimed through the computer's speaker. It was a message from Roxy, addressed to all of the store's volunteers, stating Gerald was no longer a volunteer at the store. With her usual bluntness, she informed us that we should respect her decision and 'move on'.

Move on.

Closing my laptop, I wondered how the volunteers were going to react to losing another of their own.

Chapter

16

STUFFING

(November 22, Tuesday)

O ver the weekend a massive snowstorm hit the Sierra Nevada range and the interstate was packed with holiday skiers heading east into the mountains. The colder temperatures also brought more customers into the bookstore, though many seemed to forgo purchasing in order to linger as long as possible in a warm, clean, well-lighted place.

Since Gerald's dismissal, I had been going to the store almost daily either to sort or help the twins organize the children's section. The up side was the interaction with the customers, something I'd never experienced coming in only after hours, and I found myself enjoying answering their myriad of questions. Unfortunately, the down side was I garnered the full brunt of the other volunteers' frustration over losing Gerald.

Cheryl had been the first to approach me.

"I really like you and hope you didn't have anything to do with this." She said, eyes rimmed red from crying.

"This was Roxy's decision; I don't have that kind of authority." I had told her, admitting the timing did look suspicious and not entirely in my favor.

"I hope I'm not next, especially taking in the kittens and all. I couldn't bear the thought of not working here."

Marilyn, on the other hand, didn't seem at all concerned about the dismissal.

"Stop fussing, we have books to shelve." She had told Cheryl before taking the opportunity to complain to me about the poor stacking job one of 'my sorters' had done with 'her hardcovers'.

Since Katrina had roped me into filling Gerald's cashiering spots until she could find a replacement, Evelyn was more than happy to teach me during her Monday shift. Although she didn't comment on his dismissal, she did inform me he had left a message on her answering machine over the weekend.

"He left it Sunday morning, but I was at church all day so didn't see it until that evening. It was quite rambling, something about planning to lodge a formal complaint with BARF's board members, but I don't pay heed to gossip so deleted it. Besides, from what I've heard, that would be a complete waste of time..."

"What do you mean?" I had asked.

"They're a bunch of puppets. The gentleman who did the drop before Katrina tried to contact them and they never even bothered to respond."

I had wanted to question her further but never got the chance as a steady stream of customers kept me well occupied.

This morning, while sorting books with Sarra, I'd been cornered near the cat enclosures by both Peg and Daphne.

"Please, won't you change your mind?" Peg begged as Teddy wailed in the background.

It was Roxy's decision." I repeated, my words beginning to sound like a broken record.

"The vibe in here is very negative, maybe we should cleanse the building. I think I have some sage we can burn." Daphne said, rummaging in the depths of her pink backpack. After making sure she understood burning anything inside a bookstore was a really bad idea, I escaped back to the sorting room.

"You OK?" Sarra asked.

"No, not really."

To be honest, I hadn't thought taking over for Pat was going to be this hard. The rumblings of the volunteers were beginning to make me question my own involvement with Gerald's firing, and I wasn't sure I liked the change of status from co-worker to dumping ground; maybe I wasn't managerial material after all.

"Do you think most of the volunteers will come tonight?" Sarra asked, interrupting my spiral of self-pity.

"I hope so, it will be good to get everyone together."

Since Thursday was Thanksgiving Day and the store was set to be closed, Katrina had originally planned the meeting for Wednesday evening. However, after most of the volunteers had complained about either visiting family or being out of town, she had reluctantly rescheduled it for tonight at 6 pm.

"Katrina's email sure was a piece of work." Sarra said, wrinkling her nose as she threw a book with a torn cover into one of the FRC carts.

"That it was." I agreed.

"How can you tell volunteers a meeting is mandatory? Isn't that technically impossible?"

"Probably." I laughed.

"Believe me, it was hard not to respond with something snarky, but I want to be there to support you AND ask Roxy about the cats."

"It will be interesting to hear what she has to say."

Though I wasn't sure how Roxy would react at being prodded, I had made the conscious decision not to interfere and let things go the way they were meant to flow.

"Looks like it's time for cider." Sarra said, glancing up at the old school clock hanging above the doorway. Someone had donated the relic and although it had a tendency to run ten minutes late, most of us had learned to adjust accordingly.

Grabbing our coats and purses, we headed out the back and drove together to the Belgian to catch up with Nate and Lynn before the meeting since, as Nate put it, "I'm going to need a drink before having to deal with Roxy." By the time we arrived, both were already seated along the front window and looked to be deep in conversation.

I gave Nate a kiss on the cheek before motioning to the three drinks lined up on the counter in front of him.

"Is one of those for me?"

"Yep, and the other is for Sarra." He said, smiling as I sat down next to him.

Looking over at Lynn, I noticed she seemed even more animated than usual.

"You two getting on OK?" I asked.

"Just enjoying your hubby's company." She responded with a giggle.

Nate laughed. "Lynn wanted me to recommend some books to read, but she says she doesn't like science fiction or fantasy."

"I told her she should read Harry Potter." Sarra said.

"You've never read Harry Potter?" I asked Lynn who shook her head.

"It's a very popular young adult fantasy." Nate told her.

After discussing some of our favorite books and movies for a bit, we switched gears to discuss the impending meeting.

"Did you bring your notes?" Sarra asked me.

"Yes, but I'm planning on keeping it simple. Mostly I'm hoping to get everyone to agree on organizing the nonfiction and putting up uniform signs."

"It's probably best to only make a few changes at a time." Nate said, agreeing with my cautious approach. "Though I do want to see about installing a motion-activated light out back, and possibly getting some more flashlights. With it getting dark so early, we have to think about people's safety." He raised an eyebrow and gave me a determined look, and I could tell he was referring to lurking strangers.

"Sounds like a plan." I said, lifting my glass.

After finishing our rounds, the four of us returned to the bookstore with half an hour to spare before the meeting. While Sarra and Lynn busied themselves with sorting, Nate and I carried a couple of our genre boxes out front to shelve and the gregarious retired couple who worked the afternoon shift were delighted to see us. Frank knew Nate from having sung with him in a local men's chorus and while the two of them dove into a technical discussion about some new science fiction author, June and I talked turkey.

"Is your bird thawed and ready for the big day?" She asked, following me over to the cookbook section to watch me work.

"Yep. I only bought a small one since it's just going to be the three of us."

With a heart-shaped face framed by faded strawberry blonde curls, June's appearance was as appealing as her personality and her perfume reminded me of freshly baked sugar cookies. From past conversations I had learned her greatest joy was hosting gatherings for her extensive family.

"Small birds are always tastier; don't you think? When is your son coming home?"

"He's planning on driving down tomorrow. How about you, did you get another big bird this year?"

"Of course, Frank always has to pick the largest one he can find. This year it's a twenty-six pounder."

"That's huge!" exclaimed an elderly female customer who had been browsing the nearby gardening section.

"We've got the whole tribe coming, so it needed to be big." June explained, her face beaming with obvious pride. She and Frank had raised five children, if I remembered correctly, and all of them seemed to have as many if not more kids of their own.

"I've never attempted one that big, doesn't it take a long time to cook?" The woman asked. She had come closer to be a part of the conversation and I recognized her as one of our regulars who came in several times a week.

"If you don't stuff it, only about five hours." June responded cheerfully, happy to discuss the wonders of holiday cooking.

While the two continued chatting about seasoning and the correct placement of oven racks, I worked my way through my box of books. Among the usual fare of outdated celebrity and fab diet hardcovers, I happily discovered a spiral bound community cookbook, always intriguing for those of us who enjoy good recipes. This gem was self-published in 1954 by a women's church group from Georgia, and as I leafed through the pages I came across one that was both dog-eared and covered in stains.

"Aunt Irma's Sweet Potato Pie," I said, reading the recipe's title out loud, "I've never made one of those."

June moved closer so I handed her the booklet.

"Oh, it's quite yummy. We used to make them all the time when I was a girl." She said, turning the pages to look at some of the other recipes.

Suddenly, she gasped.

"Oh my, cornbread stuffing, just like the one my gran used to make."

The customer had also moved closer to read the recipe alongside June.

"I've never had cornbread stuffing, is it good?" she asked.

"It's sublime!" June exclaimed.

"If you want that book, you better buy it before 'you know who' does." I said, looking around to make sure a distinctive tie-dye shirt wasn't in the vicinity. The wearer had the annoying habit of coming in right before closing and since she regularly purchased prodigious quantities of books, most of the cashiers silently endured waiting for her to finish shopping before locking up.

"Cookbook Kathy" June whispered, her eyes widening.

The nickname was one Evelyn had chosen since Kathy had a penchant for spotting newly shelved cookbooks, especially the community ones, which she snatched the minute I put them on the shelves. No one knew exactly what she did with all the books she purchased, though rumor had it she stored them all in her garage.

"Who's Cookbook Kathy?" The customer asked.

"Did I hear my name?" a distinctive drawl more sour than sweet called out from the end of the row, making me simultaneously jump and cringe. Even though her girth took up a large portion of the aisle, Kathy could move as stealthily as a field mouse.

"Oh!" Both June and the customer said in unison as the vivid mass approached.

"What do you have there?" Kathy asked, her voice dripping with honey while she reached towards the booklet with chubby fingers.

June clutched it tightly against her chest and dashed behind me while the customer skedaddled over to an adjoining aisle.

"Whoa!" Kathy cried out, raising both flabby arms high above her frizz of teased yellow hair in an exaggerated move. The momentum spun her slightly sideways and for a moment she looked like an inverted pyramid ready to topple over.

'Volunteers killed by falling customer' wasn't something I wanted to personally experience so I backed up a couple feet taking June with me in the process.

Kathy dramatically held a hand to her chest and leaned against the shelving, exhaling exaggerated puffs of air while locking her dark beady eyes on the booklet.

"Are ya'll going to buy that or not?"

"Yes, we are." I said, turning towards June with raised eyebrows and widened eyes. Fortunately, she instantly understood my silent facial message.

"I'll go buy it right now." She said, quickly fleeing the scene.

Although Kathy was giving me a chilling stare, I cut her off at the pass.

"We have a meeting tonight and will be closing exactly at six." I told her, having no patience for someone who could be so demanding and rude, especially toward our sweet volunteers.

Her demeanor shifted dramatically at the news.

"A meeting? Is it about Gerald getting fired? I heard he got fired. Oh, I won't be a bother at all, ya'll won't even know I'm here!"

She seemed quite exuberant at the prospect of being a fly on the wall.

"Sorry Kathy, we're closing in a few minutes and you'll need to leave."

I picked up the empty sorting box and walked away before she could get in a word edgewise.

* * *

At six on the nose, I escorted a sour-faced Kathy out the front door and locked up. Outside, the sun had disappeared behind the horizon but I could still make out an approaching thick wall of black clouds high above the shopping center's parking lot. It looked like more snow was coming to the mountains. Spotting a group of volunteers making their way towards the store, I unlocked the door and waited for them. Roxy had given me Pat's old key and, looking at it now, I wondered what she would have thought of my attempts to improve the place; I hoped to do her proud.

While Nate and Sarra carried folding chairs up from the back, Lynn set them up in a semi-circle around the desk. Someone must have brought in some coffee as the rich aroma filled the air, and Daphne was walking around with a plate of home-baked cookies. Even with the attempt at hominess, I could still sense tension in the crowd.

At twenty past six, I counted a total of sixteen bookstore volunteers gathered around the front of the store either munching on cookies or sipping coffee. Most I knew at this point by first name, but one was unfamiliar. When I asked Evelyn, she told me her name was Zina, and I recognized the name as the volunteer responsible for shelving the Politics and Business sections.

All of us, however, were waiting for Roxy.

"She should be here any minute." Katrina said for the third time, staring down at her phone. Sitting on the edge of one of the fold-up chairs and tapping the heels of her black leather boot ferociously against the hard floor, she looked like someone truly wishing they could be anywhere else.

Glancing over at Nate, who was leaning up against the end cap of one of the mystery rows, I could tell he was getting irritated. Lynn was seated next to Sarra and when she caught my gaze made a silly face that almost caused me to laugh out loud.

"Should we start without her?" Daphne asked hesitantly.

"No!" Katrina snapped, her harsh tone making Cheryl, who was sitting next to her, cringe.

"I can't wait around forever, I've got plans." Evelyn piped in. She was a vision in powder-gray wool this evening with dark purple boots that looked like suede.

"How-deee!"

An all-too-familiar voice projected itself down the main aisle, causing some of the volunteers to gasp.

Roxy approached from the back at a fast clip and came to a breathless halt by the empty chair next to Katrina.

"Dang horses, got out right as I was leavin'!"

She began to slap at the front of her dirt streaked pants causing a cloud of dust to explode outwards. Even from six feet away I could tell she reeked of 'Eau de horse'.

"We need to get this thing going." Katrina said, giving her a disgusted look.

Roxy sat down and began to rub the palms of her hands together, causing a tiny cascade of dried mud to scatter onto the floor.

"Okie dokie. Holly, why don't you start!"

The gesture seemed to anger Katrina and she exhaled loudly before crossing her arms. Glancing over towards Nate for mental support, I saw he was sporting a priceless 'what the hell?' look.

"Sounds good." I said, opening my binder.

Evelyn suddenly let out a cry, causing all of us to simultaneously look in her direction.

"Oh my Lord!" She said, staring at her phone.

"Gerald's been murdered!"

LISTEN HERE

(November 22, Tuesday)

A lthough the plastic umbrella was working better than the salad bowl, it was also more obtrusive. With night fallen, if he could continue avoiding the circles of light from the lamp posts, hopefully no one would notice. Moving stealthily through the parking lot until he was directly across from the bookstore, he hunched down between two stopping blocks separating a pair of nose-to-nose parked cars and carefully positioned the paint roller handle with one hand while tapping the ear piece with the other. Systems were a 'go'.

He was proud of his homemade parabolic microphone. It had taken some initial trial and error to figure out, but nothing a little bartering and a walk to the dollar store hadn't solved. The design was simple but effective, and his only regret was not having his partner beside him to share in the thrill of putting it to use; working alone would never feel right.

Moving slightly to the left, he found he gained a clearer view of the store's front windows but a row of paper signs covering the lower half prevented him from seeing much of anything inside. Regardless, he was picking up voices. Perfect. He took out his notepad in anticipation.

He hadn't planned on using his microphone tonight, especially since he hadn't tested it yet, but when he'd spotted his primary suspect reappearing at the store and remaining with others after six o'clock, he knew something was afoot.

A sudden increase in volume of the incoming dialogue made him jump and drop his mechanical pencil. It bounced out of sight, rolling beneath the chassis of the car to his left.

Rats.

In order to reach it he needed to put down the microphone and lie on his side against the cold ground. By the time he got re-situated, a couple of women were exiting the bookstore; one of them looked like a cop.

He watched the two walk briskly down the sidewalk a few yards before coming to a stop near a massive pickup truck. Deciding to move closer, he quickly jotted down the plate number before repositioning his contraption to try and catch their conversation. It took a little bit of maneuvering to keep the microphone pointed in the right direction while still taking notes, but he was successful.

They were arguing with raised voices. This was good stuff, he thought, catching a few phrases; the cop even mentioned his prime suspect by name.

The shorter woman abruptly turned and hopped into the vehicle. When she backed out of the parking lot and zoomed away, tires squealing against blacktop, he realized he hadn't thought to turn down his mic and his ears rang from the amplified sound. It hurt.

Looking back at the store he saw more people streaming out of the front door, some of them coming in his direction.

!!!!Abort mission, abort mission!!!

He pocketed his notepad and made a run for it.

SNICKERDOODLES

(November 22, Tuesday evening)

There were only six of us left.

Needless to say, the meeting had abruptly ended with most of the volunteers using the tragic news of Gerald's death as a perfect excuse for a hasty exit. With all the rushing about, jumbles of anxious conversations, and quick refolding of chairs, I wasn't even aware of how many of them had bailed. The bookstore suddenly felt cold and cavernous.

"Do you want to take the rest of the snickerdoodles home?" Daphne asked Nate, holding out the paper plate with the remainder of what I knew were his favorite type of cookies.

"I'd love to." He responded without hesitation, reaching for the plate while trying to balance an armful of chairs in one arm. His attempt was less than successful and several crashed to the floor.

"Here, let me help." Lynn said, taking the plate away from him and setting it on the glass counter.

While the two of them carried the rest of the chairs to the back, Sarra and I kept Evelyn company.

"I should have returned his call." She said, still holding her phone and looking visibly shaken.

"That's crazy, how could you have known something like this was going to happen." Sarra told her.

"Who was it that texted you?" I asked.

"My daughter."

"Oh my gosh, was she the one who found him?"

Evelyn shivered slightly, but shook her head.

"No, thank heavens."

"How did she find out?"

"I don't ask. People tell her things."

The typical six degrees of separation didn't apply to Evelyn; her vast network of acquaintances seemed to trend much less than five intermediaries. Apparently, this trait didn't end with her.

"Any idea what happened?" Nate asked, his deep voice resonating within the sales area. He and Lynn had returned from the back to join us, while Daphne hovered nearby.

"They found him lying in front of his opened storage unit with what looked like a blow to the head." Evelyn said, reading what I presumed was the latest incoming text from her daughter; the depth of information at their disposal truly amazing. "Since there were books strewn everywhere they think it might have been a robbery gone bad."

"Books?" I asked.

"Yes, his unit was full of them."

"Why would anyone want to steal books?" Lynn wanted to know.

"You'd be surprised what some are worth," Daphne piped in, "especially first editions."

"Poor guy." I said, trying not to imagine another dead body lying on the ground surrounded by books. This scenario was becoming something of a pattern and the thought made me more than a little queasy.

"That's it for me, I need to go home." Evelyn said, sliding her phone into the chic leather clutch she held before snapping the clasp shut.

She placed a perfectly manicured hand on Nate's shoulder and smiled up at him.

"Would you kindly walk me to my car?"

"Of course." He said, and I quickly tossed him my key.

"Me too!" Daphne called out and scrambled behind the desk for her backpack. Pulling out a purple knit cap with a gigantic pom-pom on top, she yanked it down over her ears before following Nate and Evelyn out the door.

After they'd left, Sarra let out a whistle. "Never a dull moment in this place."

"No kidding." Lynn agreed, hopping up onto the edge of the desk and letting her legs swing.

"This is beyond crazy," I said, "first Pat and now Gerald."

Sarra frowned. "Hopefully, that old saying doesn't apply."

"Which one is that?" Lynn asked.

"You know – bad luck comes in threes."

A moment of silence descended as we processed the possibilities. At the far end of the mystery hardcover section, one of fluorescent light fixtures began to flicker. After a few sputters, the tubes gave off an eerie orange glow before dying, plunging the entire area into darkness.

"OK, that was weird." I said, wondering if this was some sort of sign.

Sarra shuddered and overlapped the front edges of her fluffy white cardigan together, wrapping her arms across the layers.

"Maybe Daphne is right about there being bad mojo in this place."

Without warning, a sudden icy draft chilled the nape of my neck.

"I'm back." Nate called out as he relocked the front door.

"We can tell." Lynn quipped in return.

His smile dissolved as he approached the desk. "Why is it so dark in here?"

"We decided to have a séance." Sarra replied with a straight face.

"Did you bring your crystal ball?" He responded without skipping a beat.

Noticing my unease, he moved closer and instinctively put his hand on the small of my back for reassurance; the gesture worked.

"One of the lamps must have died." Lynn told him, pointing in the direction of the failed fluorescent.

"I'm not surprised. Most of them probably need replacing." He tipped his head back to look up at the ceiling which made everyone else do the same, and I could almost hear his engineering brain at work calculating specifics of model numbers and exact quantities needed.

"Maybe a séance would be a good idea," I said, "we could ask Pat what happened to Gerald."

My comment brought everyone's attention back to floor level.

"Do you think it was more than a robbery gone bad?" Sarra asked.

"I don't know, but you have to admit it's a bit suspicious…. First Pat, and now this."

"Hey, if you count the guy killed behind Rudy's, that would make three." Lynn interrupted.

"If you're counting murders, that's only two" Nate interjected.

"Fine, if you have to be technical." She volleyed back.

Although Nate was correct in that Pat's heart attack had been an accident, Lynn had a point. So far there had been a total of three deaths within a short period of time in the small universe of our used bookstore.

"Roxy and Katrina sure skedaddled out of here fast. So much for giving a flying fig about the welfare of your volunteers." Sarra commented.

She wasn't the only one to notice their quick departure. It made me wonder if they felt at all guilty over having fired Gerald, or if they were just bored.

Bored? - Board?

"Evelyn said Gerald wanted to lodge a formal complaint with BARF's board. I wonder if it was about being fired or something else." I said, racking my brain for any obvious clues I may have missed during the brief times I'd interacted with him. Unfortunately, there wasn't much to grasp onto as mostly I'd worked hard to avoid him.

"Maybe he figured out what Roxy is really doing down at the 'Secret Ranch'." Sarra said, moving her index fingers to indicate single quotations around the name.

"What do you think she's doing there?" Nate asked, giving me a quizzical look.

"We're not sure." I said, "Just curious, especially since we found out she's not rescuing cats anymore."

"That and the fact she acts like she's on drugs AND has been taking baggies of money out of the store." Sarra added with a snort.

"She's always acted like she's on drugs," Nate laughed, playing devil's advocate as he often did, "and she could just be making the deposits."

I knew it would take real tangible evidence to convince his logical brain that anything out of the ordinary was going on, one of the reasons I hadn't yet told him of our suspicions.

Sarra and Lynn exchanged a brief sideways glance and I wished I could have asked them what they were really thinking.

"Well, not that this hasn't been fun and all, but I'd better get a move on." Lynn suddenly said, hopping down from the desk with a thud.

"Me too." Sarra said, retrieving her purse.

The four of us left the store together, exiting out the back door with Nate taking up the rear to turn off the lights. Once Sarra and Lynn were safely tucked away inside their respective vehicles, he gave me a quick kiss.

"See you at home." He said, watching me climb into my car before hopping into his truck.

On the drive up the interstate, with Nate's headlights diligently reflected in my rear-view mirror, my mind began to wander with a bizarre swirl of images; from running kittens and Pat's smiling face, to hand prints on my car window and Gerald's strange sorting piles. I wondered if these metaphors had a deeper meaning; offering some key I should recognize, but for now the jumbled pieces seemed too isolated and impossible to connect.

After parking in the garage, I waited for Nate to pull his truck into its normal resting spot out on the driveway. As he strode inside, I pushed the button to close the rolling door.

"Damn it!" He cried out.

"What's wrong?" I asked, terrified I'd somehow hit him.

"I forgot my snickerdoodles!"

SEA SALT

(November 23, Wednesday)

B aking always puts me in a good mood.

Humming to myself, I began to work on creating a salted caramel apple pie; a time consuming process and my family's favorite Thanksgiving dessert.

After preparing the dough for the crust and putting it in the refrigerator to chill, I began to gather the ingredients for the salted caramel sauce.

"Have you seen the sea salt?" I asked Nate, who was seated at the kitchen counter opposite me staring at his phone while working on a second cup of coffee.

"Huh?" he responded, without bothering to look up.

"I'm sorry, did I interrupt you?"

"Nope, just playing a silly game."

"Have you seen the sea salt?"

"It's not in the spice cupboard?"

"No, I've looked on every shelf and it's not there."

"Sorry." He said, still focused on his screen.

"Well, that's just great."

I slammed the cupboard door a bit harder than necessary which finally made him look up, eyebrows raised.

"Can't you use regular salt?" he asked.

"No, it needs to be sea salt," I snapped, folding my arms across my chest, "or the caramel won't taste right."

So much for my cheerful disposition.

"I'd go to the store for you but I'm waiting for a call from Louisiana."

He got up from the counter and came around to where I was standing. As he wrapped his arms around me I initially kept mine tucked against my chest, but once his warm hands touched my back I quickly released them to reciprocate the hug. Nuzzling slightly into the spot below his left ear, I could feel the wisps of hair at the nape of his neck, still damp from his morning shower. As usual, his embrace worked like a charm to calm my frustration.

"Why don't you make a regular apple pie?" He murmured before letting go and reaching across the countertop for his empty cup.

"Because, I already promised Philip I was making the salted caramel." Sighing, I took off my apron and laid it on the counter. "Guess I'll have to run to the store myself."

"Sorry."

I watched him drop another pod into the coffee machine before pressing the blinking blue brew light. As a jet of hot coffee streamed down into his cup, a few brown droplets splashed onto the surrounding tiles in the process. No doubt aware of my gaze, he quickly wiped them away with his fingertips.

"Anything else you can think of we need while I'm down in Autumn?" I asked, knowing the small market in Mountain Terrace wouldn't have anything exotic as sea salt which meant I would have to make the twenty-minute drive.

He surprised me by responding with something other than the typical 'no thanks' response.

"The library has that book I wanted on hold. If you want to swing by and pick it up, that would be great."

His request would mean a longer side trip, but I agreed.

After retrieving his coffee and kissing me on the cheek, he wound his way through the family room towards the back door.

"Hey, maybe you could pick up my snickerdoodles too!" He called back to me before sliding the glass door open.

"Don't push your luck!" I told him.

He laughed and shut the door, slowly descending the wooden stairs which led off the deck to his basement office while coffee steam drifted diagonally behind him.

"Meo-owrh."

Martha knew the sound of the coffee machine meant cream was nearby. After pouring some into her bowl, I double checked the recipes I planned on using for tomorrow's feast against the kitchen's inventory. Although it looked like sea salt was the only missing item, it was important enough to make the trip worthwhile. That, and the book Nate had been patiently waiting to read. It might have seemed silly going to a library when we both volunteered at a used bookstore, but for specific books at no cost, the library was hard to beat.

It didn't take long for me to slip into some shoes, grab a jacket and head out the door. Although a few inches of snow had fallen overnight, the roads were relatively clear and I was relieved to see only a trickle of traffic heading up the interstate's east bound lanes. This would change dramatically by early afternoon as the mass exodus of city travelers descended upon the last portion of their mountain journey, but I planned on being home well before then.

The sky above me was stacked with layers of ominous dark gray clouds. According to the weather report I'd listened to that morning, the worst of this latest snowstorm was mostly shifting north. Snow flurries were possible over the pass and this had me slightly concerned for Philip who planned on driving across it later today. Although he was a capable enough driver with a vehicle well equipped for winter conditions, it was all the other people on the road that had me worried; especially the neophyte flat landers who thought having a four-wheel drive made them immune to the laws of physics.

*   *   *

After purchasing sea salt and a few other random items at the grocery store, including some hard cider that happened to be on sale, I sat back in my car and checked my phone. It was only 9:30 and the library didn't open until ten. Mulling over options on how to spend the extra time, I thought about calling the girls and seeing if they wanted to meet somewhere for coffee. I knew Sarra had invited Lynn over to her house for Thanksgiving dinner tomorrow, but wasn't sure what either of them was doing today.

No, probably a bad idea. I needed to return to my baking as soon as possible; snickerdoodles it was.

Since Marilyn and Cheryl worked Wednesday mornings, and I didn't want to deal with the former, I would need to retrieve the cookies as quickly as possible. Remembering Lynn had set the plate on the glass counter near the front door, I parked in one of the spots by the entrance and scanned the interior before making the commitment to get out of my car.

The place was dark and the coast looked clear.

Quickly unlocking the door and dashing inside, I nabbed the cookies and was about to leave when a sound from way in the back caught my attention.

"WHUMPF"

Turning, I heard it again.

"WHUMPF"

It was a muffled sort of thumping noise, like someone hitting a punching bag.

"Hello?" I called out.

Contemplating what to do next, I checked the parking lot outside just in time to see a large white car parking in one of the diagonal spots across the street; Marilyn.

If I took the time to check out the mysterious noise in back, I would be trapped.

My decision was swift and I was just opening my car door as she climbed out of her Cadillac. Unfortunately, our eyes met so I had to think of something fast.

"Cookies!" I yelled, holding the plate up in the air so she could see. "Nate forgot his cookies!"

She began walking towards me so I panicked, diving quickly behind the wheel while simultaneously tossing the cookies onto the passenger seat. By the time she approached the curb, I already had my seatbelt on and the engine started.

I could see her frowning at me as I backed away from the curb.

"Happy Thanksgiving!" I yelled through the closed window.

Driving away, I only felt a little guilty. No doubt she had several complaints that needed addressing and I was removing a perfectly good opportunity for her to vent, but I didn't care; there was an apple pie in my future and my entire family would soon be under the same roof.

*　　*　　*

As I walked along the sidewalk leading to the Autumn Public Library's main entrance, a sudden gust of wind swayed the overhead pines causing a flotilla of dead needles to fall and swirl around me. Although this storm may have been passing us by, it was still letting its presence be known.

Taking in the one-story fortress-like exterior with its predominance of exposed concrete, I suddenly recalled the 1970 era architectural style as being called Brutalism; sometimes my art degree comes in handy. Inside, I was surprised to see a queue of people already waiting at the check-out desk. Before joining the end of the line, I decided to pay a quick visit to the bathroom since, as Sarra always said, never pass up a toilet.

The restrooms were located in a small hallway just off the main lobby, and passing a cork-covered display board which hung between the two doors, something caught my eye; a flier with an image of someone I instantly recognized.

"In memorium of Pat Mulderry and her years of service as a treasured library volunteer"

Library volunteer? When did she volunteer at the library?

I inspected the photo closely. Yep, the short pageboy haircut, oversized square rimmed glasses and toothy grin was definitely the Pat I knew.

"We sure do miss her." A soft voice spoke behind me.

Turning, I saw a small woman standing behind a cart loaded with books. She had dark shoulder-length hair interspersed with threads of white, and a flawless complexion that reminded me of lightly toasted almonds.

"You knew Pat?" I asked.

"Oh yes, she volunteered here a couple of times a week." She said.

The name tag pinned to her cornflower-blue volunteer apron read Emiko, and I noticed it was adorned with a single yellow smiley sticker.

"Wow, I had no idea."

Emiko moved closer to the bulletin board and pointed to the paragraph below Pat's photo.

"She was with us nearly seven years."

"We volunteered together too, at a used bookstore" I said, no doubt sporting a puzzled expression as I tried to calculate how Pat could possibly have done both.

"Is that the one run by BARF?" Emiko asked.

"Yes." I said, cringing as always at the silly acronym.

"Pat certainly seemed focused on that particular non-profit."

"She put in a lot of hours at the store, if that's what you mean." I said, watching as Emiko moved back behind the cart to arrange some of the books so their spines lined up perfectly.

"No, there was something else," She said, pausing a moment to furrow her brow, "but perhaps I misinterpreted."

I didn't feel comfortable following up so instead asked her what Pat had done at the library.

"She helped with the computer classes. Here, let me show you."

Emiko pushed the cart out into the main part of the library and pointed towards an open area in the center. There, three large round tables had been partitioned to create five sections, each with its own computer. From the looks of it every single cubicle was occupied by a library patron.

"We get a lot of seniors and homeless coming in for the free technology classes." Emiko explained.

I took in all the gray and white hair as well as the hodgepodge of outerwear and hats. My gaze must have caught the attention of one thickly bundled man as he looked up so that we made eye contact. His eyes widened, as if in fright, and he quickly ducked down behind the partition out of view; there was something oddly familiar about the brightly colored logo on his baseball cap.

Emiko's soft voice brought me back to the moment.

"I hope you have a nice Thanksgiving..."

"Holly." I told her.

"Holly." She repeated, giving me a warm smile.

"Thank you, you too." I said, watching as she maneuvered her cart towards the fiction category.

The line at the check-out had thinned down during my diversion and it didn't take long for me to get Nate's book. On the drive home, a lovely mixture of rain and ice crystals began to hit my windshield and the outside temperature dropped to a nippy thirty-seven degrees Fahrenheit. So much for the weather report, I thought, switching on the wipers. At this rate if wouldn't take much for the droplets to turn to snow and with so many people on the road heading to vacation cabins, a winter storm could very well cause the pass to close - which was a scary thought.

The Mystery of Cabin Island

I don't know what made me think of that particular Hardy Boy mystery book, a favorite of both my brother and myself when we were children. Perhaps being inside the library had triggered some nostalgic memory, or maybe it was because the plot had something to do with staying at a cabin during a winter storm. Regardless, Evelyn and I had looked at a Hardy Boys book just the other day, right before a customer had bought it; a man with a smiley face on his hat just like the one on Emiko's name badge.

Suddenly, I thought of the computer user at the library. His cap had the exact same logo and it didn't seem likely there were many of those floating around. It must have been the same person, the one asking about his missing friend.

Why had he acted so scared to see me, I wondered.

A light snow began to fall just as I made it home. Climbing out of my car, I watched the drifting white flakes for a few minutes before closing the garage door. Although I enjoyed their beauty, I was glad to see them melt as soon as they hit the ground. Hopefully, things would stay that way until Philip got home.

Setting the bag of groceries onto the kitchen counter, my phone dinged with an incoming text. It was from Roxy; apparently Marilyn was hysterical over my rude behavior in front of the bookstore and was demanding an apology.

Pulling out the sea salt and cider, I knew which one I had to open first.

SMILEY FACE

(November 28, Monday morning)

Time always seems to speed up when things are going well, and Thanksgiving weekend proved no exception. The days whizzed by in a fabulous blur of good food and wine, walks in freshly fallen snow, and even a round of the game Nate referred to as 'monotony'. The salted caramel apple pie came out perfectly, if I do say so myself, with Philip devouring most of it in no time flat.

The festivities helped distract me from thinking too much about any bookstore drama, and also allowed me keep my earlier promise to Sarra about staying away from the place.

"You spend enough time there," she had told me, "enjoy your family!"

She was right, of course, and by the time Monday morning rolled around I felt refreshed and ready to tackle most anything the universe might throw at me.

The only other creature stirring as I prepared to leave was Martha. She conveniently decided to throw a fit when I slipped into my shoes, her shrill voice echoing through the kitchen, so I dribbled more half-and-half into her bowl as a distraction before making a quick exit out to the garage.

With the pretty white stuff mostly melted and roads merely wet with no visible signs of overnight ice, I made good time down to the bookstore. At nine-thirty, give or take a minute, I was just switching the lights on when the buzzer informed me someone else had arrived.

"Good morning!" Sarra and Lynn greeted in unison as I opened the back door.

While they shed their coats in the sorting room, I surveyed the state of affairs in the hallway.

"Things look pretty much the same as they did last Tuesday." I commented, after rejoining them. "In fact, it doesn't look like we got many donations at all over the weekend."

"Makes sense, it being a holiday and all." Sarra said.

"I don't know about you two, but I need to burn off some of this pumpkin pie." Lynn said, patting her stomach.

"You're looking sharp today." I told her, taking in the burgundy dress suit and white ruffled blouse she was wearing. It was quite the contrast to my own pair of faded jeans and ratty fleece sweatshirt.

"This old thing? I've had it for years." She twirled around so the skirt billowed outward.

"Sure you have." Sarra said with more than a touch of sarcasm.

Checking the status of the three FRC carts lined up against the back wall, I let out a whistle. Although they were five feet tall, their molded front openings dipped to my waist and each was full of books to this level.

"We can't put anything else into these." I said, "We don't want Angel getting into trouble."

Angel, the FRC pickup driver, usually showed up before eleven on Mondays to remove any of our filled carts and replace them with however many empty ones he happened to have on hand. Books stacked above the 'fill line' could cause the carts to tip over when moved, and accepting them meant a possible reprimanding by his supervisors.

"Can we put discards into something else?" Sarra asked.

"Sure, he'll take anything we give him on the side."

While the two of them searched for boxes, I went to check on the fish room and discovered it emptier than I'd ever seen it.

"This is amazing." I said, rejoining them in the hall. "I think we're actually going to be able to finish most of the sort this month."

"You've never done that before?" Lynn asked.

I shook my head. "Not since I've been here; I wish Pat could see this, she would be so happy."

"Well, unless a ton of donations come in this week or something, we should have no problem." Sarra said, sounding confident.

"Then let's get to it!" Lynn exclaimed, grabbing the handle of the nearest shopping cart and pushing it alongside one of the bins in the hall. "I'll take a couple of bags of paperbacks up front and work on them there."

"You don't fool me." Sarra chuckled, causing Lynn to break into one of her 'tee-hee-hee' giggles.

"What's going on?" I had to ask.

"She's planning on flirting with a certain customer, that's why she's all dressed up." Sarra explained.

"Oh?"

I looked over at Lynn and noticed a pale pink flush rising in her cheeks.

"I can't help myself," she said, "I appreciate a good looking man."

Her cart loaded, she pushed it towards the front, wiggling her rear end for effect as she turned the corner.

"See you later girls!"

"Trouble maker!" Sarra called out after her and we both shared a laugh.

As we focused on filling our own shopping cart, I recounted my Wednesday adventures, - everything from learning Pat had volunteered at the library to my snickerdoodle encounter with Marilyn.

"I'm hoping if I avoid her long enough, the whole thing will blow over."

"Don't let them yank your chain." Sarra said, "Say, would you consider this historical fiction or general fiction?" She held up a hardcover so I could see the front cover.

"Historical."

"Is that the fifty-year rule?"

"Yep, that's what Pat always used and it works for me."

"Pat was something special, wasn't she," Sarra said, tossing the book into the cart, "working all those hours here plus volunteering at the library."

"I still don't know how she managed to do both. Argh, looks like I have to go in."

Even though I had lowered the hinged front section of the metal bin, I still couldn't quite reach the back portion.

"Careful." Sarra commented as I crawled into the container on hands and knees across the slippery layer of books.

Grabbing four at a time, I handed them over to her. Up front, I could hear Lynn talking with someone and realized it must be after ten.

"Do you need to help cashier?"

"Are you kidding? Lynn has it under control." Sarra chuckled.

"If you feel like shelving, there's a couple of sections that need help."

"Maybe, after we finish here. Tell me more about that smiley-face hat guy, he's intriguing."

She placed the last stack of books into the cart before holding out a hand to help me up out of the bin. Steadying myself on the floor, I wiped my hands on my jeans and promptly let out a sneeze; as usual, most of the books from the barn were covered in a fine layer of dust.

"Gesundheit."

"Thanks." I said, rubbing my itchy nose on the sleeve of my sweatshirt before continuing. "There's not much to tell other than I'm pretty sure it's the same guy who was in here looking for his friend."

"Do you think he knew Pat?" She asked, pushing the cart into the sorting room and parking it alongside one of the tables.

"Possibly, especially since he was in the computer section of the library."

"Did that friend of his ever show up?"

"I have no idea, but we could ask Lynn since she's shelving the westerns now."

"Ask me what?" Lynn said, surprising us both by suddenly appearing in the doorway.

"Don't you have any customers to flirt with?" Sarra asked.

"I'll have you know I'm quite capable of working while I flirt." Lynn quipped back, her feigned indignation offset by a twinkle-eyed grin.

Although western fiction only rarely trickled in as donations, the genre's popularity warranted a small shelf space up front. Lynn had agreed to shelve them since her husband had been an avid reader, making her familiar with many of the authors.

As she walked over to check the contents of that particular box, I asked her if any customers had come in asking about them.

"No, why?"

As I brought her up to speed on 'Mr. Smiley' and his missing friend, she pulled a single vintage paperback out of the box, its cover faded and pages thin from use.

"There's a couple who come in on Mondays since they know that's when I shelve," she said, inspecting the book, "but no one else has asked about them."

"DING-DING-DING-DING"

The sound of the desk bell ringing made us pause our conversation.

"Do you want me to get that so you can shelve your book?" Sarra asked, light-hearted sarcasm dripping from her voice.

"Fine, be that way." Lynn snapped back.

"Oh, maybe I'll be lucky and it will be that cutie who always buys the coffee table books." Sarra laughed, continuing her teasing as she hustled out the door.

Lynn began to follow but paused momentarily to look back at me.

"Hopefully that missing friend isn't the guy they found dead in the woods." She said before leaving.

Her comment gave me a sharp chill; the possibility a macabre concept. If Stubby, or Stumpy, or whatever his name was, had been a customer of our bookstore, Pat could very well have known him. I wasn't sure what that meant in the scheme of things, if anything, but the idea was intriguing.

The sound of laughter echoing down the hall brought me back to the present and I looked up at the clock; it was almost eleven. Swinging the back door open, I checked to make sure the area behind the ramp was clear so Angel could park his truck below. After propping the door ajar with a brick, I turned and saw something I hadn't noticed before. It was a yellow smiley sticker stuck on the side of the desk in the alcove, and it looked just like the one on Emiko's name badge.

I had never paid much attention to the desk, other than trying to find a spot on its cluttered surface, and on closer inspection discovered it had two drawers to the right of the kneehole. Curious, I pulled the top one open and found it crammed full of a mishmash of outdated office supplies, including a couple of bottles of whiteout and some long heavy duty black zip ties.

The larger bottom drawer wouldn't budge. Looking for a possible key hole, the sound of a diesel engine followed by screeching brakes interrupted my search.

By the time I pushed the back door completely open and secured it in place with the brick, Angel was already walking around to the rear of the backed-up delivery truck.

"Good morning!" I called down to him.

"Hola!" He responded, looking up at me with a wide grin.

Releasing the latch of the truck's rolling door, Angel pushed it upwards to reveal a painfully thin man dressed in baggy overalls standing just inside the bed. His hair was the color of carrots and he was sporting the most impressive sideburns I'd ever seen, and after the lift lowered, he hopped out of the truck and jogged up the ramp.

"Can I please use your bathroom?" He asked, looking somewhat desperate.

"Of course," I said, pointing to my left, "it's over there" as he made a mad dash for the door.

Angel walked up the ramp at a much slower pace, dramatically sighing upon entering.

"Sorry about that, I told him not to drink so much coffee before we left."

"No worries."

"How many you got this morning?" he asked, strolling towards the sorting room. Although the overalls he wore were similar to his helper, his fit quite a bit snugger across the middle and the leg cuffs were rolled up to accommodate a much shorter stature.

95

"All three are full and we didn't go over the lines. How many can you leave us?" I asked, watching as he peeked into the nearest cart.

"I can leave you two today and bring you two more on Thursday. That work?"

"Great."

The man with the sideburns reappeared and began to help Angel maneuver one of the carts out the door. Leaving them to their work, I returned to the desk and resumed my search for a keyhole. When that proved fruitless, I began yanking on the drawer handle out of sheer frustration.

"You gotta hit it just right. Here, let me show you." Sideburn's voice startled me and I stepped back as he leaned over the desk and pounded the side of the drawer with his fist. Pulling on the handle, it glided open with ease.

"Wow, thanks."

"I used to have one like this and it stuck all the time. Once you figure it out, no problem. Thanks for the bathroom." Sideburns vanished out the back door just as Angel approached me with a FRC donation receipt.

"Everything OK?" he asked.

"Your partner was just helping me." I explained, pointing to the opened drawer.

Angel took a bandana out of his back pocket and wiped his brow.

"Dan showed Pat that trick too. He's a good guy, just drinks too much coffee." Shoving the cloth away, he stepped out onto the landing and moved the brick across the threshold with one foot.

"See you later!" he called out before the door clicked shut.

Alone, I quickly returned to my snooping. The bottom drawer, I soon discovered, contained a hanging file system full of multiple folders. A few of these had plastic tabs with handwritten titles, and I instantly recognized the distinctive writing as belonging to Pat. Pulling one labeled *Donations*, I found a handful of the blank forms we used when customers requested a receipt, and made a mental note of their location before sliding them back into place.

Another folder labeled *Sales* was full of loose sheets of notebook paper with handwritten lists of book titles with corresponding ISBN numbers. Some were highlighted with yellow marker and one or two had red check marks next to penciled-in dollar amounts; this must have been Pat's attempt at selling books online, something she told me hadn't been worth the effort. Near the back of the stack I found a few stapled together with **Gerald?** Written in black felt tip marker on a sticky note atop the first page, making me wonder if he had helped her with this project.

Most of the remaining folders were empty except for the last tab which held a small monthly planner. Its cutesy cover featured three fluffy white kittens spilling out of a picnic basket surrounded by flowers, and looked more like something Daphne would have chosen than Pat, but the writing inside confirmed it as hers.

Leafing through the pages, I paused on the month of October.

"Holly?" Sarra called out from the other end of the hall.

"Back here!"

She found me in the alcove and moved closer to see what I was holding.

"What's that?"

"It's Pat's planner," I said, pointing to the square below the number six, "looks like she had an appointment the day before she died."

Sarra squinted at the writing.

"I don't have my glasses, what does it say?"

"R @ SR 5pm."

"Oh wow!" She gasped.

"What?"

Grabbing my arm, she squeezed so tight I nearly dropped the planner onto the floor.

"Don't you see? R stands for 'Roxy' and SR is 'Secret Ranch'. I told you we need to find that place!"

Chapter

21

SUPER CAB

(November 28, Monday afternoon)

H ow very odd." Evelyn said, handing Pat's planner back to me.
"That's what we thought." Sarra responded as she slipped into her coat
"Now that you're here, we're going to see if we can't find the place."

Evelyn shrugged and artfully rearranged the orange silk scarf draped around her neck, its hue complementing the royal blue of her knit top.

"Better you than me. I don't much care for livestock."

"So you think it's on Gold Road?" I asked, pulling out my phone to bring up a map of the area.

"That's what I heard."

"My boyfriend and I were just looking at a rental down there." Jill, our newest bookstore volunteer, interjected. "Gold has a north and south section, so you'll have to watch for that."

Up to that point, Jill had been silently listening in on our conversation and as I enlarged the map on my phone's screen, she leaned closer to point out a specific location.

"See, the northern half ends... there, at the railroad tracks."

"Thanks." I told her.

"No problem, sounds like an exciting adventure." She said, returning my smile.

It was hard for me to correctly gauge her age, though I would have guessed mid thirty, and she was dressed in black stretch pants with an oversized purple t-shirt embellished with a colorful image of the Hindu deity Ganesh; definitely not a typical outfit worn by the foothill crowd.

"Don't get yourself into any sort of trouble, we've had plenty of that around here." Evelyn said, giving us a stern look before turning to Jill. "Come on Miss Yoga, let me show you our bell."

Jill obediently followed with a serene expression befitting her new nickname.

"Do you want me to drive?" Lynn asked, already wearing her coat with car keys in hand.

"Fine, but I don't want to leave my car here. Let's go to my house first and we can decide from there." Sarra said.

"I'm starving. Can we get something to eat first?" I asked. My stomach had been growling for the past hour, no doubt from recent holiday overindulgences, and I really needed some food.

Before long, the three of us were in Lynn's SUV heading west on the interstate happily munching on some of Burger Pit's finest. I'd been assigned navigator position while Sarra ran commentator in the back seat. Or, as she put it, "Driving Miss Daisy".

Slurping the last of my chocolate milkshake, I gazed out the window and admired the bucolic surroundings. Unlike the steep foothills covered in dark pine trees, here the landscape was golden and rolling with an occasional cluster of ancient oaks, limbs barren for the winter. Farms and ranches still seemed to be the norm as the suburban sprawl of the valley floor hadn't quite reached this elevation, and I hoped it never would.

"What are we going to do when we find the ranch?" Lynn had asked me earlier as we waited our turn in the drive-up. I didn't know what to tell her since, honestly, the odds weren't good. We were searching for a needle in a hay stack, with no clear idea of what the place even looked like, and for all I knew it was hidden behind an impenetrable gate guarded by a pack of vicious canines.

"Take this exit." I instructed Lynn and she veered right onto a divided arterial. A few left and right hand turns later down streets with names in keeping with the region's mining history, we finally popped out to a T with Gold Road.

"Left or right?" Lynn asked.

"Left!" Sarra piped in from the back.

Lynn did as she was instructed, slowing her speed to allow us adequate gazing time. Although the road was paved, there were no dividing lines painted on its surface and both graveled shoulders dropped dramatically down into deep irrigation ditches.

"I hate driving on roads like this." She muttered while keeping the SUV as close to the middle as possible.

"Sorry." I said, glancing over at her white knuckle grip on the steering wheel.

"You wanted to drive." The voice from the back chimed in, prompting Lynn to stick her tongue out at the reflection in the rear view mirror.

"How about that one?"

I pointed to a place on our right; the driveway had a small bridge over the irrigation ditch and there were multiple cars parked near the side of what looked like a manufactured house.

"That doesn't look very secret." Sarra responded.

I was beginning to regret letting her sit in the back.

Continuing to creep along Gold Road, we scoped out any driveways and buildings that might fit the bill. Although we saw plenty of ranch style houses and a few horses along the way, none of the properties looked as if they were set up to protect confiscated animals.

Two and a half miles and roughly thirty minutes later, the road came to an abrupt end at the railroad tracks.

"Guess Jill was right." Lynn grumbled as she worked to turn the car around.

"Do you want to try the southern end or call it quits?" I asked, concerned this whole ranch search was getting to be a bit of a stretch.

"We can't stop now!" Sarra cried out from the back.

"That's right, we've got to see this thing through." Lynn stepped on the gas hard, causing both her passengers to hit their heads against the back of their seats.

As we approached the 'T', a large black truck suddenly appeared and nearly clipped our front end as it squealed around the corner heading north.

"What the heck!" Lynn exclaimed, swerving left to avoid an impact.

Holding onto the grab handle for dear life, I suddenly recognized the super cab.

"That's Katrina!"

"Follow her!" Sarra yelled and Lynn responded quickly, straightening out the steering wheel while applying more pressure to the accelerator.

Lynn's lead foot helped us gain some ground until the truck's tail lights began to flash red.

"She's stopping, watch out!" I cried out and Lynn instantly eased off the gas.

We watched as the truck swerved left past a lime green mailbox and disappeared up a narrow dirt drive, churning a cloud of fine dust in its wake.

Following, Lynn drove a few yards past the mailbox and came to a stop in front of an opened chain-link gate; a large red NO TRESPASSING sign hung off the top rail.

"Now what?" she asked.

"Stay here, I'll walk up the drive a bit and check it out first. If I see anything I'll text you." I said, hopping out of the car before anyone could argue with my decision.

A wall of tall grasses obscured a clear view of the property from the entrance, but as soon as I walked past it and up a slight rise, the landscape opened up to pastureland. Pausing at the top of the hill, I surveyed what looked like a ten-acre field which dipped down in the center, the grass freshly mowed except for a narrow buffer around a small pond. The drive followed the curve of the land and ended near a cluster of buildings set near the upper right-hand edge. Although the distance was too far for me to garner much detail, I could make out Katrina's black truck parked near a white one.

Clouds suddenly moved across the sun, casting everything into dark shadows, and the air became chilly enough for me to see my breath. Hoofing it back to the car, I climbed into the warm interior and shut the door.

"Well?" Lynn and Sarra asked simultaneously, their anxious voices blended together.

"There are some buildings at the back of the property and I saw Roxy's truck, but it's too far away for me to see much of anything else."

"I've got binoculars in the back!" Lynn exclaimed, undoing her seatbelt.

"I'm coming too." Sarra said and both scrambled out of the car before I could respond.

Lynn opened the hatchback and rummaged around in a side compartment, eventually locating a worn leather case.

"These were Lenny's." She explained as she pulled out an ancient looking pair of binoculars and handed them to me.

"Definitely better than nothing." I said, and the three of us retraced my steps up to the top of the hill.

"I can't believe we actually found the secret ranch." Lynn whispered into my left ear as I struggled to figure out the best position for the binocular's focusing knob. Everything was blurry, which was frustrating.

"Do you see anything?" Sarra's voice asked from my right.

"I'm not sure. Oh, wait, there's Roxy. She's moving around in front of Katrina." I said, fiddling with the knobs.

"Let me look." She said, and I was more than happy to hand the glasses over to her.

"They look like they're arguing... I think Roxy went back into the house... Here, take these back, they're driving me nuts." She handed the binoculars back to me.

With the eye cups stuck back against my face, I closed my left eye and refocused my right eye onto the black truck. As I watched, Roxy marched out of the house and began throwing something at Katrina. The clouds must have shifted as the entire scene was suddenly bathed in golden afternoon light, causing the objects to glisten as they fluttered between the two women.

"Katrina's getting into her truck, we have to go!"

Quickly jogging back to the car, we clambered into our seats.

"Where to?" Lynn asked breathlessly, putting the car into reverse and backing onto Gold Road.

"Right, right!" Sarra yelled at the top of her lungs.

"She won't see us if we go that way!" I agreed, checking the front window for any sign of the black truck.

With a dramatic flailing of elbows, Lynn rotated the steering wheel as far as it would go and hit the gas, swerving the SUV dangerously close to the edge of the ditch before straightening it down the center of the road.

"Damn, woman!" Sarra wailed as her entire body rolled and smacked against the door panel; I didn't fare much better.

After covering at least half a football field of distance, Lynn finally eased off the accelerator.

"Are we safe?" she asked, cheeks flushed from all the excitement.

Shifting around to look through the rear window, I saw the tail end of Katrina's truck skidding past the mailbox heading north.

"Yep!"

"Thank goodness. I need a drink." Lynn exhaled.

"The Belgian?"

Sarra's quick suggestion made us all laugh.

*   *   *

Tall glasses of cold cider did a good job of soothing our frayed nerves. Sitting along the front window of the Belgian, we drank in collective silence as the late afternoon sun cast long shadows across the counter and into our laps.

"You ladies doing OK?" The bartender called from behind the bar. His forehead was wrinkled and there was genuine concern in his voice.

"Yeah, we're good. Just calming down after a little adventure." I said, swiveling slightly on my stool to give him a smile.

Sarra rolled her eyes and looked past me over to Lynn. "Yeah, fine... other than needing to visit my chiropractor."

"Wimp." Lynn responded, taking another sip of her cider.

"No more issues with your vehicle, I hope." A familiar voice made me turn around to discover Sean, the sheriff, ordering at the bar. His gray sweatshirt and worn jeans was such typical attire for the majority of pub customers I hadn't even registered him coming through the front door.

"Come join us!" Lynn called over to him, pulling out another stool from beneath the counter and situating it between us.

"Thanks." He said, settling himself down before taking a swig of his beer. "So, anything to report?"

"Uh..." I stammered, glancing over at Sarra's widening eyes.

"Just out for an afternoon drive, officer." Lynn piped in as cool as a cucumber.

Sean set his glass on the counter and took on a more somber expression.

"Sorry to hear about what happened to your fellow volunteer."

It took me a second to figure out he was referring to Gerald.

"Thank you." I finally responded, realizing it made perfect sense he would have heard about the murder, especially it being a small town and all.

"Speaking of which, do you have any new information about his murder that you can share?" Sarra asked.

Sean raised his eyebrows slightly, but shook his head in the negative.

"Nope."

I wasn't surprised at the response; I'd read enough murder mysteries to know cops weren't allowed to talk about ongoing investigations, especially with civilians. Sarra's inquiry, however, did make me think of something else.

"Did you ever find out the identity of the homeless man killed behind Rudy's?"

Sean's face instantly lit up at my inquiry.

"Yes, his name was Francis Smith. The Journal did a nice piece about our findings."

"I don't get the Autumn paper," I explained, not willing to delve further into the reasons why, "did you ever find out what happened to him?"

"Pretty much." Sean said, taking another sip of his beer.

"What exactly do you mean by 'pretty much'?" Sarra asked, sounding every inch the English major turned teacher. Thankfully, Sean was nonplussed and continued freely sharing information.

"He died of blunt force trauma to the back of the head. At first it looked like he had fallen, but the coroner concluded the body had been moved after death which points to homicide. Unfortunately, as is the case with many of these types of situations, unless someone comes forward with evidence it will remain a mystery."

A tingling sensation began working its way up the back of my neck.

"DUH-DA-DO-DO"

A bubbly, sing-song sound made Sean reach for the back pocket of his jeans and pull out his cell phone.

"Gotta run, ladies, was nice chatting with you."

We said our goodbyes and watched as he returned his glass to the bartender before quickly exiting the pub.

"I didn't want to say anything while Sean was here," I said, once we were alone, "but if Francis Smith is the person Mr. Smiley was looking for, then that would mean a connection to the bookstore..."

"Oh my gosh!" Lynn interrupted, "Didn't Evelyn say Gerald died from a blow to the head?"

Sarra's eyes widened. "Should we have said something to Sean?"

"There's nothing to tell that he doesn't probably already know." I said.

"What do you think Roxy was throwing at Katrina?" Lynn asked, changing topics.

"I have no idea," I responded, suddenly feeling very tired, "it could be any number of things."

"Maybe it was drugs." She continued. "If they are doing something fishy down there, Pat could have found out and that was the reason for the meeting."

"But why did she go to the bookstore?" Sarra countered.

The two began to volley conspiracy theories back and forth until my head began to spin from more than just the cider.

"You ladies want another round?" The bartender called out.

Glancing at my phone, I was shocked to realize it was nearly five o'clock.

"Not for me, I have to go." I told him, standing and reaching for my jacket.

"See you Friday." Sarra said, "Stay out of trouble until then."

"Yeah, because who knew volunteering could be so dangerous." Lynn added, before erupting into a cascade of giggles.

VAMPIRES

(November 30, Wednesday evening)

"How long will you be gone?"

Nate looked into the rear view mirror and moved over a lane before answering.

"Like I said, my flight home is scheduled for the sixteenth."

"So three weeks?"

"No, that's only two weeks."

"But what about Christmas?"

"I'll be back before then."

His words didn't help console my anxiety; the last time he had worked on an overseas project his return had been delayed for nearly a month.

"I don't understand why they couldn't wait until January." I pouted; the realization I would need to cut and trim a tree, hang outdoor lights and wrap presents all by myself having put me in a foul mood.

Nate sighed before responding. "They need this portion finished by the end of the year."

Glancing over at his profile, I suddenly felt a tinge of guilt; there were bags under his eyes and he looked exhausted. Although my better instinct told me to back off, my little monsters switched gears as his impending work trip wasn't the only recent bombshell.

"When are you going to talk to Philip?"

"You already know my answer."

Looking out the passenger window, I decided to employ the silent treatment for the duration of the drive.

Once Nate had parked behind the bookstore and turned off the ignition, he shifted in his seat to face me.

"Look, I'm sorry I have to go to Australia." He said softly, reaching over to take hold of one of my hands. "You could always go with me."

"You know I can't, not with the holidays and everything. Damn it, now you're going to make me cry." His gesture had made my eyes well up and I could already feel my nose beginning to drip.

"Sorry."

He squeezed my hand slightly before letting go so I could rummage through the glove box for a packet of tissues.

"About Philip," he continued, "it's better to talk with him in person when he's home, you know that. For all we know he's already changed his mind about quitting."

"He better." I said, before blowing my nose.

"Do you want to go to the Belgian and have a cider?"

"No, I'm OK. Besides, if we do that I won't want to come back here."

I pocketed the tissue and began to exit the car just as a large droplet of rain smacked against the windshield. It wasn't the last, and Nate hustled behind me up the ramp as the torrential downpour hit full force. Since the security light still hadn't been fixed, I fumbled with the key before he came to the rescue and illuminated the door with the flashlight on his phone, and we soon plunged into the bookstore with streams of water dripping off our bodies.

The inside lights were blazing as it wasn't quite six o'clock, and it took a few seconds for my eyes to acclimate.

"I'll go tell them we're here." I said, shrugging out of my wet jacket and hanging it over the edge of one of the metal bins while Nate disappeared into the sorting room.

Informing the cashiers of our presence was more necessity than courtesy. Mary, one of the ladies who worked the Wednesday afternoon shift, had recently walked in on us while we were sorting unannounced in the back room and nearly had a coronary; needless to say, we didn't need another one of those around here.

"Do you have anything with vampires?" A smooth feminine voice with a hint of an accent interrupted my beeline for the desk. Turning, I saw a slim woman wrapped in a sleek black raincoat that hung nearly to the floor.

"Yes," I replied, "that's one of my sections. If you want, I can show you where it is."

She followed as I spun on my heels, deftly maneuvering around a leaning carousel filled with maps and taking a left at an end cap filled with military fiction. Striding down to the middle portion of the aisle, I came to a stop in front of the section entitled *Horror*. Although it was small compared to Nate's *Science Fiction and Fantasy* category that ran to its right, I was especially proud of the sign printed in a font aptly named 'Creepier'.

"Why are they in horror?" The woman asked, giving me a somber look from beneath blunt cut bangs. I noticed the tips of her dark hair were dyed a unique shade of purple that looked almost iridescent beneath the fluorescent lights.

"Well, we figured it was the best place even though some of them should probably be in a paranormal romance section, but we don't have one of those." I explained.

"What's paranormal?" She asked, making the word sound almost erotic.

"Not normal?"

"What do you mean?" The tone of her voice had noticeably changed to defensive.

"Well, vampires aren't exactly normal..."

"That depends on the vampire." She interrupted, her expression darkened into a frown.

Although a part of me wanted to continue arguing my point, I decided it was best to call it quits; vampires were clearly a touchy subject for this customer.

"OK, well, sorry I can't help more." I said, quickly retreating to let her deal with the undead on her own.

I found Mary and Sharon seated side-by-side behind the front desk with their noses in books, doing their part in reinforcing the stereotype of the typical used bookstore volunteer.

"Howdy. Must be nearly six." Sharon said when she saw me, checking her wristwatch for the time.

"Just about," I laughed. "busy day?"

"Pretty typical." Mary said as she slowly rose to her feet. She closed the newer looking hardcover she had been reading and studied the back cover.

"You going to buy that?" Sharon asked her.

Mary shook her head. "No, I'm not sure I like it and don't want to waste a dollar."

"Harrumph," Sharon said, making the universal sound of disapproval. "this new policy is for the birds."

"What new policy?" I asked, confused as to what she meant.

"You didn't get the email from Katrina?" Mary asked, looking at me from across the bridge of her reading glasses.

"No, I don't seem to get her emails."

"She officially informed us we're no longer allowed to borrow books without paying for them, even if we bring them back." Sharon said, folding her arms across her chest and leveling her gaze at me. "Pat never had a problem with us doing that but it seems Roxy is worried we'll abuse the privilege and start stealing or something. Does this have anything to do with Gerald getting fired?"

It was my turn to shake my head. "This is the first I've heard of this and believe me, I don't agree with it either."

As far as I knew, no one had ever betrayed Pat's trust in bringing back books they didn't want or putting a dollar in the till for those they did. She felt people were good by nature, especially those who volunteered, but this new policy set the tone for a completely opposite viewpoint.

Sharon seemed satisfied with my answer and asked me to lock up while they closed out the sales for the day. Making a quick sweep of the store floor for any straggling customers, I was surprised not to find the vampire lady, even though I was pretty sure she couldn't have walked past the desk without my seeing. After rechecking everywhere twice, including the fish room and Roxy's office, I went ahead and locked the front door.

The deluge outside had intensified; shimmering sheets of water were spilling over the building's front edge and rivers flowed across the parking lot, gathering into black pools in every indent.

"It's coming down like crazy." I warned Sharon and Mary as they began to gather their belongings.

Sharon merely waved her unopened umbrella in the air and laughed. "I'm prepared."

"You'll turn off the lights?" Mary asked, zipping into her rain shell.

"Definitely."

After locking up behind them, I turned to see Nate pushing a shopping cart loaded with boxes down the main aisle.

"I've got your horror books." He called out to me and I met him halfway, helping him maneuver it towards our sections.

Shelving was much easier for Nate without customers in the store. Since taking over the Science Fiction and Fantasy genre six months ago, his meticulous culling of non-sellers and overall organization had resulted in a steady growth of loyal customers, and recently he'd been getting three or four boxes of donations in per week. With shelf space limited, this required him to shift large sections of already shelved books around in order to accommodate newly acquired series or popular authors, and without customers to worry about, he could use the entire length of floor in front of his shelves to separate books into alphabetical piles.

My own Horror section was a much slower seller and, more often than not, duplicative titles were donated that already sat on the shelves. Since some of the genre's better known authors were known to churn out exceptionally thick hardcovers, I could rarely make room for more than a few copies.

"I'm finished," I told Nate about fifteen minutes later, "how are you doing?" I asked Nate about twenty minutes later.

He was sitting cross legged on the floor intently studying the back cover of a paperback, and mumbled "OK" without looking up.

Leaving him to take care of my discards, I noticed a forlorn looking Teddy sitting near the front of his enclosure. Although he tracked my movements with his saucer shaped eyes, he didn't make a sound, and I made a mental note to ask Daphne if his appetite had improved.

About twenty minutes later, after shelving my cookbooks, I returned to the sorting room to find Nate stacking his discards into one of the FRC carts. This time he looked up at me with a grin.

"The place looks great. I can tell how hard all of you have been working."

"Thank you." I said, returning his smile; the compliment reminding me how good it felt to bask in the light of a positive achievement.

"Since we're done here, can I take you out for a drink?"

Before I could respond, a loud rattle followed by a cringe-worthy howl echoed down to us from the ceiling.

"Whoa, what was that?" I asked, moving closer to Nate.

"The wind must have picked up."

Above us, the clattering continued while the lights began to flicker.

"I think I just want to go home." I told him.

Since it wasn't uncommon for us to lose power whenever high winds came through, Nate agreed and we decided to pick up some wine and groceries before heading up the hill.

Out on the ramp, the rain was still coming down hard as we sprinted to the car, and after parking in front of Rudy's, we reversed our mad dash for the dry interior.

"Good evening folks, although it's a nasty one." An employee greeted us as we passed through the sliding doors. He was judiciously laying carpeted floor mats down onto the already wet tile to prevent possible slippage, even though the store looked pretty empty.

While Nate stayed near the front to peruse the wine department, I ended up having to visit both back corners in order to pick up a loaf of bread and some half-and-half.

"Which sounds better, Petite Sirah or a blend?" He asked when I rejoined him, and my dramatic sigh prompted him into making a quick decision. "OK, we'll try the blend."

Back in the car, Nate suddenly slammed on the brakes while backing out of the parking spot.

"Crap!"

"What's wrong?" I asked, terrified he had hit something without my realizing.

"I forgot my books."

"You scared the heck out of me! What books?"

"I picked out a couple of paperbacks for my trip and left them on the table in the back." He explained as he turned the steering wheel sharply to the left and drove over to the bookstore. Parking near the front door, he asked to borrow my keys.

"I might as well go with you," I said, "I forgot to pee."

Since the sidewalk was well lit by the overhead lot lights, Nate didn't have to use his phone's flashlight until we got inside.

"Did you pay for them?" I asked, holding onto his wet jacket sleeve for guidance as we walked through the dark interior.

"Yes, I already put a couple of dollars and a note inside the ledger. Why are you whispering?"

"I don't know."

A thumping sound made us both stop in our tracks.

"Was that the wind?" I asked, still keeping my voice low.

"I don't think so; it's coming from the back." Nate raised his phone to illuminate the end of the main aisle and the light reflected off the steel meshing of Teddy's enclosure.

When the noise repeated, I was suddenly reminded of what I'd heard while retrieving his snickerdoodles. Cautiously moving towards the hallway, we spotted a light coming from beneath the closed mystery room door.

"Should we call 911?" I asked.

Before Nate could answer, the door exploded open and we were temporarily blinded by a glaring spotlight.

"Ahhh!"

The person let out a screech and the heavy-duty flashlight they were holding dropped to the ground.

"Roxy!" Nate cried out, aiming his light directly into her startled face.

"Jesus Christ!" she responded, "Ya'll scared the 'livin daylights outta me!"

"I'm so sorry!" He said, rushing over to switch on the store's breakers. "I forgot my books and we were coming back for them."

"I forgot you two are night owls." she said, forcing a laugh while her face flushed a deep crimson.

While the two bent over to pick up the other items she'd dropped, I noticed they included a couple of hardcover mystery books and several plastic baggies filled with cash, their clear surfaces gleaming under the fluorescent lights.

Roxy stood up and stared silently at me for a moment, as if calculating what to say next.

"Well, gotta git these to the bank."

She hugged the books and baggies close against her chest before dashing out the back door.

"What a flake." Nate said after the latch clicked shut.

I didn't comment as I was too busy thinking about what she had thrown at Katrina down at the ranch.

Chapter

23

MIRRORS

(December 1, Thursday morning)

Holding his breath, he slowly moved his head from side to side. This was no good; the small craft-mirrors were still sliding.

He blamed the trouble on the recent rain as dampness was no doubt making the white glue not want to set properly, but there really hadn't been another option. The salvaged glue gun had made a popping sound and emitted a horrible odor when he'd plugged it into the outlet behind the gas station, compelling him to ditch his first adhesive of choice and try something different.

Carefully moving the thin mirrored disks up to the inside corners of the sunglasses' frame, he clamped them into place between his thumbs and index fingers and slowly counted to twenty. When he let go, he realized the mirrors didn't offer much field of vision to the rear, but at least they seemed to be staying in place.

The idea for this particular apparatus had been a hasty one. Since he wasn't as skilled at electronics as his partner, the web instructions for the covert spy glasses had proven much too complicated. Additionally, a spy camera with a nine-volt power clip had been impossible to purchase for a price he was willing to pay.

Walking past Rudy's, the strong aroma of freshly brewed coffee wafting through the sliding doors teased his nostrils. He paused for a moment and closed his eyes, visualizing steamed milk foam artistically swirled within the circumference of a pristine white ceramic cup. His partner would have laughed at the concept, deeming anything not poured into a paper cup a 'sissy' drink, so he quickly abandoned the daydream and readjusted his sunglasses.

"Good morning!"

A woman in a white turtleneck cheerfully greeted him from behind the glass counter as he entered the bookstore. This wasn't what he had planned. He had been hoping to scope out the place in peace, left alone to his own devices to see about gathering more information to further his investigation.

"Can I help you?" The woman called out.

She had rounded the desk and was heading straight for him.

Instinctively, he tucked his chin towards his chest and veered to the right only to stumble over an upholstered armchair, his fingers tangling in the loops of a colorful crocheted afghan draped across the back.

"Are you OK?" She asked.

He disengaged from the yarn and rushed down the nearest aisle lined with books, swaying his head from side to side in an attempt to see if she was following. The dark tint of the sunglasses made it extremely difficult to see things clearly inside the store, a factor he hadn't considered.

Suddenly, the small mirrors reflected a glowing visage that seemed devoid of color, it's ghostlike quality filling him with sudden dread. As it approached, he panicked and increased his speed to outdistance the apparition, taking a sharp right at the end of the aisle and hurrying up an adjacent row towards the front of the store.

"Did you need help finding the large print section?"

The specter had cut him off at the pass and was blocking his exit. He came to an abrupt halt and put his hand onto his chest, forcing himself to take a couple of deep breaths to slow down his heart rate.

"Oh my, I didn't mean to startle you."

The elderly woman had one hand cupped over her mouth and didn't look nearly as frightening when viewed up close. She moved to one side and he slipped past, coming to a stop near a table covered with children's books. One of the mirrors slipped and fell, bouncing off his cheek, and he fumbled for it as it disappeared onto the floor; that's when he saw the book.

"Would you like help getting that?"

The woman moved incredibly fast and reached the box beneath the table seconds before him.

"Oh my, a detective handbook, this looks fun. Don't worry about paying for it, hon. Children's books are only twenty-five cents and I feel so bad about scaring you."

He left the bookstore with both the book and a renewed sense of purpose; this clearly was a sign from his partner.

Chapter

24

COFFEE BREAK

(December 2, Friday morning)

H e's lonely."

Daphne and I continued to watch Teddy stare at his bowl. Even though she had filled it with his favorite kibble several minutes earlier, he still hadn't made a move.

"But he doesn't even like other cats." I reminded her, thinking back to an earlier attempt at providing him with a cage partner. The outcome had been chunks of missing fur and a trip to the vet for the other unfortunate feline.

"I know, but I'm certain he picks up on their vibrations. Now that he's the only cat in the store..." She trailed off.

I was glad she didn't bring up the lack of new adoptees. With our last meeting aborted, and Katrina yet to reschedule another, Sarra hadn't had her opportunity to ask Roxy, and although I probably could have done so myself, compared to the other questions I wanted answered, getting more cats wasn't a priority.

Daphne had tilted her head to one side and was looking at me with a puzzled expression.

"Did you want me to watch the front so you can shelve?" I asked, quickly changing the subject.

"No, it's cool." She shrugged, causing the sea shells hanging from her neck to clatter together.

"All right, I'll stay back here and sort. Let me know if you need any help."

Her next question came from out of the blue.

"Do you think we should consider having a braille section?"

"Why? Did someone ask?"

"No, but Peg said she had a visually impaired customer come in yesterday which made her think we should consider having one."

"If someone donates some then sure, we could look into that."

Daphne seemed pleased at my response. "Groovy, I told Peg you would be open to the suggestion. See you later." She turned and trotted towards the front, her necklace creating a sound reminiscent of the classic beach wind chime.

Back in the hallway, I surveyed the bins. My hope was to empty them as soon as possible in order to give us some time to clean and organize before next weekend's drop. Looking at the light amount of donations piled atop the remaining barn books, the goal seemed easily accomplishable, especially with three of us working.

Right on cue, the buzzer rang.

"It's about time!" Lynn declared as I pushed the door outward.

Although the rain had let up, it was cold and breezy and she hurried inside.

"Is Sarra here too?" I asked, scanning the parking lot for her car.

"Nope, just me."

Letting the door swing shut, I followed her into the sorting room and watched as she set her travel mug of coffee down on the table. She was dressed much more casually today, with dark jeans and a green sweatshirt featuring a pair of kittens wearing red Santa hats.

"You look ready for the holidays." I commented.

"I love Christmas, even though my silly kids always muck it up."

"How do they do that?"

"Oh, they're always at each other about where I should spend Christmas, and with my daughter up in Idaho and my son moved to Houston, it ends up putting me in a pickle. This year I'm going to tell them I'm staying home, especially since Sarra invited me over to her house for prime rib."

Although I smiled at the spunky show of independence, it also reminded me of another family holiday dilemma. My newly divorced mother had recently decided to stop traveling, including taking the hour flight to our house, and since she lived in a one-bedroom condo with three small dogs whom Nate referred to as the 'pack of terrors', going to her place was out of the question.

The buzzer rang again.

"Finally!" Lynn reacted, quickly rushing back into the hallway.

"You're late!" I heard her say and within seconds Sarra came strolling into the room, a disposable coffee cup in one hand and a store-bought package of baked goods in the other.

"I brought muffins." She said.

Gazing at the four large golden-crumbed muffin tops nestled beneath clear plastic, I wished I had thought to bring my own mug of java.

"Isn't that Nate's truck out back?" She asked me.

"He had some errands to run in Sacramento so took the car." I explained.

"When does he leave for Australia?"

"Tomorrow."

"Don't worry," she said, patting me on the shoulder, "I'm sure he'll be home before Christmas."

"And if not, you can always have prime rib with us." Lynn giggled.

Although it was a kind gesture, it didn't make me feel any better.

"I'm going to get myself a cup of coffee." I told them.

Extracting a muffin from the container, I brought it up to Daphne.

"Oh, yummy!" She exclaimed, clapping her hands together in excitement.

After taking her order for some hot herbal tea, I headed over to the coffee bar inside Rudy's. Exiting the sliding doors and walking along the sidewalk a few minutes later with a piping hot beverage in each hand, a familiar tingling sensation ran along my jawline and made me pause. Scanning the area, I didn't see anything out of the ordinary so continued in the direction of the store. Then, in the shadowy back section of the covered walkway between Rudy's and the Laundromat, I saw a familiar looking figure leaned up against the wall. Before I could react, he disappeared around the corner.

"Did you see that guy?" Daphne asked, holding the door open for me as I approached the store. "He came by and was looking into the window right after you left, but I told him we didn't open until ten."

I didn't tell her I had the distinct feeling he wouldn't be returning.

Back in the hallway, Sarra and Lynn were pulling books out of a bin and tossing them into a shopping cart.

"It's about time you decided to join us." Lynn quipped as I passed them on my way to the sorting room.

"Hey, I have my priorities." I said.

Leaning against one of the tables, I took a few minutes to enjoy both my coffee and the lone remaining muffin. Peeling off bits of crust to pop into my mouth, I thought about the mysterious would-be customer who I was certain was Mr. Smiley. Perhaps another trip to the library was in order. If not to see about cornering him, then to ask Emiko some questions; her comments about Pat being concerned about the bookstore had me more than a little curious, especially if it had something to do with money in baggies being thrown around.

Sarra interrupted my musing. "Here you go Missy, something for you to do." She said, pushing the book-laden cart through the doorway and parking it alongside me.

Laughing, I set my coffee aside and the three of us soon fell into an efficient sorting system, with Sarra and me identifying the books' genres and placing them into appropriate boxes while Lynn transported any of those needing to go outside the room.

The sound of clanking sea shells interrupted our work.

"There's a woman up front who says she's Gerald's niece." Daphne told me, "She wants to talk to someone about making a donation."

While Sarra and Lynn groaned at the news, I tried to maintain a more neutral demeanor as I followed her to the sales area.

Gerald's niece was glancing into the display cases, her nose wrinkled in apparent distaste at our selection.

"You wanted to make a donation?" I asked, silently calculating that the enormous designer handbag hanging from her arm was probably worth more than an entire bin of our used books.

"Yes. They belonged to my Uncle Gerald." She explained. "Now that the police have released the contents of his storage unit we want to get rid of them as soon as possible. I figured this would be a good place to donate them since he volunteered here."

"Of course, thank you." I said, all the while feeling her eyes scrutinize my disheveled hair, flannel work shirt and worn jeans. I guess I wasn't the only one judging a book by its cover.

"We're so sorry about the loss of your Uncle." Daphne piped in from the side.

"Thanks." Gerald's niece said, briefly looking at Daphne before turning her attention back to me. "So, can you pick them up today?"

"Today?" I was confused.

"Yes, I need to drive back to Napa and need this taken care of immediately."

Oh, I thought, that explains everything.

"How many books are there?" I asked, hoping it would be something we could handle on our own.

"I'm not exactly sure, but it's a small unit, so maybe only a dozen or so boxes."

"That's not much," I said with relief, "We should be able to handle that no problem."

Gerald's niece, who let me know her name was 'Ms. Foster', gave me the address and code for the storage facility along with a key for unit's padlock, indicating she didn't need it returned.

"Did you want a receipt for your donation?" Daphne asked.

"No, that isn't necessary." Ms. Foster said before leaving.

After she'd gone, I made the executive decision for Sarra to stay with Daphne and Lynn to join me in picking up Gerald's books.

This time I'm driving." I told her, grabbing Nate's truck keys.

DONATION

(December 2, Friday morning)

OakLeaf Self-Storage & Rental was located about a fifteen-minute drive north of the bookstore, right on the edge of the city limits. Stopping at the main gate, I punched in the entry code Ms. Foster had given me and watched as it swung open. Uncertain of where to go, I ended up taking several wrong turns within the maze of narrow lanes and identical roll-up metal doors before finally locating Gerald's unit.

With the truck parked alongside, I unlocked the padlock and Lynn pushed the door open to reveal a ten-by-twenty-foot interior. Other than a small table and chair set up against the right-hand wall, the rest of the space was stacked floor-to-ceiling with lidded banker's boxes.

"This is way more than a dozen." I said.

Lynn whistled. "Guess we can forget about finishing the sort today."

"They can go into the fish room for now and we can sort them later."

"Thank goodness."

"Yeah, but we still have to get them to the bookstore."

Inspecting the wall of boxes, I calculated we'd need at least two trips.

"Come on then!" Lynn said, rolling up her sleeves before grabbing the nearest box.

As we worked, the two of us couldn't help sneak a peek at what kinds of books Gerald had been storing. Most looked to be historical nonfiction with a heavy emphasis on world religions, which wasn't a big surprise.

"Hey, this one has some mystery hardcovers." Lynn said, extracting a book from the box she had set on the tailgate. "Won't Marilyn be excited."

"Darn." I said, pausing to check the time on my phone. It would probably be well after two o'clock by the time we finished a second run, which meant I would have to face said individual in person.

Although the truck's canopy limited us stacking boxes more than three levels high, between my dogged determination and Lynn jumping into the bed to help maneuver, we ended up loading a good portion into the first load. Before leaving for the bookstore, I texted Sarra to let her know we were on our way and when we arrived, she already had the back door propped open with an empty shopping cart waiting.

"Holy crap, that's a lot." She commented as I swung open the canopy.

"There's more." Lynn told her.

"How much more?"

"Another trip should do it." I said, handing her a box.

Once the cart was full, it took two of us to roll it up the ramp and get it over the threshold. While Sarra finished pushing it the rest of the way into the fish room to unload, I brought another empty cart down to the truck. We continued to work in tandem like this, switching places on each run.

On one of my turns loading at the bottom of the ramp, Sarra suddenly came trotting down and called out my name. She looked upset.

"Marilyn is in the fish room and wants to go through all the boxes."

"Seriously? Why is she here so early?" I asked.

"I don't know, but somehow she found out about us getting Gerald's books."

"Oh my gawd," I moaned. "I don't have time for this right now."

"Help me get this last load up the ramp and then you guys can take off." Lynn said, hopping out of the truck. "I can handle Marilyn."

With the afternoon slipping by and plenty of work left to finish, I decided not to argue. As Sarra and I climbed into the cab, I hoped I hadn't made a big mistake.

"She'll be fine." Sarra said, reading my silent worry as she buckled in the seatbelt.

"I hope so. I still haven't apologized to Marilyn and the last thing I need is for Lynn to get into it with her."

"I wish Lynn had a smart phone so we could text to see how it's going. What is up with Marilyn and her stockpile of hardcovers anyway?"

"I don't know." I said, starting the ignition. "She can be a pain about it, for sure, but she works hard and does a great job taking care of the mystery section."

"Maybe, but she's still a hoarder."

During the drive back to OakLeaf, I recounted Nate's and my late-night run-in with Roxy, and Sarra agreed that it had to have been baggies of the store's cash she was throwing at Katrina.

"But why would she be giving her money?" Sarra asked.

"Good question. Maybe Lynn is right and they are dealing drugs."

"Doesn't the board of directors have anything to say about how money is handled?"

"You would think so, but according to Evelyn they're nothing but a bunch of figure-heads, and I have no reason not to believe her."

Coming to a stop at OakLeaf's main gate, I typed in the four-digit code. Suddenly, something obvious occurred to me.

"I wonder..." I mumbled.

Sarra gave me a puzzled look. "Now what?"

"Whoever killed Gerald," I elaborated, "How did they get in here?"

"Thanks, Nancy Drew, I'd almost forgotten we're about to work where someone was recently MURDERED." She said, emphasizing the last word.

"Sorry, but you have to admit it is a good question."

"I don't know," she said, looking into the side rear-view mirror, "that thing closes really slowly. There would be plenty of time for someone to slip in behind."

"That's a freaky thought." I shuddered, the possibility giving the entire scene an even more macabre feeling.

Back inside Gerald's unit, Sarra promptly inspected the card table. Other than a couple of yellow number two pencils and a battery powered calculator with an extra-large display window, the surface was clear.

"What do you think he was doing in here?" She asked. "Getting books ready to sell?"

I lifted the lid off the nearest box and pulled out a book. Inside its front cover, a dollar amount was written in pencil in the upper right-hand corner, the typical way to price a used book.

"Holy Cow!" I exclaimed.

"What?"

"He was asking fifty dollars for this."

"For a book he paid a dollar for? What a schmuck." She said. "Oops, sorry, probably shouldn't be speaking ill of the dead."

Working our way through the last row of boxes, Sarra found something of interest in the back corner. Moving closer I saw what looked like a stack of hardcovers partially concealed by a black plastic trash bag. As Sarra pulled it off, I could see the colorful spines of a popular and all-too-familiar mystery series.

"Evanoski!" Sarra exclaimed. "Why would Gerald be hiding these back here?"

I picked up the top book and looked inside, but instead of a dollar amount there was a strange sequence of random numbers and letters.

Checking the other books in the stack, I discovered a similar code in each.

"What do you think these mean?" Sarra asked.

"Haven't a clue," I said, "maybe Nate will know."

Pulling out my phone, I snapped a couple of photos of the codes while Sarra searched for an empty box to transport the books.

*   *   *

At exactly three-thirty-four, with the last of Gerald's books loaded in the canopy and a take-out order of a double cheeseburger and French fries for Lynn on the seat between us, we finally arrived back at the bookstore. After opening the rear door, she was nowhere to be found.

"Lynn? Lynn?"

Searching everywhere in back, we eventually found her seated behind the front desk looking white as a sheet.

"What's going on?" I asked her.

"Marilyn is in the hospital."

Chapter

26

ILLUMINATION

(December 2, Friday afternoon)

There are times in your life when you make a quick decision and it ends up biting you in the rear; this was fast becoming one of those moments.

"She wanted me to go through the boxes for her and I said no." Lynn explained. "The next think I know Cheryl's telling me they need to go to the emergency room."

I suddenly felt nauseous and was pretty sure it wasn't from the hamburger I'd just eaten.

"Oh my gosh, was it her heart?" Sarra asked, instinctively placing a hand on her chest.

"Have you heard from them?" I asked.

"No, but it's only been about twenty minutes since they left. I offered to drive but Marilyn was pretty insistent Cheryl take her, that's why I'm up here at the desk."

Lynn sounded as exhausted as she looked.

"Oh man, I feel awful putting you into this position."

Lynn leaned back in the chair and gave me a stern look. "This isn't your fault, kiddo. I'm a trouble maker, remember?"

"Here, eat something." Sarra said, setting the greasy fast-food bag onto the desk.

"Thanks, but my appetite is shot."

"This has been a hell of a day," I told her, "why don't you go home?"

"No way! I'm going to help you finish the job."

"OK, but let me see if I can get a hold of Cheryl first."

Much to my surprise, she answered on the second ring.

"Hello?"

"Cheryl, its Holly, is Marilyn OK?"

I heard her say something muffled to someone else before answering.

"Yes, but they want to keep her overnight for observation. I was just about to leave and come back to the store."

"All right, see you when you get here."

Hanging up, I gave Lynn firm instructions to remain at the desk until Cheryl returned, especially since there were customers milling about. She wasn't happy but stayed put while Sarra and I returned to the truck.

We had just finished stacking our first load into the fish room when I got a call from Roxy.

"Katrina just called, what the HELL happened?!" She yelled, her voice piercing through my phone's speaker.

Although I tried to explain what little I knew of the situation, Roxy quickly interrupted.

"This is not good, NOT GOOD!" She shrieked, "We can't have volunteers a-saltin' each other! We need to deal with this as soon as possible!"

The connection suddenly went dead.

Sarra raised an eyebrow. "I couldn't help overhearing. What the heck does she mean by a-saltin'?"

Even though Roxy had mangled the verb, the meaning had been perfectly clear; either Katrina had embellished the story to get back at Lynn for some reason, or Marilyn had accused Lynn of attacking her.

"That woman is certifiable." Sarra commented, but I knew her well enough to know she was as concerned.

"Cheryl is here." Lynn said, rushing into the room.

Sarra and I exchanged looks but didn't breathe a word about Roxy's phone call. For my part, until I knew more about the situation, I didn't want Lynn feeling any worse than she already did.

At a quarter to five, with everything finally unloaded, I told an exhausted Sarra and Lynn to go home and for once neither argued. Helping Cheryl deal with a line of customers I kept an eye on the time, and when six o'clock finally arrived, breathed a massive sigh of relief to finally be able to lock up; this crazy day was officially over.

"Thanks for staying with me Holly, I really appreciate it." Cheryl said with a weary smile.

"No worries."

I watched as she struggled with a small calculator to total the sales for the day.

"This thing isn't working right." She said, banging it against the palm of her hand.

"Maybe the batteries are dead." I suggested.

"I put new ones in last week but it still isn't working. We used to have a better one but it disappeared."

I wondered if the calculator inside Gerald's unit was the one she was referring to, but didn't mention it as we had decided to leave it behind.

"Do you want to use the one on my phone?" I offered, reaching into my back pocket, but she shook her head.

"No thanks. Marilyn has one of those fancy things too, but I don't trust myself with them."

I treaded carefully with my next question as I wanted to get an honest answer.

"Speaking of Marilyn, thanks again for taking her to emergency, that was really sweet of you. Was she not feeling well?"

Cheryl gave this some thought, rubbing at her chin with a finger and looking off into the distance before answering.

"She seemed fine when I got here."

"Did something happen between her and Lynn?"

"I don't know, I was helping customers and... well, when Marilyn came up here and started complaining about feeling woozy, I thought I better take her to the hospital."

She didn't look at me directly and instead turned her attention back to the calculator.

"DOO-DOO-DOO-DOO-DOO"

The unmistakable X-Files theme song blasted from my phone, immediately reminding me I hadn't let Nate know what was going on.

"Is everything OK?" he asked, his voice full of concern.

I apologized for not calling earlier and gave him a quick summary of the day's excitement as I walked towards the back of the store, careful not to mention Roxy's phone call until I was well out of Cheryl's hearing.

"We're closing up now so I should be home soon." I told him, envisioning a long hot shower, a big glass of wine and some snuggle time in front of the fire.

"Shouldn't you stop by the hospital and check in on Marilyn first?" he asked, instantly deflating all my happy thought balloons.

He was right, of course, in that it was the politically correct thing for me to do, especially if she hadn't been the one to lie about Lynn.

After ensuring Cheryl made it safely to her car parked up front, I turned off the lights and exited through the back of the store. Seated inside the truck's cab, I paused to let the engine warm up while considering how best to approach Marilyn; this was not going to be easy.

Chapter
27

PILLOW TALK

(December 2, Friday evening)

Autumn's Sierra Hospital advertised itself as a twenty-five bed acute care facility nestled in the beautiful Sierras. I had to admit the location was charming, even in the dark, with the parking lot rimmed by massive red oaks and a sweeping landscape of native plants lining the walkway towards the main entrance.

It had been nearly five years since I'd last visited the place, under more urgent circumstances, when Nate accidentally nicked his thumb while operating a chop saw. Luckily, the cut hadn't been deep enough to cause any nerve damage and had only required a few stitches.

"Can I help you?" A man sitting behind a desk in the lobby asked me.

I noticed he was wearing a laminated photo ID which read "Thomas – Information & Guest Services".

"Yes, I'm looking for a co-worker who checked in a couple of hours ago. Marilyn Stokes?"

He punched a few buttons on his computer's keyboard before writing a room number down onto the corner of a detailed hospital map, then spent the next several minutes giving me verbal instructions on how to locate the room. A bit overkill for such a small hospital, for sure, but I wasn't about to complain.

When I located the room and knocked on the opened door, I could see Marilyn propped up in the lone bed staring intently down at her phone. Since she wasn't wearing her glasses, she didn't recognize me at first.

"Holly, what a surprise." she said, pursing her lips in what I took to be a cool reception.

"Hello Marilyn. I hope I'm not bothering you, just wanted to check and see if you were OK."

"Thank you for your concern."

She placed her phone face down on the tray table hovering above her lap before continuing. "Now that you're here, there's something I need to talk to you about."

I could feel my cheeks begin to flush as I prepared myself for Lynn being thrown under the bus.

"Someone went into my closet and rearranged my hardcovers."

Her voice faltered as she spoke, as if this were a truly traumatic occurrence.

"Wow, OK," I said, taking in the news, "when did this happen?"

"I don't know, but when I finished my shift on Wednesday I distinctly remember having everything perfectly alphabetized and today it was in total disarray."

There were tears welling in the corners of her gray eyes, and I suddenly found myself feeling sorry for her.

A nurse holding a pillow walked into the room.

"Here you go, hon, found you another one."

Stuffing it behind Marilyn's back, she fluffed it up a bit before turning towards me.

"Your mum is a such a dear," She said, speaking with a slight Australian accent, "a real pleasure to take care of.

I decided it wasn't worth the effort to correct her assumption.

"Just press your button if you need anything else." She told Marilyn before heading out the door.

"Thank you Belinda."

The attention melted Marilyn's face into a glowing smile, so I decided to focus on something other than the bookstore.

"Cheryl tells me they're keeping you overnight for observations?"

"Yes, they want to make sure everything is all right with my pacemaker."

"My Mom has one of those too. The last time I visited her she was feeling dizzy and I had to take her to emergency, so I know how that goes. No fun."

Bringing up my mother seemed to put Marilyn in better spirits and we spent the next several minutes discussing the frustrations of living far away from loved ones.

"What's your mother's name?" She asked.

"Dolores, but everyone calls her Doris."

"I love that name. I couldn't get enough of Doris Day when I was young and had a scrap book of every magazine and newspaper article mentioning her I could find. I even had a signed photo of her hanging up on the wall of my shop in Marin."

"I like Doris Day too. What was that movie she was in with Rock Hudson...?"

"Oh, you mean Pillow Talk!" Marilyn interrupted, clapping her hands together like a thrilled teenager.

The conversation was going so well I worried about my next step, but decided to segue into what I really wanted to find out.

"Did you let Katrina know what happened?" I asked, treading carefully.

"Of course. I called her right after I found out I had to spend the night. Cheryl will sub for me tomorrow so it's all taken care of."

"Oh good, I would have offered but I have to take Nate to the airport. He's flying to Australia for a couple of weeks."

"I'm sure you'll miss him terribly."

"That I will. Oh, Lynn sends her regards, she was worried about you." I said, playing the last card in my deck while carefully watching her reaction.

"I appreciate that." Marilyn responded, with no visible change to her composure. "Please tell her thank you."

Belinda returned and I took it as my opportunity to say goodbye and exit the room. On the drive home, I had a lot to think about. From what I could tell, Katrina had interjected herself into this drama and was fabricating a scenario. She seemed intent on creating another problem with one of 'my sorters', someone she had already dubbed a trouble maker, and I had no doubt her goal was to get Lynn fired.

Marilyn, on the other hand, seemed way more concerned about her books being messed with than anything else; books stored in a closet where I had heard Roxy rummaging on possibly more than one occasion.

What the heck was going on in our used bookstore?

Chapter
28

WORD WUMP

(December 5, Monday morning)

A massive beast swung into the spot adjacent my own, filling the entire side view with a wall of glossy jet black. The driver revved the engine a couple of times before shutting it off, making me wonder what kind of person does that in a restaurant parking lot. Squeezing out from between our sandwiched vehicles I called over to the dark clad figure climbing out of the pick-up truck's super cab.

"Katrina!"

"Roxy's going to be late." She said with a face devoid of any expression, positive or negative.

"Should we wait for her inside?" I asked, forcing a fake smile; there was no way I was going to let her see my own level of discomfort at having to attend this meeting.

"Sure."

Katrina marched towards the entrance and I followed, watching her long hair swish back and forth across her back like a thick ebony tongue.

The tantalizing odor of frying bacon and Big Buck's signature vanilla pancakes greeted us as we pushed our way through the front doors. Waiting for the hostess, I noticed that the top of Katrina's head only came to my chin even though she wore two inch heels. Somehow, this trivial fact helped calm my anxious 'taller than average' nerves.

After we were seated in a booth and handed menus, a waiter came by to fill our coffee mugs with steaming hot brew and leave a bowl of creamers on the table.

"She'll be here soon." Katrina said in a raspy voice while tapping something on her phone. She slipped it inside her leather jacket and shivered slightly.

"You sound like you're fighting something." I said, deciding to make small talk to fill the time, though still very much aware she was intent on causing me problems.

"Yeah, I'm taking care of my Dad and he gave me his cold."

"Is he ill?" I asked, realizing I knew very little about her personal life.

"He was paralyzed in a hunting accident."

"I'm so sorry to hear that. Was this recently?"

Katrina seemed distracted and pulled her phone back out to type something before answering.

"No, it happened seven years ago. My Mom died last year so it's been my job to take care of him now."

The waiter interrupted to see if we were ready to order, but quickly left when Katrina told him we were still waiting for someone.

"That must be challenging." I said, pulling the lids off two creamers and pouring them into my coffee.

Katrina shrugged her shoulders. "It's not too bad, he sleeps most of the time." She picked up the menu and glanced at it briefly before pulling her phone out, again.

"Everything OK?" I asked, wondering who she was texting.

"No, just getting my ass kicked on Word Wump."

"What's that?"

"It's an online game I'm addicted to." She explained, turning the phone around so I could see the screen. Various words were appearing and disappearing within three dimensional boxes floating around a colorful background; it looked like something an elementary student would play.

"If you hit the matching words on time it makes this cool 'wump' sound."

"OK." I responded, trying hard not to judge her choice of entertainment.

Katrina swore under her breath and shoved the phone back into her pocket before picking up her coffee. After taking a sip, she focused in on me.

"Marilyn told me you visited her at the hospital. She's such a dear and wanted to work yesterday but I insisted she take a couple days off. I don't know what we would do without her." Her demeanor had visibly changed as she spoke about Marilyn, softening slightly with the corners of her mouth rising upwards. This positive emotion was fascinating, and I couldn't help wonder if this was what a panther would look like if it could smile.

Suddenly, she began to wave her arms in the air and within seconds Roxy bounded into view, sliding onto the bench alongside her.

"Boy could I use some java!" she exclaimed, squirming around to look for the waiter. Her knees bumped the bottom of the table in the process, the impact causing some of my coffee to slosh out onto the table and across my hand. Fortunately, I had added enough cream to make it more lukewarm than scalding.

The waiter reappeared and, after filling Roxy's mug, once again asked if we were ready to order.

"I'll have the Miner's Special with a side of bacon, extra crispy." Katrina said before handing her laminated menu over to Roxy who stared at it with blood shot eyes.

"How about you, Ma'am?" The young man asked me.

I was finishing wiping up the spill with a napkin when I read his name badge, suddenly realizing why he looked so familiar.

"Martin?"

I slid out from behind the table to stand and give him a quick hug.

"Oh my gosh, you've grown a foot since the last time I saw you!"

"Hello Mrs. Singer." He said, grinning ear to ear. "There's a couple of us in the kitchen who recognized you."

Sitting back down I noticed both Roxy and Katrina staring at me.

"Martin was one of my students." I explained before turning back to him. "How is your art going?"

"OK, I guess. I took a class down at Starline, but the teacher sucked."

"Well, don't give up, you're too good."

"Thanks, what can I get you?" he asked.

Since I didn't think there was any way I could eat anything while dealing with whatever was about to unfold, I simply opted for the coffee.

He nodded and turned back towards Roxy who had gone back to looking at the menu.

"Get what you got last time." Katrina hissed at her.

"The Big Buck combo?" Roxy asked, looking confused.

There were bits of straw and what I assumed to be horsehair embedded across the front of her nubbly fleece jacket, and she had stopped fidgeting somewhat, which was good, especially since she was now in possession of her own steaming cup of coffee.

"You want sausage or bacon with that?" Martin asked her.

"She'll take the bacon, extra crispy like mine." Katrina interjected, abruptly pulling the menu out of Roxy's grip to hand over to him.

I couldn't believe Roxy was allowing Katrina to boss her around like this, and noticed Martin raise his eyebrows in a definite 'WTF' look before leaving.

"I didn't know you were a schoolteacher." Roxy said, even though I'm sure I had told her.

"Well, single subject. I taught visual and performing art up in Mountain Terrace for ten years." I explained.

"Oh, so you're one of those CREATIVE types." Katrina said in a mocking tone which caused both of them to laugh. My stomach tightened at the obvious attempted slam, and I was really glad I hadn't ordered any food.

Before I could get onto the subject of why we were meeting in the first place, the two began talking horse; something I know nothing about. After a few minutes of listening to their rambling conversation, I decided I'd had enough.

"So, you wanted to talk about what happened Friday at the bookstore?" I asked Roxy.

"Dang straight!" She responded, leaning forward with a furrowed brow. "Sounds like we have a real trouble maker on our hands with this Lynn."

"Lynn didn't do anything wrong and..."

"She threatened Marilyn." Katrina interrupted.

"No one was threatened." I countered, feeling my blood already begin to boil.

"That's not what I heard."

Roxy waved her arms in the air as if to get our attention, "I don't know," she said, "maybe she's gotta go."

Shocked at her blunt statement, my mind raced at how best to respond when Martin suddenly appeared to distribute their plates of food.

"There's no way this is extra crispy." Katrina said, holding up a slice of bacon which looked plenty fried to me.

Martin leaned slightly forward to inspect the piece before straightening.

"If it was any crisper it would be burnt." he responded with a perfectly deadpan expression, and I made a mental note to give him an extra-large tip.

After he left, I glanced over to see Katrina folding the bacon into a napkin. When she caught me watching, she quickly slipped the packet into her jacket before turning towards Roxy.

"Lynn also went into Marilyn's closet and messed around with her books."

"What?! Didn't you tell her not to go in there?!" Roxy screeched, causing the family seated across from us to look up from their pancakes.

"Yes," I said, keeping my voice as low as possible, "but we both know other people go in there too."

Roxy's eyes bulged as she caught the gist of my meaning.

"But nobody should be going in there except Marilyn." Katrina protested.

"You know Marilyn," Roxy chuckled, obviously changing gear, "she's always thinkin' people are messin' 'round with her books." She stuffed a huge piece of pancake into her mouth in order to end the discussion.

Unfortunately, the tactic didn't deter Katrina.

"But Lynn sent Marilyn to the hospital!" She insisted.

"That's ridiculous!" I snapped back.

"Did you ladies want some more coffee?" Martin asked, reappearing at the table with the glass carafe.

"Darn tootin'!" Roxy said through a mouth full of dough as she held out her mug.

Katrina continued her tirade after Martin had left. "We know Lynn's a trouble maker."

"I don't know what your problem is, but saying Lynn's responsible for Marilyn going to the hospital is, well... unbelievable." I grabbed my purse and began to scoot across the bench, deciding it was best to put as much distance as possible between us.

"Whoa now Holly," Roxy said, waving her palms over the table in an attempt to calm things down, "Katrina's just worried about Marilyn, that's all."

Clutching my purse against my chest like a shield, I reluctantly remained seated.

"So you're going to take care of this?" Katrina asked Roxy; she was starting to remind me of a rat terrier, and not in a nice way.

Roxy surveyed the remains of her half eaten breakfast.

"I'll discuss it with Marilyn first." She mumbled.

Katrina frowned and began to stab at her own food with a fork.

"Some of the volunteers have been asking about the meeting." I said, taking the sudden turn of events as an opportunity to push some of my own buttons. "Any idea when it's going to be rescheduled?"

"What?" Roxy looked up from her plate, "Didn't we already have one? Whatever, I don't care. You two figure it out."

Katrina's responding smirk told me everything I needed to know.

"OK, fine, I need to get going." Standing, I shrugged into my coat.

"But we're still eating." Roxy said.

Ignoring her, I said goodbye and headed for the register.

"Everything OK, Mrs. Singer?" Martin asked as he rang up my tab.

"Yes, it's all good. Keep doing art, OK?"

"Definitely."

I left the restaurant and climbed back into my car. Driving to the bookstore, my contacts began to float across the surface of my eyeballs, and by the time I parked behind the ramp, tears streamed down both cheeks.

This is stupid, I was allowing a bully to turn me into a pile of mush when what I really needed to do was pull myself together and stand firm; There was no way I could allow Katrina to succeed in getting rid of Lynn or prevent the volunteers from having a meeting.

"Well, at least I'm not addicted to Word Wump." I told my reflection in the vanity mirror while checking for running mascara.

"Inquiring minds want to know." Sarra quipped as I walked into the sorting room.

"Is it too early for a cider?" I responded while hanging my purse behind the door.

"That bad?"

"Yep."

"Marilyn better tell the truth so this whole thing with Lynn gets dropped." She commented, after I relayed the highlights of the meeting.

"BAM"

A shopping cart filled with boxes slammed into the room's doorframe, making us both jump.

"Did I hear my name?" Lynn asked as she parked it next to a table.

Sarra gave me a 'what are you going to do now' look so I decided to go with an honest approach.

"Katrina is saying you threatened Marilyn last Friday, even though I visited her at the hospital and she didn't say a word about it. I'm pretty sure it's just Katrina being a bitch."

Lynn's eyes widened and her complexion paled, making me instantly regret my decision.

"Don't worry," I said, quickly attempting to patch up the damage. "Roxy is going to talk with Marilyn and clear it all up."

"Marilyn doesn't like me any more than Katrina does." Lynn said with a defeated expression. "If it comes down to their word against mine, Roxy won't believe me – I'm too new."

"If she fires you then I'm quitting too." Sarra said, slamming the book she was holding down onto the table before crossing her arms defiantly.

"Nobody's getting fired." I told them.

"We'll see." Lynn said before hustling out the door.

For the next hour, Sarra and I sorted in relative silence while my overactive imagination went into overdrive with possible worst case scenarios. If Lynn did end up getting fired it would probably mean Sarra would quit too, which would leave me with the difficult decision of either quitting myself or working at the bookstore without friends.

Right on cue, the next book I pulled out of a bag made the perfect statement: *The Care and Feeding of Volunteers.*

"You should put that on Roxy's desk" Sarra said when I showed her the title.

Playing with the idea momentarily, I eventually chickened out and tossed it into the business genre box.

"I know, I'm a wimp." I told Sarra who was rolling her eyes at me.

At a quarter of two, Evelyn sashayed into the sorting room wrapped in a fawn colored trench coat cinched tightly at the waist. Her white hair was pulled back into an impressive ponytail, and when I commented on the length, she merely laughed.

"It's fake!"

Although I had no doubt she had already heard about Marilyn being in hospital, she didn't bring it up and instead gave us some other interesting news; apparently, the store's bookkeeper had quit.

"Maybe the woman finally got tired of the whole baggie situation." Sarra chuckled.

When I asked Evelyn if she knew the reason why, she didn't have an answer.

"I need to go back to the library and talk to Emiko," I told Sarra, once we were alone, "maybe she can help fit some of these puzzle pieces together."

Lynn strode into the room and grabbed her jacket and purse from behind the door. "I'm not feeling up to going to the Belgian today, you gals go without me." She told us as we walked down the ramp to our cars. Before we could dissuade her, she slipped into her car and drove away.

"I hope she's OK." Sarra said.

"Me too."

Although we hadn't known each other long, Lynn already felt like a good friend and her uncharacteristic decline of cider and favorite sandwich had me worried. My only conclusion was the situation with Marilyn really had her upset, and I could have kicked myself for spilling the beans.

Approaching my car, I noticed it was leaning slightly to the left and quickly discovered one of the rear tires was flat.

"Dang it!"

Sarra stayed with me until the road service showed up fifteen minutes later.

"You must have really pissed someone off." The driver told me, breaking into a fit of laughter after inspecting my tire.

"What do you mean?" I asked.

"Someone cut your stem, see?" He pointed to the valve which had clearly been severed in half.

"How?"

"Probably wire cutters."

I'd read somewhere that the first person you think of when something bad happens is usually the person responsible, and since this was the kind of petty vandalism you would expect a bully to engage in, Katrina fit the bill.

In the time it took to replace my damaged tire with the spare, Sarra and I decided to forgo the Belgian and call it a day. Later, having settled onto my living room couch with cat in lap, the home phone rang. Martha squeaked in protest as I disengaged her to scramble for it.

"Hello?"

"Holly? It's Lynn."

Her voice was solemn and I could tell right away something wasn't right.

"I wanted to let you know I've emailed my resignation to Roxy and Katrina."

Chapter

29

STRIKE ANYWHERE

(December 5, Monday night)

One last trip to the dollar store was all it took.

Thanks to information revealed within the newly acquired detective handbook, he had decided to ditch the gadgets entirely. His coat pockets were now filled with only the most essential of items; pocketknife, flashlight, handkerchief, small magnifying glass, notebook, mechanical pencil and a Zippo.

The lighter had been a bit of a compromise, mostly because he couldn't find any 'strike anywhere' matches, but it would do. Besides, as a gift from his partner, having it near made him still feel somewhat connected.

"Sift through the evidence, look for clues." He muttered to himself as he made his way to the parking area behind the bookstore.

His well-documented observations had revealed that the store's trash was regularly emptied Monday afternoons by the tall, dark skinned volunteer. She reminded him of the superhero character that could manipulate weather so he did his best to avoid her gaze as lightning, in particular, terrified him.

With dusk descended and the bookstore now closed, he felt relaxed and ready for the task at hand as he approached the dumpsters. Turning on his flashlight, he lifted one of the lids and peered inside.

Suddenly, everything went dark.

He banged the flashlight against the palm of his hand a couple of times but it refused to respond and remained dark.

Rats, must be the batteries.

Shoving it back into his pocket, he scrounged around in another for the Zippo. It sputtered to attention at the first click, and he carefully lowered the small flame down into the depths of the bin.

An over-stuffed white trash bag lay on the bottom with its orange draw-string handles off to one side. Bending at the waist to reach for them, the sound of an approaching diesel made him freeze his position. Although semi-trucks often parked in the adjacent lot for the night, instead of hearing crunching gravel, tires squealed onto the asphalt behind him and headlights swept across the front of the dumpster, startling him into dropping the lighter.

Double rats.

From the sound of it, the vehicle had stopped directly behind him.

Quickly extracting himself, he scuttled behind the dumpster wall and huddled against the brick, listening to the sound of a door creaking open and slamming shut. Forcing himself to take a peek, he saw the outline of a person standing next to a large pickup truck, something oddly familiar about both.

"Look for clues, find connections." He whispered across a tongue suddenly gone dry as sand.

Connections, what were the connections?

Behind him, a car had pulled into the restaurant's drive-thru and the menu board intercom crackled to attention, offering him a perfect opportunity to make a run for it; better safe than sorry.

Chapter
30

WHAT A HOOT

(December 6, Tuesday morning-early afternoon)

The sound of an owl woke me from a restless dream.

I had been chasing kittens down the main aisle of the bookstore, trying to grab their scampering bodies before they disappeared beneath shelves while Roxy yelled in the background for me to hurry up. Following one around a corner, I came upon Nate helping Marilyn shelve mystery books; both of them wearing baseball caps embellished with smiley face logos.

Separating myself from the strange images, I focused in on the pair of Great Horned Owls performing a duet of alternating calls in the woods outside. The female sounded like she was stationed in one of the oak trees in our back yard, while the male's deeper hoot echoed from across the low-slung valley behind our property; his distance a bittersweet reminder of the empty spot next to me on the bed.

I checked the clock on the nightstand, estimating the time in Sydney to be around ten PM. After doing my business in the bathroom, I slipped into my robe and slippers and headed for the kitchen to make some coffee. Once a dollop of half-and-half was splashed into both my cup and Martha's bowl, I sat down at the counter and opened my laptop to click on the Skype logo.

"What are you doing up so early?" Nate answered almost immediately.

His computer screen cast an eerie glow across both his face and the portion of hotel wall behind him where a black and white photo of the Opera House hung.

I told him about the owls and my strange dream.

"You should have gone back to sleep," he said, taking a sip of what looked like a glass of red wine, "I would have called you in an hour or so when you normally get up."

"This way you can go to bed sooner."

"I haven't been able to sleep. For some reason it's taking me forever to get acclimated to the time change."

"Is that Shiraz?" I asked, knowing how much he liked certain Australian wines.

"Yep, it's from Margaret River and is really good."

Alternately sipping our wine and coffee, like the owls and their calls, we briefly talked about the progress of his job before switching gears to bookstore gossip.

"Are you going to try and talk her out of it?" He asked, referring to Lynn's decision to quit.

"I hope so. Sarra and I are going to meet her at the Belgian this afternoon."

"Let me know how it goes."

"Will do. Hey, did you get a chance to look at those photos I sent?"

He yawned before answering. "Nope, not yet."

"No worries, I was just curious if you knew what those codes were."

He finished the last of his wine and yawned again, prompting me to say farewell and end the call.

Snapping the laptop closed, I carefully moved Martha off my lap and went to look out into the darkness beyond the back window. Even though I didn't hear the owls anymore and the sun wouldn't be up for at least another hour or so, thanks to daylight savings being in effect, I was too awake to think about going back to bed and decided to make more coffee.

Between holiday cards to finish, emails to answer, and an obligatory hour long phone call with my mother, the morning sped by in a flash. I thought about working on the painting propped up on the easel in the family room, but for some reason the creative spark just wasn't happening for me at the moment.

At noon, with a pile of addressed and stamped envelopes nestled on the passenger seat beside me, I took a left at the bottom of our drive and headed south on Placer Ridge Way toward Mountain Terrace. The winding two-lane road was an enjoyable route offering serene views of meadows fringed by dark forests of Ponderosa pines, the asphalt covered in places with leaves and needles drifted into soft fiber rolls. Houses were few and far between along this stretch, with most hidden at the end of long, private driveways like our own.

Pausing at the only stop sign along the way, I saw an elderly couple raking leaves in their front yard, and they waved at me as I coasted past; the gesture making me smile.

Mountain Terrace's 'main drag' runs a mere quarter of a mile, and has only one stop light which rarely turns red. With only a few businesses to boast of, including a small grocery store, a bank, and a hardware store, it's really more of a village than a town.

After stopping at the post office to drop off my mail, I continued driving south past the abandoned school where I used to work. Shifting demographics and severe budget cuts had caused it to close a couple years ago, with students and teachers transferring to surrounding schools, and my position had been one of many to fall through the cracks.

"And now I'm working at a used bookstore." I said to myself, wondering if I had been a hypocrite for telling Martin to keep doing art when my own focus was torn.

Fifteen minutes later, I pulled into the library's main parking area only to find it full. After nabbing the last available space in the graveled overflow lot across the street, I couldn't help wonder if this was normal for a Tuesday afternoon.

Walking past a stroller packed forecourt, I soon had my answer. The lobby was teeming with toddlers running in all directions across the carpeted floor while weary looking parents with armfuls of picture books stood in the check-out line; I'd evidently arrived at the end of story-time.

I wasn't at all surprised to discover the elusive Mr. Smiley was a no-show in the computer area; the roar of kiddies was enough to make anyone want to head for the hills. With librarians focused on customers, I opted to search for Emiko myself and was relieved to find her working far from the madding crowd. She smiled in recognition as I approached, straightening from a bent position in front of the graphic novels.

"Hello Emiko. Did you have a nice Thanksgiving?" I asked.

"Yes, and you?"

"Mine was great, thanks."

Bowing her head slightly in acknowledgement, she turned back to her book cart.

"If you're not too busy I was hoping to ask you some questions." I said, watching her shelve a Manga novel I recognized as one my son had read.

"Of course, we can go to the Sierra Room. No one is using it now."

If she was surprised at my request she didn't show it, and I wondered if she had already guessed my queries would concern Pat.

Emiko began to push her cart towards the front of the library and motioned me to follow. Up by the checkout, she swerved to avoid the queue and suddenly came to a complete stop. When I looked around the cart to see the cause, I saw a little girl clutching a large picture book blocking our path.

"Excuse us Miss." Emiko said, but the child didn't budge and kept both feet planted firmly on the carpet.

Glancing over at the adults in line, I hoped one of them would call her away, but none seemed to be looking in our direction.

"Miss?" Emiko asked again, still with no luck.

Approaching the girl, I crouched to eye level and gave her my biggest smile.

"Did you find a good book?" I asked.

The ploy worked and she instantly relaxed.

"It's about owls," she said, showing me the front cover, "I like owls."

"Cool. I like owls too." I told her, thinking about the pair that had woken me that morning.

A woman's voice called out a name and the girl scampered away.

"Fukuro," Emiko said, smiling as she pushed the cart forward, "in Japan, owls are a sign of good luck."

Sounds good to me, I thought, following her past the restrooms. I noticed Pat's memorial flyer had been replaced with a holiday party notification, and somehow this alteration made me even more determined to continue my investigative efforts.

At the end of the hallway, a doorway led to the library's Sierra Room; a large rectangular shaped space with tall banks of windows at both ends. While the left faced the entry forecourt and the dwindling number of strollers, the right overlooked a paved path bordered by a wall of lush evergreen shrubs. Framed photos of local landmarks lined the walls, and a baby grand piano took up the back right-hand corner, its shape distorted by a thick quilted cover.

Emiko parked the cart near the entrance and walked to the opposite corner of the room where an alcove revealed a small kitchenette.

"Would you like something to drink?" She asked. "There's coffee and tea."

"Coffee would be great." I replied, following her into the cramped space.

I watched as she swung open a cupboard above a stainless steel sink and removed two white cups, setting them down next to a coffee machine that looked a lot like the one in my kitchen back home.

"I prefer drip but everyone here seems to love this thing." She said, selecting a pod from a table top carousel and dropping it into the machine's yawning holder.

"They're definitely convenient." I offered, thinking how great it would be to have one of these at the bookstore; convincing Roxy to pay for one, however, would be next to impossible.

With coffee in hand, we settled into a pair of leather upholstered chairs beneath a black and white image of the County's courthouse.

"Thanks for taking the time to talk with me." I said.

Emiko took a cautious sip of her coffee before responding.

"Of course. I take it this is about Pat?"

144

I paused, suddenly feeling tongue-tied; the questions fluttering around in my brain might very well sound idiotic if I said them out loud.

Emiko surprised me by lightly patting me on the knee.

"You've lost someone you obviously cared about," she said, "it's understandable you want to know more about their life."

Her reassurance comforting, I decided to continue. "The last time we spoke, you mentioned Pat was concerned about something having to do with BARF. Can you tell me more?"

"Pat wasn't one to complain, but it was easy to see she was troubled. At first I assumed it had something to do with Roxanne, especially having heard her reputation for being difficult to work with, but when Pat began to question me about non-profits specifically, I knew it had to be something else."

"What do you mean?" I asked.

"Pat knew I worked at a law firm before retiring and had some experience dealing with them. Unfortunately, I learned the hard way that finding out more than what is legally required of them to reveal can prove challenging."

Emiko paused for a moment, as if trying to recall something.

"However, sometimes when they apply for grants they are required to list all their major donors. There are websites that can help you access that information, and Pat got all excited about one in particular that she even printed out some pages."

"Do you know what she found?"

"No, she seemed to want to keep it private."

My interest piqued, I asked Emiko how to access the sites myself and she obliged, typing my contact information into her cell phone with a promise to send me the links.

For the next few moments we quietly sat and sipped our remaining coffee. My thoughts soon turned to the secrets Pat seemed to be holding, particularly why she hadn't told me she volunteered at the library. When I shared this with Emiko, her demeanor changed.

"I'll always wonder why she left Ruth's party so abruptly." She said with a sigh, "When I heard she died all alone in the bookstore, it nearly broke my heart. If only she would have stayed here, surrounded by people, we could have possibly saved her life."

"Pat was here the night she died?" I asked, confused.

"Yes, one of our librarians was retiring and we threw a party here in the Sierra Room." Emiko glanced over at the far window which faced the paved walkway. "Pat seemed distracted and left not long after the party started."

I sat momentarily stunned; the reality that 'R @ SR' wasn't 'Roxy at the Secret Ranch' hitting me like a splash of cold water.

"Do you have the cart?" A librarian called from the hallway, prompting Emiko to quickly rise and reach for my empty cup.

"Excuse me for needing to leave, but I should get back to work."

"That's quite all right." I said, standing as well. "Thank you so much for taking the time to talk to me, and for the coffee."

"Best of luck with solving some of Pat's mysteries, and I hope to see you again soon." She said before disappearing into the kitchenette.

Back out in the main part of the library, I scanned the computer area one more time but Mr. Smiley was still absent; so much for luck.

As I walked to my car feeling frustrated at now being in possession of more questions than answers, a group of stroller-pushing joggers caught my attention. They were on the paved pathway that curved around the library past the Sierra Room window, no doubt making their way to the adjoining park. A few feet behind them, a white-haired women wearing a bright pink tracksuit followed their course, and for a brief second I thought she looked a little like Marilyn.

"I really need a cider." I said, to no one in particular.

CIDER GIRLS

(December 6, Tuesday afternoon)

S andwich boy was out in the Belgian's side lot smoking a cigarette and talking with someone dressed in a long trench coat. At first glance I thought it was the vampire obsessed customer I'd encountered at the bookstore, but on further inspection this individual looked much younger. Walking past them on the way to the entrance, she ignored me but he raised a long arm in the air in what I assumed was a gesture of hello; people never cease to amaze me.

Inside, the pub was relatively empty except for a few lone customers seated along the main bar.

"Hey Holly, looks like you're the first one here." The bartender said.

He filled a goblet with cider and slid it across the counter in my direction, it's faceted exterior catching the light and shimmering like a golden jewel.

"What's this?" I asked, "It's beautiful."

He grinned, obviously pleased with himself. "We just got those in and I thought they would be perfect for you cider girls."

Thanking him, I paid and headed for the back room's corner table, figuring it would offer us plenty of privacy just in case we needed it. Seated so I faced the front, I waited for my friends while sipping cider and listening to the calming metronome of the overhead fans.

Sarra was the next to arrive and soon descended the ramp with her own golden goblet in hand.

"Aren't these fancy." she said, setting it down opposite my own.

"Guess we're officially the 'cider girls' now." I said with a chuckle.

"You know, we really need to figure out his name."

Agreeing, I looked over her shoulder to see Lynn approaching with a third goblet.

"What's this about you quitting?" Sarra demanded before she even had the chance to sit down.

"Now don't you start in on me too." She said, plopping into a chair. "Like I told Holly, I've made up my mind. Besides, there was no way I was going to let you two quit because of me."

Sarra looked over at me for support, but I didn't have much to offer.

"I already told her this wasn't necessary. Roxy said she was going to talk with Marilyn and..."

"Never mind all that," Lynn interrupted, "I've already found something better and it's a doozy." She giggled in way that made me think trouble was brewing.

"What have you got yourself into?" Sarra asked, her eyes narrowing.

Lynn moved closer to the edge of the table and lowered her voice in a conspiratorial manner.

"You know how you guys get those books from the barn down in Jefferson? Well, I went down there yesterday to check it out and got to talking with Liz, the lady who runs the place. We hit it off right away and when I told her I had quit working at BARF, she let loose on how Roxy doesn't know HOW to treat volunteers."

As she paused to take a sip of cider, I wondered where this was going.

"Then," she continued, "Liz tells me her husband does odd jobs over at the Secret Ranch but she's not happy about it because she feels Roxy abuses his good nature. That got me to thinking maybe he's seen some of what is going on over there, so I signed up to be a volunteer and I start this Sunday."

"You're unbelievable." Sarra laughed.

"Speaking of the Secret Ranch," I said, "there's something you both need to hear."

My news about Pat attending a retirement party at the Sierra Room, however, didn't seem to faze Lynn.

"Regardless, we all saw that something fishy is going on down at the ranch and I think my volunteering at the barn will help us figure out what."

"OK, fine, but I think we need to find out what Pat was investigating."

"You're both starting to sound like Nancy Drew." Sarra said.

Looking at Lynn's determined face, a new concern popped into my head. "Will you be working at the barn during the drop?" I asked.

"Yes, Liz says we have to load up all the bins because she doesn't trust Katrina's biker friends to do a good job."

"Please do me a favor and stay away from Katrina," I warned, "I don't trust her."

"And be sure your phone is charged so you can call us if anything happens." Sarra added.

"I can take care of myself." Lynn snapped back.

Sarra sighed and distorted her mouth into an exaggerated frown. "So you're really going to quit on us? Mondays won't be the same without you flirting with all the customers."

"We can still meet here for cider."

While the two of them continued to banter back and forth, I pulled out my phone to check the time and noticed a message from Nate.

"Hey," I interrupted, "remember those strange codes we found inside the books in Gerald's storage? Nate says they look like DigiCoins."

"What the heck are those?" Sarra asked.

"Oh! I watched a documentary on that just the other day," Lynn said, "they're a new form of money that uses crypto-currency."

Sarra looked confused. "Crypto what?"

"Codes instead of cash. It's a way of digitally transferring funds." I explained further.

"So those codes are worth something?"

"Possibly, if they haven't been used yet."

My mind began to swirl with possible reasons Gerald might have had for hiding the code filled Evanoski's; either he was saving them because he knew their potential value, or, he was the one creating them in the first place.

"Gerald was supposedly killed in a robbery gone bad, right?" I asked, "What if the DigiCoin codes were what the thieves were looking for?"

Sarra and Lynn both stared at me with mouths agape.

"We need to find that box of books and take it to the police right away!" Sarra exclaimed, pushing her chair back from the table to stand.

Lynn and I quickly followed suit, grabbing our empty goblets and hustling up to the bar.

"Hey ladies, ready for another round?" the bartender asked.

"Nope," Lynn told him as we set our glassware onto the counter, "we're off to solve a murder."

* * *

With all of us piled into my car, I had us parked behind the bookstore in under ten minutes. After jogging up the ramp, I unlocked the door and Lynn slipped inside while I waited for Sarra, who was a bit slower on the ascent. By the time the two of us entered the hall, Lynn had already disappeared around the corner.

"It looks like someone's gone through them!" she informed us when we joined her in the fish room.

"Shit!" Sarra and I responded in unison.

Although the boxes we'd hauled from Gerald's storage were still stacked against the wall where we had left them, they were no longer in neat rows and many had lids askew.

"Who would do this?" Sarra asked.

"I don't know," I said, feeling suddenly deflated.

After a good half hour of searching and reorganizing, we reluctantly had to concede that all coded Evanoski books were gone; so much for possibly finding a clue to help solve Gerald's murder.

After confirming with the afternoon cashiers that they hadn't seen a thing during their shift, the three of us convened in the sorting room.

"There's no way this happened while we were here, and Evelyn would definitely have noticed someone messing around back there." Sarra commented.

"Guess I need to talk with Peg or Daphne." I agreed, "If they didn't see anything this morning, then it had to have happened sometime last night."

Lynn gave me a questioning glance. "Do you think it could have been Marilyn looking for her stupid mystery hardcovers?"

"I don't see how, especially with her just getting out of hospital."

Although the thought had briefly crossed my mind, I had quickly nixed it as impossible; Marilyn was obviously in no shape to rifle through a wall of boxes and re-stack them.

"I'm going to check her closet anyways," Lynn declared, "they can't fire ME anymore!"

She dashed out into the hall and by the time Sarra and I reached the mystery room, had already disappeared into Marilyn's inner sanctum.

The space looked to be nothing more than an oversized walk-in closet at only six feet wide, but ran a good twenty feet back. Mystery hardcovers were packed into an assortment of bookcases lining the left side, some reaching nearly to the ceiling, while others were stacked on the floor along the right-hand wall.

Lynn was at the farthest corner, looking up at a unit full of glossy neon colored spines.

"Bingo." She said, extracting an apple green book and handing it over to me.

Scanning the inside front cover, I found it clear of any codes.

"Might as well check the rest." I told her.

We had nearly finished searching the rest of the volumes when a voice in the adjacent room made us all freeze.

"Marilyn? Is that you?"

Turning, I saw Cheryl.

"What the heck?" she exclaimed, eyes wide in a startled expression, "What are you doing in there?"

Before I could explain, she erupted in anger.

"Marilyn was right; you are messing with her books! I didn't want to believe it but now I see it for myself! You should be ashamed of yourselves!"

Her cheeks had turned blotchy and her hands were clenched into fists; this was a side of Cheryl I'd never seen before.

Lynn snorted from behind me. "It was my idea to come in here so don't blame them, I already quit."

She pushed past me and stomped out into the hallway, and Sarra and I quickly followed. Behind us I could hear Cheryl slam the closet door shut.

"Meowrrrrr"

Teddy screamed from his cage and I began to laugh; something I'm prone to do at the most inopportune of moments. A friend studying psychology once told me it comes from a need to project dignity and control during times of stress and anxiety, but usually it results in my getting weird looks like the one I was getting from Cheryl at the moment.

"What do you have against poor Marilyn?" She said, her voice still raised, "Why would you want to do this to her after all she's been through?"

"For goodness sakes, Cheryl, we weren't doing anything to Marilyn, just looking at her books." I responded, trying to regain some composure. Her overreaction was starting to piss me off and I could see by the expression on Sarra's face she echoed the sentiment.

A sudden click from the back door made me realize Lynn had already left.

"Come on Sarra, let's go. I need another cider."

Turning to leave, I took Teddy's follow-up howl as a declaration of encouragement.

CONNECTIONS

(December 7, Tuesday early evening)

A crow balanced on the top edge of a dumpster gave him the stink-eye. The sight made him uneasy, so he waved it away with his arms. Rising into the air without a sound, the creature caught the evening breeze and disappeared into the network of trees beyond the dead-end road like a black ghost. Usually he didn't mind crows, but after the strange events from the night before he wasn't in the mood for anything dark.

The loss of the lighter had stressed him out; as much for its nostalgia as for the desire to keep his detective kit complete. Although he had tried looking for it at first light, the shopping center's new security guard had hung around longer than expected and thwarted his plans. After purchasing more batteries and some much needed aspirin at the dollar store, he had taken sanctuary in the woods to reflect over his notes.

Scanning the area for any watchful eyes, he moved around to the front of the dumpster and lifted the lid. With the trash due for pick up the next morning, he had to retrieve the items before the others who utilized this location showed up. It was a balance of timing: just after the store closed, but not much later. Luckily, through his keen observations he had learned the volunteer couple who worked the afternoon shift never parked in back.

With the flashlight now working, he instantly spotted the white plastic trash liner along with a flash of silver on the floor beneath; it had to be the Zippo.

He tugged at the bag but it wouldn't budge. Further inspection showed the culprit, a heavy cardboard box, was pinching it in place. Hefting this out took some time as his upper body strength wasn't in the best of shape, and once he had finally maneuvered it onto the ground, a loose lid revealed the contents: hardcover books, the expensive kind, with brightly colored glossy covers.

Abandoning the box, he successfully extracted both the bag and the Zippo before making for the woods.

Time to look for clues.

Chapter

33

30 MINUTE WORKOUT

(December 9, Friday morning shift)

T hat's funny, I didn't get the email. When did she send it?"

"Tuesday night." Daphne said, twisting the end of one of her long white braids.

"Interesting."

Apparently, Katrina had notified all the volunteers about a meeting scheduled for this evening; everyone, that is, except me.

"Do you think maybe she doesn't have your correct address?" Daphne asked.

"No," I said, "that's not the problem."

Her eyes widened slightly at the irritation in my voice, though she didn't respond.

I went to unlock the store's front door. Outside, droplets of rain were creating dark splotches on the sidewalk and the wind had picked up, even though the forecast hadn't mentioned anything about a storm.

"It's starting to rain." I told Daphne before heading to the back.

Sarra had offered to come in and shelve Nate's Science Fiction books this morning and I was looking forward to her company. Ever since the run-in with Cheryl, I had been stressing over possible repercussions via Roxy, most of them ending with my having to quit, but so far all had been quiet on the western front.

On a more positive note, we had finished the sort. Other than a few miscellaneous walk-in donations scattered among the shopping carts and bins, the hall looked bare.

The buzzer rang and I ran to open the door for Sarra, who bustled inside holding a Starbuck's take-out tray containing two coffees in one hand and a pastry bag in the other.

"You're awesome." I told her.

"I know." She said before making a beeline for the sorting room.

"Did you get Katrina's email?" I asked, following her and the irresistible aroma of freshly brewed coffee.

"Yes."

"I didn't."

"She's just playing games with you because you intimidate her." Sarra said as she handed me one of the coffees, "This is her attempt to exert control."

"Thanks. Well, whatever it is, she can't stop me from going."

"Good girl. I have to say her statement about Lynn's resignation being 'unfortunate' struck me as rather hypocritical." She rustled the bag. "Scone?"

"Wow, thanks. Unfortunate? What a bitch, she's probably just pissed Lynn quit before she could get her fired."

I pulled a blackberry scone out of the bag and took a bite.

"Say, did you ask Daphne about Gerald's books?" Sarra asked, forcing me to swallow fast in order to answer.

"Yes, but she didn't notice anything and neither did Peg, which isn't saying much. I'm thinking it had to have happened Monday night."

Sarra's eyes widened. "That means it has to be someone with a key."

"Or someone who knows the combination to the lockbox, which is pretty much every volunteer who has ever worked here. I did find out something interesting about those codes though." I said, filling her in on what I'd learned from a website Nate had suggested. Although the personal information of the DigiCoin transactions was encrypted in such a way to keep their users anonymous, both had been cashed Monday night and each had been worth a whopping five thousand dollars.

The news made Sarra whistle. "My goodness, if all those codes were as valuable it would certainly explain someone wanting to steal them."

"That's what I thought."

Sarra leaned up against the table and took another sip of coffee.

"What about Roxy, have you heard anything from her?"

"No, and to tell you the truth, if she does make a stink about us going into Marilyn's closet I'm about ready to tender my own resignation." I said, letting out a deep sigh as a lump began to form at the back of my throat.

For the past two days, I had been doing some heavy thinking about my role at the bookstore. Although I wanted to focus on improving the place as a whole, between

Katrina's negative attitude and Roxy's strange behavior, I felt I was fighting a losing uphill battle.

Sarra patted me on shoulder.

"Don't bail on us quite yet. Regardless of what Roxy or anyone else says, you're doing a fantastic job and those of us who actually work here appreciate everything you do."

"Thanks, I needed that."

With the combination of caffeine, sugar, and pep talk helping boost my spirits, I decided to shelve some cookbooks while Sarra focused on Nate's section.

"Holly!" Daphne called out, beckoning me over to the desk as I walked past. "That lady who just left said she nearly slipped on our mat."

Setting down my box, I inspected the rectangular piece of carpeting laying just inside the entry and discovered the rubber backing was practically threadbare.

"We need a new one," I told her, "especially with the rainy season starting."

"Can you talk to Roxy about it? For some reason she keeps ignoring me." Daphne pouted.

Agreeing to take care of it, I picked up my box and headed to the opposite side of the store.

The cookbooks were housed in a pair of massive wooden bookcases standing side-by-side smack dab in the middle of the second aisle. While the majority of the store's shelves were metal wire units salvaged from an out-of-business video store, these monstrosities were built out of particle board by a former volunteer and weighed a ton a piece. They had been secured together with screws, thanks to Nate, since he didn't want me getting squished in case of an earthquake.

The volunteer who had shelved the section before me hadn't spent a lot of effort organizing. When I had taken it over, I created sub-categories and discarded any books that didn't sell over time and also began to display some of the newer books face forward to draw customer's attention. The result was one of the more popular, and highest selling, nonfiction sections in the store.

Sitting cross-legged on the cold cement floor, I was just pulling out some microwave recipe collections I'd decided to discard when a shadow moved across my field of vision. Looking up I saw bright swirls of tie dyed color feathering outward into a sunburst pattern.

"Mornin' hon!" Cookbook Kathy bellowed down at me.

"Morning." I responded, quickly turning back to my books; the faster I could finish, the faster I could leave.

"Don't ya'll look cute down there, busy as a bee."

"Yep."

"What do you have there, anything that might interest me?" She bent over to inspect the book in my hand, but when she saw the cover, instantly recoiled. "Oh, no thanks, those aren't REAL cookbooks."

Apparently, we shared a similar dislike for microwave cooking.

"So, I hear ya'll got Gerald's books in the fish room. Can I take a peek for old times' sake?"

She leaned up against a shelf and draped one exposed arm across it for support, the wobbling pink skin beneath reminding me of a molded gelatin concoction.

"You know the rule, Kathy." I told her.

There were several reasons why customers were no longer allowed in the back, and she was one of them. Not only was it annoying to have to deal with customers tearing through donations in search of certain titles, it also created potential conflict. When a book buyer from San Francisco got into a physical tussle with a sorter over a book both wanted to purchase, Pat had laid down the law citing liability issues as reason enough for enforcement.

"Can't you bend it just this once, for lil' ol' me?" Kathy whined.

Ignoring her, I continued to work.

She sighed dramatically. "Well, maybe I need to start volunteering here so I can get first dubs on all the good books like some OTHER people I know."

"What do you mean?" I asked, unable to stop myself from taking the bait.

"Oh, you know," she teased, "OakLeaf storage?"

"What are you talking about?"

"Gerald and me aren't the only ones with a unit there." She said, looking pleased with herself.

"Who?" I demanded.

My voice had risen slightly and she seemed taken aback.

"No need to get upset. If ya'll don't know who it is, I'm not gonna be a tattletale."

A sly smile stretched across her pudgy face and when it was obvious she wasn't going to divulge a name, I picked up my empty box and headed for the back. It was either that or stay and throw a copy of *The Joy of Cooking* at her, an idea almost worth getting fired over.

Mulling over this new bit of information, I wondered if it had any significance. OakLeaf storage was a large facility and the odds against another volunteer having a unit there couldn't be too high. Still, with everything that had happened recently, the coincidence felt worth looking into.

Sarra wasn't in the sorting room so I assumed she was still shelving. After drinking the last of my now-cold coffee, I grabbed the four books out of the Horror genre and went to find her. Rounding an end cap in my usual haste, I nearly ran into a browsing customer.

"Oops, sorry!"

"Is that King?" The man asked, unfazed.

Looking at the massive volume in my hands, I nodded my head. "Looks like it."

"Actually it looks like *Under the Dome*." He chuckled.

His comment made me laugh; this was definitely a King fan.

Handing him the volume, we briefly discussed a recent film adaptation before I went to shelve the remaining books. To my surprise, Sarra wasn't in the Sci-Fi section.

"Have you seen Sarra?" I asked Daphne.

Her eyes widened and she quietly pointed an index finger to an area behind my left shoulder. Turning, I saw Sarra straddling what looked like Marilyn's rolling step stool half way down the main aisle. As I walked towards her, a sick feeling suddenly washed across me; she was parked in front of Katrina's VHS tapes.

"Ummm... what are you doing?" I asked.

"On Monday a customer complained how unorganized this section was but I didn't have time to check it out." She responded, pulling a couple of tapes out and placing them on top of some others already stacked on the floor near her feet. "Have you seen the shape it's in?"

"I know it's bad, Katrina shelves them."

"Harumph." She snorted, "It's ridiculous, no wonder customers can't find anything. Everything is all mixed together and there's stuff in here no one in their right mind would want. I mean, come on, would you buy this?"

She held up a pink colored box featuring an image of a woman sporting a circa 1980's headband and leg warmers while holding dumbbells and doing the splits.

I couldn't help laughing. "What do you mean, you don't want to give that a try?"

"Not in this lifetime."

"You know," I said, getting serious, "Katrina's going to be pissed."

"Tough."

The firm response made me realize her motive wasn't purely altruistic, but at this point it didn't much matter as there was no way the tapes could be put back to the way they were.

"Promise me you won't get too crazy and don't throw anything away, OK?"

"Yes ma'am." She promised.

Heading to the fish room to tackle Gerald's books, I could feel a knot of apprehension begin to form inside my gut; poking Katrina was risky. Her reaction would no doubt be negative, and my biggest concern was that another of my friends was going to get the axe.

HO, HO, HO

(December 9, Friday after six)

There were deviled eggs.

"Did you make these?" I asked Evelyn, though I already knew the answer.

"Don't be silly," she said, "my daughter made them."

Gently picking one up, I admired the small slivers of green olives and dots of red pimentos artistically arranged to look like flowers atop the golden filling.

"They're beautiful." I said before taking a bite.

"The devil is in the details."

Her raised eyebrow made me think she was alluding to something other than the egg in my mouth, but before I could swallow and ask, Peg interrupted.

"Do you think we should set up the tree in the same place as last year?"

"Sure, I guess."

Nodding her head enthusiastically at my answer, she floated off to watch two other volunteers slide a massive oblong shaped box down the main aisle. The torn and duct-taped cardboard was splitting even further in the process, leaving a stream of dark green plastic needles in its wake.

Evelyn shook her head at the sight. "We should have thrown that old thing out years ago."

"Where's Nate?" Daphne asked, setting a plate of snickerdoodles down on the counter next to the eggs.

"He's still in Australia," I said, "but he'll be home the end of next week."

Sampling one of her cookies, I watched as more volunteers carrying containers and plates of food flowed into the store. After placing their goodies onto the counter, they drifted towards the artificial Christmas tree being assembled across from the sales area. From the look of all the pieces being pulled out of the box, it was going to be a major undertaking.

"Nifty idea to combine a decorating party with the meeting, looks like everyone is showing up." Daphne commented before heading towards the others.

"Yeah, nifty, who thought of it anyways?" Sarra asked, having strolled in behind the last wave sans any offering.

"Guess." Evelyn said, rolling her eyes towards the upholstered chair across the aisle. Marilyn was seated on it like a queen on a throne; overseeing all the activities while Cheryl hovered nearby.

"Figures." Sarra chuckled, "I contemplated bringing some hot chocolate and peppermint schnapps, but decided I might need both later."

"I'm glad you didn't." I said, thinking as good as that sounded right about now, I needed my wits sharp for whatever might happen during the meeting.

A few cookies and pieces of fudge later, cheers erupted from the tree group as the last twisted branch was snapped into place.

"There's my cue." Evelyn approached the tree and the volunteers parted like the sea, watching in silent admiration as she worked her magic transforming the metal and plastic boughs into something that looked like the real deal.

Katrina strode in a quarter past six with a single bag of chips she unceremoniously dumped onto the counter. A collective sigh of relief rippled through the crowd after she informed us Roxy would be at least a half an hour late.

Soon, someone located the plastic bins full of holiday decorations in the fish room and hauled them up front. A jovial spirit quickly descended as volunteers spread out to drape gaudy tinsel garland along counters and end caps or hang ornaments on the tree. Everyone was talking and laughing and sharing in the fun. Everyone, that is, except Katrina. She was slumped behind the desk with eyes glued to her phone, no doubt playing Word Wump while she finished off the rest of the deviled eggs.

"She hasn't noticed." I whispered to Sarra as I clambered up the rickety wooden stepladder to attach another portion of lights to the front windows with a piece of duct tape.

"I'd ask if you two need any help, but you seem to have things well under control." An unfamiliar woman's voice said from behind me.

Glancing back, I saw a person with short cropped spiky gray hair and a large red scarf grinning up at me.

"I don't think we've been properly introduced. I'm Zina." She said, and I climbed down to shake her hand, recognizing her from the first meeting as the volunteer responsible for shelving the foreign language and politics sections.

"Those need to be higher." Marilyn's whiny voice drifted our way, and her wagging index finger made me realize she was referring to the section of lights I'd just hung.

"They look perfectly fine." Zina told me, loud enough for Marilyn to hear, and I instantly felt she was someone I would like.

"Evelyn tells me you're the one responsible for all the fantastic signs. Would you be able to make some for my sections as well?" She asked.

"Of course" I said.

"And I love that new check-in log, did you make that as well?"

"That she did," Sarra piped in before I could respond, "and she's got even more ideas on how to improve this place."

"Fantastic! I'm looking forward to them." Zina said before meandering off.

A little after seven o'clock, with the bins empty of their treasures, I stood back and admired our collective handiwork; the place felt festive, with even the old artificial tree looking down-right charming covered in an eclectic mix of animal themed ornaments.

"Holly? Can you take a photo of everyone around the tree?" Evelyn asked as everyone quickly gathered together.

"You too!" She hollered over at Katrina, who surprised me by getting up from behind the desk to come squeeze into the frame.

I had just taken a couple of shots of the group with my phone when the front door burst open.

"Howdy!" Roxy hollered in typical fashion, making a beeline for the food. "Yowsa, I'm starvin', anything left for me?"

While she loaded up a paper plate, a couple of us began to arrange fold up chairs near the desk area in order to get the meeting started. Looking around at faces turned suddenly somber, I realized I wasn't the only one ready to head for the hills; something about Roxy seemed to put people on edge.

Hearing a gasp, I turned to see Katrina staring at the VHS section. She must have felt my gaze because she swung around to approach me with a look that can only be described as murderous.

"Who touched my tapes?" She hissed through clenched teeth.

"Let me explain..."

"No one should touch my section, NO ONE. If YOU did this..."

"Come on now, let's git this meetin' going. I've got critters to feed!"

The booming announcement made Katrina hesitate, and we both turned to see Roxy perched on the corner of the desk staring directly at us.

While Katrina quickly withdrew behind the desk to sit near Marilyn and Cheryl, I opted to move over to the counter where I had left my folder. With my heart pounding a mile a minute, I was sure my face had turned as red as a tomato; conflict always plays havoc with my complexion.

"Hey, ya'll." Roxy said, opening the meeting with a brief acknowledgement of the bookstore's recent losses. "I know it's been a tough couple months, but ya'll have pushed through. Why don't you go over your stuff now Holly?"

The abrupt segue caught me completely off guard.

"OK, thanks."

I could feel Katrina's eyes bore a hole into the side of my face as I rustled through my notes. "First of all, a big thank you to everyone for working so hard. I'm happy to report that, for the first time ever, the sort has been finished."

Several volunteers clapped at this bit of news, so I paused a moment before continuing. "As you probably already know, the back area has been cleaned up and organized and I'm hoping we can agree on uniform signs and, um..."

"Excuse me." Marilyn's distinctive voice interrupted my brief hesitation with razor accuracy, and all eyes instantly focused in her direction.

"I don't think it's right for other volunteers to tamper with our sections," she said, "we work too hard to have to put up with unnecessary stress." Her voice wavered slightly, as if she was on the verge of tears.

"What? Who's messin' with, what?!" Roxy pivoted on the desk to face me, her brow furrowed.

"I'm not the only one having problems," Marilyn continued, "Others have also been complaining." She glanced briefly at Katrina before staring straight at me, "Plus, your sorters are continuing to throw away perfectly good books."

This last dig was hard to miss.

"Look, Marilyn, I don't know who is moving your books around, maybe it's customers, but saying the sorters are throwing away good books is just not true." My attempt to respond to her dump of complaints sounded overly defensive, even to my own ears, and the pleased look on Katrina's face told me she had obviously added fuel to this fire; my next statement was directed at her.

"I agree no one should have their sections organized without their permission and I apologize for the one time that happened, but..."

Roxy cut me off.

"No one should be touchin' anything that ain't theirs, and that's final!"

A moment of awkward silence was broken by a distinctive voice from the back row of chairs.

"I don't know what you all are talking about, but I for one think some organization is exactly what this place needs."

Evelyn's statement resulted in a majority of the volunteers nodding their heads and murmuring in agreement.

"Things have been doing fine." Katrina said, her voice now also raised. "We don't need to change anything."

Both twins simultaneously raised their hands as if asking permission to speak, and when Roxy acknowledged them, Trey spoke in a quiet voice.

"We really appreciated Holly helping us organize the kid's section. Both of us have noticed we've been selling a ton more books."

"Ditto for my classics!" Daphne piped in.

Others followed, sharing positive feedback they'd received from customers as well as upticks in sales. With what looked like a majority of volunteers giving their thumbs up, I was confident organizing the store wouldn't be an issue if we put it to a vote.

"I agree with Roxy; things are fine the way they are." Marilyn chirped in, and I wasn't surprised to see Cheryl nodding her head in concurrence.

"Isn't our goal to sell as many books as possible to make money for the animals?" Sarra asked, causing one of the volunteers to call out a "Hear, hear."

"Having a uniform system for the whole store makes sense. Why don't we put it to a vote?" Zina suggested, and all eyes focused back onto Roxy.

"That's not how it works!" She snapped. "This is NOT a democracy!"

Her retort didn't seem to affect Zina. "Well, that just ludicrous," she responded, "maybe we need to bring this up with BARF's board and see what they have to say."

"Yes, and why aren't we taking cats anymore?" Sarra blurted out, causing Daphne to jump up and down in her chair and wave both arms in the air.

"Yes, yes! What about our cats?" She exclaimed.

This last question seemed to hit Roxy like a brick. Her entire body began to shake and rosy streaks flushed along her jawbone.

"THAT'S IT!" She screamed, exploding into a fit of rage and turning to point an index finger in my direction. "WE'RE DONE HERE!"

Hopping off the desk, she stomped towards the front door and yanked hard on the handle, causing the window panels to quiver. Swearing, she quickly unlocked it and exited just as a section of lights detached and dropped, swinging across the surface of the glass like a pendulum.

Everyone sat momentarily stunned until Evelyn broke the silence.

"I take it the meeting's over?"

Chapter

35

IT GOES BUMP IN THE NIGHT

(December 9, Friday evening)

Some idiot with super-bright headlights was tailgating me. The beams were aimed high, like those from a large SUV or truck, and I had to adjust my rearview mirror in order to keep from being blinded. As they followed me off the interstate exit down Timber Hills Road, I tapped on my brakes several times to let them know to back off, but they didn't get the hint.

A mile later I came to a stop at the T with Placer Ridge Way and the driver pulled up inches from my back bumper, revving their engine.

Jerk

I was about to turn left when suddenly my car lurched forward; the massive beast had tapped my rear bumper with its grill.

My heart raced hard against my chest as I gripped the steering wheel. The flight-or-fight response had kicked in, but I'd heard too many stories of road rage to even think about getting out of my car along a lonely stretch of woods to deal with this aggressor. Besides, for all I knew they probably owned a gun - like many of our foothill neighbors.

Accelerating instead, I began to speed along the winding road in hopes I could shake them, but they stuck like glue. I was beginning to panic; going home was out of the question, there was no cell service, and the closest town was five miles away.

Suddenly, the glaring lights from an open garage door caught my attention. Tapping on my brakes, I signaled left in hopes the truck wouldn't crash into me before making a sharp turn up the short driveway. Parking behind the two cars inside the garage, I held my breath and looked into the rearview mirror. The vehicle had come to a stop on the road behind me and seemed to hesitate, the filtered light silhouetting its shape as a truck. I could hear the engine rev a few times and then it was gone, red tail lights smearing away in the darkness.

"Are you OK?" A voice called out.

Rolling down my window, I greeted my neighbors.

"Yes, sorry for bothering you. Someone was tailgating me and it kind of freaked me out."

After reassuring them I was alright to go home on my own and really didn't need to come inside for a cup of coffee, I backed out onto the main road and drove the last hundred yards to my own driveway.

Quickly closing the garage door once my car was safely parked inside, I hurried into the house and made sure all the windows and doors were secure before finally taking my first full breath.

"Meowrr."

I scooped up Martha and plopped down on the sofa, burying my face into her warm fur. She took the abuse for a few minutes, then squirmed away and headed to the kitchen in hopes of a late night snack. Following her, I filled her bowl with cream before pouring myself a much needed glass of wine.

Why would someone do that?

It had been too dark to make out the color of the massive truck, but it had definitely been a diesel. The only people I knew with trucks like that were the two women I'd just seen down at the bookstore – the two who were currently angry with me and knew where I lived.

An involuntary shiver ran up my spine.

THE DROP

(December 11, Sunday morning)

O ne...two...

Lynn counted the mail boxes along the edge of the road and took a right-hand turn as soon as she passed the third.

Bingo

She would have to thank Liz for the suggestion; last time she had missed the driveway entirely and had been forced to travel nearly half a mile further down the country lane before finding a safe place to turn around.

Maneuvering cautiously around deep potholes, she followed the dirt road past a yellow rambler to where it ended in a mown pasture behind a barn. Miscellaneous farm equipment and a couple of junked cars occupied the center so she pulled around to an outer edge and parked near a large patch of blackberry brambles.

As she locked her car, she noticed two deer grazing in a frost-tinged field on the other side of a broken-down fence. The sight triggered a memory of her kids feeding tame ones in a park somewhere, but she quickly brushed it aside; this was no time for sentimentality. Walking briskly across the stretch of dead stubbled grass, she entered the barn through a side door.

The massive corrugated-tin covered barn was of pole construction set on a concrete slab. With no apparent insulation or heating, Lynn was glad to have followed another of Liz's tips to dress in multiple warm layers. She also wore one of Lenny's old baseball caps, even though she hated hats, hoping it would help disguise her from Katrina.

A handful of people were already inside the barn milling around the extensive network of banquet tables. These lined the walls and were arranged into long rows, surfaces covered in trimmed cardboard boxes packed with books, spines facing upwards; the place was truly a bibliophile's paradise.

Lynn made her way towards the opposite end, near the main entry and giant overhead rollup garage door, where a woman was folding brown paper bags on tables set up to create an 'L' shaped cashier area.

"Morning Liz!"

"Good morning Lynn! You're early." Liz replied, a cheery smile spreading across her heavily wrinkled face.

"That's the bird that gets the worm."

Liz laughed. "You want to help fold these?"

"Sure." Lynn responded, rubbing her hands together in response to the chilly air.

"It's a cold one, I know. Once you get moving, you'll warm up."

Lynn noticed the older woman was wearing fingerless gloves and a thick overcoat, even though there was a space heater glowing red hot near her feet.

"When do we start packing up the books?" She asked.

"I'll let the customers shop another fifteen minutes or so, then we'll start to clean the place out. The big sale was yesterday, but I like to have some hours open on Sunday for those who can't make it." Liz explained. "First thing we do is pull out all the paperbacks and put them into these bags. You can start doing that now if you want. When the BARF truck gets here we'll load the hardcovers directly into their bins. They usually get here around eleven, so we have about an hour."

"Does it matter where I start?

Liz laughed again. "No, not at all, most like to start at the back and work their way forward, but you can do whatever you want. Bring them back here and we'll stack them on the tables."

Grabbing a couple of the bags, Lynn headed for the far right-hand corner. When she carried her first full load up front, Liz whistled in amazement.

"Whoa, you're a fast one."

By eleven, all the customers were gone and Liz's regular group of volunteers had trickled in, all six of them convening around the cashier area. After Liz briefly introduced them to Lynn they grabbed some bags and spread out to the far corners of the barn. As they worked their conversation flowed freely, including everything from the weather to local volunteer gossip.

"Liz says you worked at BARF?" A man with a bushy salt and pepper beard asked Lynn as he worked his way near her.

"Yep," she told him, noticing that he also sported fingerless gloves. "for a grand total of one month."

"I filled out an application but never heard back." A woman wearing a bright pink knitted headband called over from the adjacent row.

"Consider yourself lucky." The man responded. "You didn't have to deal with Roxy."

"Oh, please don't ruin this wonderful day by talking about HER!" Liz cried out from the front, making everyone laugh.

After things calmed down, Lynn moved slightly closer to the bearded man.

"Did you have a bad experience with Roxy?" she asked with voice lowered, trying not to sound too nosy.

He chuckled. "She's a complete nut. I honestly don't know how she got Pat to agree to work with her."

Lynn was about to inquire if he knew anything about the Secret Ranch, when the deep rumble of an approaching vehicle made everyone look towards the front of the barn.

"They're here!" Liz called out.

Abandoning his bag, the bearded man hurried over to the garage door and hoisted the chain. As the door lifted, the opening revealed the rear end of a large rental truck slowly backing up to park just over the threshold with only a foot and a half to spare on either side. When the driver hopped out of the cab, Lynn saw it was Katrina and instinctively moved behind taller volunteers who had gathered to watch.

The thundering roar of approaching motorcycles reverberated within the confines of the barn. These must be Katrina's biker friends, Lynn thought to herself, and watched as they parked in various positions around the front of the truck; with their thickly padded leather jackets and full face helmets, they definitely made a dramatic entrance.

"Here we go." The woman with the pink headband said to her.

Katrina, decked out in a black beanie and work gloves, unlatched the truck's roll-up door and pushed it upward. Immediately following, one of the bikers hopped into the bed and began to work a pallet jack beneath the nearest bookstore bin, guiding it atop the lift. As soon as Katrina lowered the gate with the controls, he rolled the bin into the barn and parked it down an aisle before repeating the process.

When the truck was empty, Liz's volunteers broke into action pulling hardcovers off the tables and stacking them into the bins. At one point, while helping the pink headband lady bag the remaining paperbacks, Lynn walked right past Katrina, but if she recognized her she didn't let on.

All in all, there wasn't much interaction between the two groups. Three riders remained outside, while Katrina and her helper only left the rear of the truck when a barn volunteer indicated a bin was full and ready to be lifted back into the truck. Liz, meanwhile, stayed in position behind the cashier tables and watched the entire process like a hawk.

When all the paperbacks were gathered, Lynn asked Liz if there was a bathroom she could use.

"Sorry for not explaining earlier, but you'll have to use the one in the house. The back is unlocked and it's right off the mudroom."

Lynn hesitated, knowing that getting to Liz's yellow rambler would mean walking directly past the bikers. For a moment she contemplated squatting somewhere behind the barn, but that only made her think of how Lenny would have teased her for being afraid.

Come on, girl.

Pulling the brim of her cap low over her eyes, she slipped outside.

Two of the riders were leaned against their bikes with arms crossed and both completely ignored her as she walked past. The third was a standing in the middle of the road a few yards beyond smoking a cigarette, and he smiled broadly as she approached.

"Hey there little lady, how's it going?

There was something about his swagger that made her nervous, so she lowered her head and increased her stride in order to sidestep him. His laughter echoed in her ears as she hurried into the house and, once inside the bathroom, quickly locked the door behind her.

Don't let them intimidate you, they're just punks.

After taking care of business and washing up in the sink, she carefully slid open the bathroom's tiny frosted window to sneak a peek outside. Although there were a few shrubs in the way, she could still make out the bikers through the foliage. It looked like they had gathered around the smoker on the driveway, voices carrying clearly through the brisk air.

"Did you get the drop?" One of them asked.

"Yeah, it's all good." The smoker said, throwing his cigarette down and grinding it into the dirt with the toe of his boot. "Kat says we need to make a stop at the ranch first."

"Hey! Get your asses over here!" A voice she recognized as Katrina's called from the direction of the barn, and the group quickly scattered.

The ranch. They were going to the ranch first.

Lynn left the house and hurried past the bikers who were putting on their helmets. Inside the barn, all the bins were loaded and Katrina was closing the back of the truck.

"There you are, find the bathroom OK?" Liz asked as she approached the front tables.

"Yes, thanks. Say, is it all right if I get going?"

"Sure thing, thanks for your help. You can come down anytime you want as far as I'm concerned."

"Will do, bye!"

Lynn hustled out the side door and sprinted across the field to her car, reaching it with plenty of breath to spare. The truck had just pulled away from the barn when she zipped around the corner, so she slowed to a crawl to watch it navigate its way up the bumpy drive. Two of the motorcycles led the way while the other two remained in the rear, the sight of the obvious motorcade giving her an uneasy feeling.

Rats.

The bikers had mentioned a drop which, to Lynn, meant something nefarious. She pulled out her phone and dialed Sarra's number, leaving a message after the beep.

"Hey, it's me, just letting you know I'm following the BARF truck to the ranch."

Tossing the phone back onto the passenger seat, she ignored it when it rang a few seconds later; the truck was turning left at the end of the drive and she wanted to keep visual contact.

Lynn tracked the group for several miles when the truck suddenly swerved off the asphalt onto a widened section of graveled shoulder and came to a stop, the motorcycles following suit. With little time to react or inconspicuous place to pull over, she had no choice but to drive past. Traveling no more than a hundred yards, the roar of engines made her look into the rear view mirror.

"Shit!"

Two of the motorcycles were on her rear bumper.

Slamming her foot hard against the accelerator, she lunged forward but the bikers remained close. When one of them began to pull alongside, revving their motor as they drew parallel, she panicked and jerked the steering wheel to the right. Her car jumped the curve and began to descend at an angle down the steep slope into the flooded irrigation ditch.

Chapter

37

PEPPERMINT SCHNAPPS

(December 11, Sunday afternoon)

I was on the phone with my mother when the call-waiting tone beeped.

"Mom," I said, interrupting a lengthy narrative on one of her dog's recent experiences at the groomer, "I need to go. There's another call coming in and it might be Nate."

"Well then." She huffed in annoyance, but I hung up anyways.

Much to my surprise, it was Sarra.

"Lynn got run off the road this morning."

"Oh my gosh, is she OK?" I asked.

"A bit winded, but she's all right. I just dropped her off at her house."

"What happened to her car?"

"They towed it to the shop to check the alignment. Oher than being covered in mud, it seems OK. She's more upset that she'd just had it washed."

Sarra then went on to relay all the details.

"Wow. Hopefully the cops throw the book at them." I said.

"She didn't file a report." Sarra sighed. "Apparently the tow-truck driver told her it was pointless, especially since she didn't get their plate numbers."

"But that's ridiculous, we know they're Katrina's friends!"

Sarra chuckled at my outburst. "I told her the same thing but she got all stubborn about not wanting them to think she's intimidated. Those were her exact words."

Although I could appreciate the perspective, I also knew road rage wasn't something to be taken lightly.

"Unfortunately, she's not the only one. Someone decided to scare me Friday night."

"Did you tell Nate?" Sarra asked upon hearing my story.

"No. Besides, it's only a small scratch on the bumper and not worth reporting. The worst part is I can't shake the feeling it had to be Roxy or Katrina."

"I wouldn't put it past either of them." Sarra said. "Oh, that reminds me, I need to leave a bit early tomorrow to take Lynn over to pick up her car. Do you want to meet at the Belgian after?"

"Sounds good, see you in the morning."

I hung up and rubbed my sore ear; after being pressed against the phone for several hours it felt hot and tender to the touch. Although my computer's world clock indicated it was 7 AM tomorrow morning in Sydney, I hesitated calling Nate. Up until now I had been keeping details of our fledgling investigation vague, mostly because I didn't want him to worry, but I couldn't trust myself not to spill the beans on these latest incidents.

Leaving my phone on the kitchen counter, I walked into the living room where a five-foot-tall Douglas fir patiently waited for me to finish stringing lights. Decorating the bookstore had motivated me to purchase the precut tree at White Feather Farm the day before, even though it meant breaking a nearly twenty-year tradition. Holiday spirit aside, I hadn't felt like trudging through the woods by myself.

"At least I have you." I told Martha who was busy sniffing the fragrant needles. She chirped a happy response before crawling under and disappearing beneath the green tree skirt to play hide-and-seek with one of her toys.

I had just begun rehanging lights when my cell phone rang.

"Now what?" I said, jogging towards the kitchen. When I read the name on the screen, I inhaled sharply.

"NO MORE CHANGES!" Roxy screamed without so much as a greeting or howdy-do. She was breathing heavily, as if from exertion, and I could hear the sound of whistling wind which made me assume she was outside somewhere on the ranch.

"Things are FINE the way they are!" She continued, repeating the words Katrina had used at the meeting. "People are gitten' upset!"

"I don't understand." I said, finally getting a word in edgewise. "What people? Other than Marilyn and Katrina, all the other volunteers were pretty positive..."

"And that's ANOTHER thing!" Roxy interrupted. "Why are you so hell bent on pickin' on poor Marilyn? Every dang day it's somethin' else! You need to stop intimidatin' her, UNDERSTAND?"

She was gasping for breath and I could hear dogs barking off in the distance.

"Intimidating Marilyn?" I was confused as to her choice of wording. If anything, Lynn and I had been threatened, for real, but I held my tongue.

"Git back here!" Roxy yelled away from the receiver at what I assumed were canines before returning. "Tell your sorters from now on no more books are gonna be thrown away, period! I've had 'nuff of this! Do your dang job or I swear you'll end up just like Gerald!"

The connection suddenly went quiet and I realized she had hung up.

"MEOWRRR"

I turned to look down at Martha, her eyes wide with feline concern; she's a sensitive soul and gets upset whenever I do.

"It's OK girl, I'm not going to let her ruin our day."

She blinked up at me once before strolling over to sit by the refrigerator. After compensating her leap of faith with a liberal splash of half-and-half, I made myself a cup of hot chocolate and fortified it with my own liberal splash of peppermint schnapps in hopes it would help me calm down.

Back out in the living room, I put on a CD and tried to refocus my attention on the tree. Soon, Tchaikovsky's Nutcracker Ballet helped push the memory of Roxy's phone call into the furthest corners of my brain; the schnapps didn't hurt either.

"I know it's not as good as Dad does, but it will do." I told Martha as we surveyed the twinkling tree.

Popping the lid off the plastic storage container I'd hauled in from the garage, I carefully began to remove the various boxes of ornaments. Over the years, we had collected quite an assortment; from miniature glass Santa Clauses to German straw creations formed to look like stars and delicate snowflakes. Memories of Christmases come and gone were held within these objects, and I began to descend into bittersweet nostalgia as I hung them on the tree.

Nuts.

Either I was going to sit here and start crying about being on my own, or I better focus my attention on something else. Choosing the latter, I let my mind wander back to bookstore drama.

I had to give major kudos to Pat; she had done a stellar job keeping us volunteers insulated from Roxy. Now, with her gone, a strange power vacuum had been created between Roxy acting more erratic and angry by the day and Katrina intent on taking more control, even though she rarely spent time at the bookstore. Her strange sway over Roxy had me stumped, and I was torn as to what to do next. Though part of me wanted to continue to fight the good fight for both the store and the volunteers, another just wanted to throw in the towel and go back to being an off-hour sorter and shelver with no other responsibilities.

"Phisht!" I hissed at Martha who was swatting at a low-hanging snowflake. She stopped and gave me a defiant look before licking her paw.

"Trouble maker"

I suddenly thought of Lynn; Katrina and her crew had to be up to no good, why else run her off the road? Also, why go to the Secret Ranch after picking up the books from the barn? Maybe Lynn was right in that they were cooking drugs in one of the out-buildings and Pat had caught wind of it, and that was the reason she was researching BARF's financial state...

"...you're gonna end up like Gerald!" Roxy had said.

A chill crept up my spine; I'd assumed Roxy was talking about getting fired, but now wasn't so sure. Was there more to her threat? If she and Katrina were dealing drugs, there could be a connection with Gerald and the DigiCoin codes he was hiding. Both women had keys to the bookstore and could easily have snuck in late at night to take the coded books. Were they capable of murder?

So many puzzle pieces, and I still had no idea how any of them fit together.

The distinctive sound of an incoming Skype call interrupted my rumination and I once again headed for my cell phone.

"Hello Beautiful." Nate's voice came through after a slight delay for his image to pop onto the screen.

"I thought you'd be at work by now." I told him, glad to see his face.

"I haven't gone in yet, been answering a ton of emails."

"Everything OK?"

His responding sigh confirmed my suspicions.

"Looks like I'm going to have to stay a couple of extra days, at least until the twentieth."

"Oh no!" I moaned.

"Sorry. At least Philip will be home, he called me yesterday."

"Why didn't he call me?"

"He knows you're upset about him wanting to quit school."

"Of course I'm upset, but he could still call me."

"Sorry." Nate repeated.

"I have to go. I'm decorating the tree."

I tapped the 'end call' button and he disappeared. Guilt swept over me like a wave but, instead of calling him back, I went into the kitchen and made myself another mug of cocoa. This time I added a double splash of peppermint schnapps.

WARRIOR POSE

(December 12, Monday morning)

The recent snowfall had turned the Sierras into a brilliant slash of white smeared across the horizon. Cresting the hill with my car, I had only a brief moment in which to admire their beauty before swinging onto the west-bound interstate on-ramp. A cloudless sky confirmed the clear weather report, and I hoped the trend continued; although a white Christmas was appealing, I wanted both my guys home safe and sound before another storm hit.

Nate accepted my apology. I'd returned his call yesterday, after a couple of sips of fortified hot chocolate, and told him I was sorry for being so grumpy. He was frustrated about the extended trip too, of course, and our conversation soon focused on the logistics of his return, though I did bring up Roxy's recent phone call.

"What is her issue with improving the bookstore?" He asked, though I obviously didn't have an answer.

Later that evening, with the tree decorated and a glass of wine poured, I decided to get proactive. A love of mystery books featuring clever detectives motivated me as I created a document listing everything that had transpired since Pat's death, from the closed sorting room door and where her car was parked to Roxy's recent threat. Once finished, I printed out three copies: one for each of the cider girls.

Sarra and I arrived at the bookstore minutes apart. With the drop complete and volunteers eager for more books to shelve, we had agreed to meet an hour earlier than normal to sort before having to deal with customers. When we entered the store and turned on the lights, both of us gasped.

"Whoa," I said, "this load is way bigger than last month."

"We can blame Lynn." Sarra chuckled.

Teddy made a plaintive sound the minute he caught sight of us coming around the corner. Much to my surprise, Sarra bent down to put her fingers through his cage, and the old man stretched out his neck and closed his eyes while she scratched him under the chin.

"I've never seen him do that. He must really like you." I told her.

"Yeah, we have an understanding." She smiled.

Turning our attention to the loaded bins, we sorted until the store opened, at which point a steady flow of customers required one of us to constantly work the front desk. An hour later, while I was in back, Angel dropped off two empty carts, and Evelyn showed up an hour before the shift ended while I was cashiering. She sashayed through the front door decked out in a hunter green ensemble with a glimmering gold belt and matching heels.

"You look amazing." I said, before asking if she could take over so I could run to the bathroom. She sighed but agreed just as another customer with an armful of books approached the desk.

When I told Sarra our back-up had arrived, she quickly grabbed her purse.

"See you at the Belgian!"

Returning to the front after my break, I discovered Jill sitting behind the desk instead of Evelyn.

"My class was canceled so I decided to pop on over," she explained, "I don't mind working up here if you need to sort."

Her yellow t-shirt featured a purple figure doing a unique yoga pose, but before I could ask about it, another book-laden customer appeared.

I found Evelyn in the sorting room, stacking hardcovers into a cardboard box.

"What are you doing?" I asked.

"Well," she responded, "after Miss Marilyn's remark at the meeting last Friday, I've decided to give her every single mystery book that comes in, regardless of what state it is in."

Peering at the books she'd collected, I could see all were in poor shape.

"You have my permission to toss these Evelyn."

"Are you quite certain? She raised an eyebrow for dramatic effect. "I don't want to get into trouble with 'you know who'."

"I'm still in charge back here, regardless of what anyone else says."

"Glad to hear." She said before dumping the entire box into the nearest FRC cart.

Over the next hour, the two of us worked our way through the top third of a bin full of barn books. While pushing a freshly loaded shopping cart into the sorting room, I hit my knuckles on the doorframe and let loose with an expletive, resulting in a thoroughly disapproving glare from Evelyn.

"Sorry." I apologized, rubbing my sore hand.

She set a book atop a pyramid of others stacked high against the back corner and made a 'tsk' sound. "Someone needs to start shelving religion, and it's not going to be me."

Since Gerald's death, no volunteer had been willing to tackle the section and I could understand why; the genre was large, encompassing both fiction and non-fiction, and received an excessive amount of donations.

Thinking about Gerald suddenly reminded me of something.

"Do you know of any other volunteer that has a unit at OakLeaf Storage?" I asked, relaying only the gist of what Cookbook Kathy had said.

Evelyn wrinkled her nose in distaste at the mention of my source. "No, can't think of anyone. If you don't mind my asking, why does it matter?"

"No specific reason," I fibbed, not wanting to divulge the jumble of suspicions rumbling around inside my brain, "just an intuition."

She looked at me intently before pulling her cell phone out of her apron.

"Never ignore your instincts." She tapped a message and, within seconds, got a response. "My daughter says you should ask her friend Todd, the assistant manager, who found Gerald's body."

"Thanks." I said, mentally adding this new item to my growing investigative 'to do' list.

At two o'clock we called it quits and while Evelyn headed over to check on her boutique area, I went up front to say goodbye to Jill.

"Oh Holly, good!" Her face lit up when she saw me. "Maybe you can help this lady." She gestured toward a grumpy looking woman standing near the glass display cases.

"There's something wrong with this video." The woman said as she thrust a VHS towards me, and I almost laughed out loud when I recognized the exercise tape Sarra had wanted to toss.

"Oh?" I said, sliding the cassette out of the cardboard sleeve to take a closer look. The plastic casing was warped along the edges, like it had been left out in the sun too long, and there was a sticky substance oozing from the opening.

"It wouldn't play and I think it screwed up my machine. Don't you guys check these things before you sell them?" She sounded angry.

"I'm so sorry." I told her, "You can pick out another tape or we can refund you the fifty cents, whichever you prefer."

The woman opted for the cash and, after she exited the store, I took the opportunity to ask Jill about her t-shirt.

"This is where I work." She explained, stretching the ends of the fabric away from her body so I could read the entire logo clearly. "It's the Warrior 1 pose, one of my favorites; it helps teach us how to be strong in the face of challenges but still remain poised."

"Very cool." I said, thinking it might be a move to consider mastering.

"We offer some great classes." She added, as if reading my mind. "If you'd like, I can bring you a brochure."

Thanking her, I returned to the back and tossed the damaged tape into the trash can before grabbing my jacket and purse. The afternoon sunshine felt good against my face as I walked down the ramp, and across the street a motorcycle rumbling through the Burger Pit's drive-thru made me realize how hungry I was; a sandwich and cider sounded amazing.

While backing up to leave, a strange thwacking sound made me slam on my brakes and put my car back into park. Hopping out to investigate, I rounded the rear bumper only to discover one of my rear tires was flat. Again.

When I walked into the Belgian an hour later, I could see Sarra and Lynn already seated at the back corner table. I'd called to let them know I would be late and texted once the road service had finished changing my tire, so was glad they hadn't postponed enjoying their cider on my account.

The bartender was over at the wall taps pouring a familiar tripel into a mug; the image instantly making me miss my husband.

"Hey Holly, when's Nate getting back?" He asked when he turned and caught sight of me.

"Next week." I replied, amazed at yet another skill he seemed to possess; mind reading.

After delivering the beer to a customer, he pulled a bottle of cider out of the corner cooler and opened it with a swift flick of the wrist before pouring it into one of the goblets. When he handed it to me I realized his t-shirt had the same logo as Jill's; the coincidental symbolism more than a little striking.

"Warrior 1 pose, right?" I said, pointing to the image.

He seemed impressed. "That's right. You do Yoga?"

"No, but I probably should." I laughed before ordering my usual sandwich.

"Was the stem cut again?" Sarra asked when I joined them in the back.

"No, this time the tire was slashed." I said, sitting down and taking a much needed drink.

"Holy cow! Someone really has it in for you!" Lynn exclaimed.

"Seems that way."

I told them about seeing the motorcycle before getting into my car, the fact it matched the description of Lynn's aggressors only occurring to me on the drive over.

"Maybe you shouldn't park in the back anymore." Sarra said, a concerned look on her face.

"No way. Just like Lynn, I'm not going to let anyone intimidate me." I pulled the pages I'd printed out of my purse and handed one to each of them.

"What's this?" Lynn asked as she unfolded it.

"Uh-oh," Sarra said, squinting at her copy. "looks like things are about to get serious."

"That's right." I told them. "These are pieces of a puzzle we're going to solve — it's high time we became warriors, ladies."

SNOOPING

(December 13, Tuesday)

I swear one of the chocolate muffins was calling out my name. It sat there on a plate in the middle of the kitchen table, taunting me.

"Should I make more coffee?" Sarra asked.

"Not for me." I responded, doing my best to ignore the cheeky little devil while Lynn helped herself to a second.

The three of us had decided to meet this morning at Sarra's house, since it was centrally located, and had already consumed a pot while reviewing the day's investigative itinerary and travel logistics; it's always good to have a plan.

"It makes sense to go to OakLeaf first, especially since they open at nine." Sarra said, checking the clock on the wall for the current time.

"Sounds good." Lynn agreed between bites. "And while you two do your thing at the bookstore, I'll go down to the barn."

Our plans set, at a quarter of nine, the three of us piled into my car and headed north to OakLeaf Storage. The office was located kitty-corner to the main gate and, after parking in a designated guest space, we entered the small space to find a thirty-something man seated behind a tall counter. His name badge confirmed him as Todd, the assistant manager.

"Morning ladies, how can I be of help?" He asked, glancing up from his computer screen.

"Good morning, we're friends of Evelyn..."

"Oh, yes!" Todd interrupted, jumping to his feet.

Slightly taken aback at his exuberance, I continued. "...she said her daughter suggested you might be able to help us determine whether or not someone has a storage unit here?"

I handed him a sheet of notepaper listing the names of all the bookstore's volunteers. While he perused it, I caught Sarra giving me a sideways glance and could guess what she was thinking: we were witnessing, firsthand, the power of Evelyn.

After squinting back and forth between the list and the computer screen a few times, Todd handed the paper back to me. "Sorry, none of these names seem to match anyone on file."

"Are you sure?" Sarra asked, but he merely shook his head and grinned sheepishly.

"Darn it." Lynn responded and I shared her frustration. Even though it had been a long shot, I was hoping this particular puzzle piece had potential.

"Sorry about your friend being killed." Todd said, "I recognized him because he came in here all the time." He shuddered slightly, no doubt remembering the horror of finding Gerald's dead body.

His words, however, gave me an idea and I pulled out my phone.

"Can you look at this photo and see if you recognize anyone?" I asked, showing him the group shot I'd taken of the volunteers standing around the Christmas tree.

Looking at the screen, he pointed at a distinctive figure. "There's Miss Evelyn."

"Yes, we know who she is." Sarra said, rolling her eyes.

"Oh – her... I know her too." He said, moving his finger to the opposite side of the photo. "She's the one who picks up the rental truck every month."

Turning the phone to look, I realized he meant Katrina.

"Does she have a unit here too?" I asked.

"I'm not sure, but I see her going in there all the time. You can't miss that rig of hers. What's the last name again?"

"Bale"

While he searched on his computer, I exchanged silent raised eye-brows with Sarra and Lynn.

"No, ... no Katrina Bale..." he muttered more to himself than us, "just a Joseph Bale in unit 55 "

"That must be her Dad." I said, remembering she was caring for him.

"Can we look at it?" Lynn asked.

Todd's eyes widened. "Sorry, can't do that. I probably shouldn't have even told you the unit number."

"That's OK," I told him, quickly ushering the girls toward the exit. "Thanks so much for your help, we'll say 'hi' to Evelyn for you."

"Now what?" Lynn asked as we climbed back into my car.

Starting the engine, I put it into reverse and swung around to the main gate's key pad entry system. Typing in the code Ms. Foster had given me, the screen responded with a *Welcome, Gerald* and the gate slid open.

"Aren't you the sly one." Sarra commented from the back seat while Lynn giggled beside me.

From experience driving around looking for Gerald's unit, I had a pretty good idea where to find number 55 and located it relatively quickly. Parking alongside, we exited the car and gathered in front of the padlocked door.

"I hate to play Devil's advocate," Sarra said, "but it could just be her Dad's stuff."

She was right, of course, but I couldn't shake the feeling there was something slightly more illicit hiding behind this door. Cradling the lock in my hand, I looked at the four dials along the side and wondered if I could figure out the combination.

"Maybe this is where they keep their drugs." Lynn said, pushing against the aluminum of the door so it flexed and made a wobbling sound.

"This is just plain silly." Sarra retorted, "We aren't getting anywhere standing here. Let's go to the library."

She climbed back into the car, forcing Lynn and me to reluctantly follow suit.

*   *   *

Story time must have had the week off as the library's parking lot was nearly empty. Since Mr. Smiley wasn't sitting at any of the computer stations, we split up to scope out all the other seating areas and cubby corners just in case he was holed up somewhere else.

Striding past the juvenile section, I caught sight of a familiar volunteer.

"Emiko." I called out, walking down to the end of the aisle where she was shelving books.

"Hello Holly." She responded with a smile. "Did you need help finding something?"

I told her about our search for the elusive Mr. Smiley, and she nodded in recognition as I described his cap.

"Like my sticker." She said, pointing to her name badge. "Yes, I know him. He comes in regularly."

Sarra and Lynn joined us and I introduced them before asking Emiko another question.

"Do you know if he took one of Pat's computer classes?"

"I believe so. Does your search for him have something to do with her?" She asked.

"Possibly, he spends a lot of time around the bookstore, so we were curious if he might have seen something the night she died."

"We're pretty sure the homeless man found murdered in the woods behind Rudy's was his friend." Sarra added.

"Yes, and between another volunteer being murdered and some of us getting run off the road by drug lords, there's definitely something fishy going on at the bookstore." Lynn said rather breathlessly, helping build the drama.

"It does have a fish room." Sarra muttered beneath her breath.

After giving my friends a stern glance, I looked over at Emiko hoping this flood of information wasn't too overwhelming, but she seemed to be taking it in her usual stride.

"Oh my, that is curious." She responded, "Speaking of which, I must apologize for not having sent you those links I promised. It's been a busy week."

"No worries." Came out automatically as my reply, along with the realization I'd completely forgotten this potentially important puzzle piece.

A librarian called for Emiko's help and she began to gather up her cart, but stopped and pulled out her cell phone.

"Why don't you let me look into those websites for you, Holly. I'll let you know if I find anything." She said, typing a note, before bidding us adieu.

After making another fruitless sweep for Mr. Smiley, the three of us left the library and drove back to Sarra's house. Parking in the driveway, I kept the motor running while Lynn climbed out of the passenger seat.

"Are you sure you'll be OK going down to the barn by yourself?" Sarra asked her.

"Don't be silly, I'll be fine." Lynn laughed, waving us goodbye before getting into her own car.

*   *   *

With Sarra now beside me, I drove the short distance to the bookstore and parked up front. Our plan for the next several hours was two-fold; get some sorting done and also do some clandestine snooping inside Roxy's office. Since I knew she was avoiding Daphne, Tuesday mornings seemed the perfect opportunity to sneak in there uninterrupted.

"Is that for the entry?" Daphne asked when she saw us, pointing to the roll of carpeting under my arm. She was seated behind the front desk while Peg hovered nearby in the animal section.

"Yep, it's got a slip-resistant backing which should help solve the problem." I told her, pulling the old mat away before positioning the new one into place.

Both of them clapped their hands in approval and I didn't bother revealing the purchase had been my own; based on my last conversation with Roxy, asking for a reimbursement seemed a stretch.

"So what's the game plan?" Sarra asked, once we were alone in the back.

"Let's sort some general fiction and romances." I said, a plan forming in my head. "While you pretend to stack them on the tables, I'll go into the office. That way if you see anyone coming, you can text me."

"OK, sounds good. I'll also put together a box of animal books to keep Peg busy, just in case."

Sarra's idea was prudent; although I wasn't too worried about Daphne leaving the front desk, especially with how many customers were milling around the store, one could never tell where Peg might end up roaming.

Within half an hour, we had a shopping cart full of the books we needed. With Sarra stationed behind the tables, I quickly slipped into Roxy's office and closed the door behind me. Switching on the light, I waited for the fluorescent bulbs to illuminate the small space before moving towards the filing cabinets. Unfortunately, it didn't take long to discover all four of them were securely locked.

"Damn it." I swore under my breath, yanking the handles in frustration.

Turning, I eyed Roxy's desk. It was identical to the one by the back door with two drawers to the right of the knee hole. The top drawer contained only a handful of pens and pencils rolling around and, like it's twin, the bottom wouldn't budge. I smacked the side with the palm of my hand like the man with the sideburns had shown me, and it slid open to reveal a familiar filing frame with hanging folders. Much to my dismay, after spending the next several minutes rifling through them, their contents offered nothing more intriguing than some old utility bills.

I plopped down on Roxy's chair and let out a discouraged sigh. So far, instead of finding any useful clues, our entire morning of sleuthing had been a bust. Glancing over at the still-opened bottom drawer, something shiny caught my attention. It was shoved behind the filing frame and in order to reach it, I had to pull the drawer out as far as it would go, causing the sliders to make a horrible screeching sound in the process. The object appeared to be cylinder inside a clear plastic bag, bound tight by a thick rubber band. Unwrapping it, I discovered an orange plastic prescription container full of pills, the pharmacy label made out to Patricia Mulderry.

My hands shaking, I texted Sarra.

Take a photo! She responded, but then my phone rang and startled me into nearly dropping the bottle onto the floor.

It was Roxy.

Chapter

40

PANTS ON FIRE

(December 13, Tuesday afternoon)

"This is the last straw!" Roxy shouted into my ear.

"Wuh?" I mumbled, trying to cradle the phone to my ear with my shoulder while quickly rewrapping the prescription bottle.

"Are you even listenin'?!"

"Uh huh."

Shoving the bag behind the files, I closed the drawer slowly in an attempt to generate minimal noise.

"What's goin' on?!" Roxy demanded.

Exiting the office, I closed the door and waved at Sarra, her eyes growing wide when she realized who was on the phone.

"Nothing, I needed to get somewhere where I could talk." I explained to Roxy as I slipped into the fish room for privacy.

"I thought I made it clear 'bout not throwin' any books away and now Marilyn found a whole box of 'em in one of the FRC carts!"

"That can't be right." I said, trying to process what she was saying.

"Are you callin' her a liar?"

"I... it's just... when did she find them?"

"Yesterday, and she says Evelyn threatened her when she tried to pull them out. I can't for the life of me understand why ya'll are continuously pickin' on a poor 'lil 'ol white-haired lady!"

The idea of accusing Evelyn of wrong doing was the tipping point, and I could feel my anger swelling like a dam ready to burst. "This is ridiculous." I snapped. "Evelyn would never threaten anyone and besides, I saw that box and the books were in bad shape - so Marilyn is wrong!"

"Well, SOMEONE sure is lyin' and I'm pretty sure it ain't Marilyn! I'm callin' Evelyn next to get to the bottom of this!"

She hung up and I stared at my phone, infuriated over what had just transpired.

"Everything OK?" Sarra asked, entering the room to check on me.

"Not really."

"What a bunch of poppycock." She snorted after hearing Marilyn's latest accusation.

"She's lying, I'm sure of it. But why?" I racked my brain trying to come up with a reason, but so far was coming up empty-handed.

"Maybe she's one of those people who needs to be the center of attention all the time. Evelyn will straighten this out, no doubt." Sarra said, giving me a concerned look. "Did you take the photo?"

"No, Roxy interrupted me."

Making sure the coast was clear, I slipped back into the office and took my shot. After, we studied the image in the safety of the sorting room.

"I recognize the prescription." I said, "My Mom takes these for her heart."

"Why in the world are they in Roxy's desk?" Sarra asked.

"Good question."

I thought back to the morning I'd found Pat's lifeless body. At the time, it seemed odd for Roxy to so quickly claim it was a heart attack, but now made perfect sense; she obviously knew about Pat's condition, but why hide her pills?

Sarra was looking at me with furrowed brow and asked what I was thinking.

"I'm thinking this looks mighty suspicious."

* * *

At a quarter past two, we left the bookstore and drove over to the Belgian. Sarra's phone dinged with an incoming text just as I was parking in the side lot, so I waited for her to read it before opening my door. Her sharp intake of breath instantly indicated something was amiss.

"It's Evelyn, she says she's going to quit!" She exclaimed.

"What?"

"She says she's not going to volunteer where people think she's a liar."

"Oh no."

This was not good news. I leaned my head against the backrest and closed my eyes, trying to absorb this recent twist of events; Roxy had no doubt kept her mindset that Marilyn was telling the truth, even alongside someone like Evelyn.

"Now what?" Sarra asked.

"We should probably go inside."

Feeling downtrodden, we entered the pub to see Lynn waving at us from the back corner while our familiar bartender looked to be absent. His replacement seemed to know who we were, however, and quickly retrieved the special goblets from under the counter before pouring us our usual brand of cider.

As we paid, I suddenly had an idea.

"Say, what's the usual bartender's name?" I asked her.

"It's cool, he knows I'm here." She clipped in response, eyeing me suspiciously before turning away to help another customer.

"Nice try." Sarra chuckled as we made our way down the ramp.

Approaching Lynn, I noticed a half empty glass of beer opposite her goblet. Before I could ask whose it was, Sean nearly made me spill my own drink when he suddenly appeared out of the hall leading to the bathroom.

"Hello ladies." He said with an amused expression before sitting down. "Lynn was just telling me about a drug operation going on at some secret ranch."

"Really?" I responded, looking over at Lynn who avoided my gaze by ducking her head down to concentrate on what was left of her drink.

"You don't actually believe that, do you?" Sean asked me.

An awkward moment of silence followed as Sarra and I joined them at the table.

"Yes, actually I do." I said, deciding to go for broke.

Even though Sean was a good listener and didn't interrupt the summarization of my puzzle-piece bullets, his persistent smile had me more than a little worried. When his only comment after I'd stopped talking was "That's interesting." my heart sank.

"This isn't fiction." Sarra frowned at him.

"Liz's husband says Roxy's got a ton of outbuildings on the property she could be using to hide things." Lynn interjected in an attempt to pique his interest, "What do you think? Can you go down and check it out?"

Sean merely shook his head. "You don't have any evidence to work with, let alone hard facts to establish probable cause."

"But what about Holly being followed and Lynn getting run off the road?" Sarra asked.

"Lynn admitted she ran herself into that ditch, and Holly's truck driver was probably just buzzed and driving stupid." He said, exhaling sharply before continuing. "Look, I appreciate your sharing this information with me, but I think you should stop taking unnecessary risks and let us do our job."

I couldn't help cringing at his less-than subtle patronization, and Sarra and Lynn's expressions told me they shared the sentiment.

"It's been great catching up with you ladies," Sean said, suddenly rising from the table and grabbing his empty glass. "but I really need to get going. Happy Holidays."

After he'd left, the smirk on Sarra's face was priceless.

"So, are we going to do what he suggests?" She asked.

"No way." I responded, making Lynn break into a fit of giggles.

Chapter

41

SQUIRREL

(December 13, Tuesday early evening)

One of the bags had a hole. It wasn't big, only a few inches across, but there were little flakes of plastic and paper scattered across the ground so it looked like it had snowed.

Dang squirrel.

The dull ache already throbbing in his left temple amplified when he realized how much time it would take to pick up all the shredded pieces. The effort would be necessary, however, since keeping his campsite immaculate was essential.

He searched the network of pine boughs stretched across his camp, but saw no telltale sign of a fuzzy flicking tail. Before moving to California, he had always assumed squirrels hibernated during the winter months, but had quickly learned that Western Grays didn't follow that rule; this one in particular had been trying to get into his cache of food for weeks.

Satisfied he was alone, he turned his attention back to the bookstore's two garbage bags: one from last week and the second retrieved Monday night. With the ground fairly dry after several rainless days, he had chosen this afternoon to sift through them and look for clues, but now the squirrel had ruined his plans; the hole would force him to work out of chronological sequence.

After spreading a tarp across the forest floor, he reluctantly pulled Monday night's bag on top and ripped the existing hole wider, letting the contents spill into a pile. Sitting cross-legged in front of the mound, he thought of his partner; this was the mundane type of job necessary for a good investigation and one Stumpy would have loved.

Years of reading whodunits had taught him that clues are funny things; they can be a sign, a pointer, or an indicator, but they can also merrily lead you down the wrong path. Working his way through the bag's offerings, most of it looked to be a whole lot of nothing: heaps of brown paper grocery bags with torn handles, ripped plastic bags, disposable coffee cups, paperback books without covers, and empty cans of cat food, the stench from the latter confirming how much he hated seafood.

He was about to give up and move on to last week's bag when something unique caught his attention. It was an old VHS tape with a woman on the cover that reminded him of his ex-wife, only with less makeup. Pulling the cassette out of the cardboard sleeve, he noticed something oozing from the tape head and instinctively touched it with a finger. When he placed the sticky substance on the tip of his tongue, hairs on the back of his head began to tingle.

Where is that screwdriver?

It took him several minutes to find the tool, another gift from Stumpy, and a few more to locate the five screws holding the casing together. Once open, he unwound a bit of the video tape off the left reel to reveal a micro-thin cellophane film attached to the original Mylar. It was well done, with edges perfectly aligned, and he couldn't help being impressed at the delicate handiwork; whoever had done this knew what they were doing.

This isn't a clue, this is evidence.

Standing, he began to pace back and forth across the edge of the tarp. The handbook was clear: a good detective must struggle against the forces of evil and seek to right wrongs, sometimes out of the field of established channels of authority. Stumpy's death had been a wrong, of that he was sure, but this piece of proof now put things in a new perspective; should he continue pursuing the investigation on his own or should he go to the police?

Where is that thing?

Fumbling through his coat pockets, he searched for the business card of the cop inquiring about Stumpy's murder. Suddenly, something dropped onto the brim of his cap and a chattering drew his attention to a branch high above his head.

Squirrel!

Chapter

42

NIGHTMARE

(December 14, extremely early Wednesday morning)

I could feel the cougars watching me. They were crouched on the ground a few feet beyond the glass like frozen statues, glinting eyes and tawny coats reflecting the moonlight. Their presence made it impossible for me to leave the tiny cabin for fear of being attacked, so I anxiously paced the floor, checking and rechecking the window to see if they were still there.

Martha meowed behind me and I turned in time to see her slip through a crack in the door. I had been certain it was securely locked moments before, but now I was frantically chasing her down a dark wooded trail while both cougars snarled at my heels. Panicking, I forced myself awake, emerging from the dream to find myself lying in my own bed with Martha securely rolled into a furry ball at my side.

Blinking at the ceiling, I tried to interpret the meaning of the dream. The cougars had to represent two women I obviously feared more than I wanted to admit: Roxy and Katrina. Both were unpredictable, to be sure, and if they were involved in Pat or Gerald's death, the concern was justifiable.

Martha's escape, on the other hand, forced me to leave a comfort zone and the trail could very well represent the path our investigation was taking. Unfortunately, my forced awakening had removed the opportunity to glimpse a possible outcome.

Carefully rolling over so as not to disturb the sleeping cat, I reached for my cell phone on the nightstand. The glaring screen informed me it wasn't quite one o'clock in the morning, and my mail indicated a single message. Assuming it was from Nate, I was slightly surprised to see it was from Roxy; her message short and to the point:

Your service is no longer required at the bookstore. Turn in your key as soon as possible.

I read it twice to make sure I wasn't still dreaming.

Martha whined in protest as I abruptly sat up to turn on the bedside lamp, her discomfort the least of my worries.

I needed to talk to Nate.

NOT MY PROBLEM

(December 14, Wednesday- almost afternoon)

S arra slammed her blue bag down onto the counter dangerously close to my drink.

"I quit too." She huffed.

"Maybe we should start a club of ex-bookstore volunteers." Lynn said with a grin.

"Only if we can meet here." I said, quickly moving my goblet to safety.

I had to admit it felt good to have these two near me, especially after my morning of intense roller coaster emotions. I'd texted Sarra as soon as I figured she was awake, and she in turn had called Lynn, both insisting we meet at the Belgian before I even thought about turning in my key.

"Roxy shouldn't be able to get away with this. Can't you demand a hearing with the board or something?" Sarra asked as she rummaged in her purse for what I assumed was her wallet.

"It's done and I'm not going to fight it." I shrugged, feeling slightly numb. Of course it could have been the goblet of cider I'd already consumed on top of no breakfast.

Sarra gave me a skeptical look before heading over to the bar. She returned a short while later with two ciders and set one down in front of me.

"This is from our friend. He's worried about you and says it's on the house."

Swiveling on my stool, I caught the eye of the bartender and gave him a friendly wave before turning to face the window.

"What did Nate say?" Sarra asked.

"He thinks Roxy's an idiot and the bookstore is a lost cause, especially while she's in charge." I sighed before reaching for my second drink. "Even though I hate to admit it, he's probably right."

"This is unbelievable." She said. "When everyone hears what's happened, more are going to quit. You know that, right?"

"You think so?"

"Definitely. Evelyn just texted me three others have already sent in their resignations."

"Wow, that's going to hurt. The place is already short staffed."

"I don't think you should quit." Lynn told Sarra. "We need someone to stay on the inside."

Sarra made a harrumph sound. "There's no way I'm going back there."

"But what about our investigation?" Lynn insisted.

"We don't have to be volunteering to continue with that." I said, "In fact, at this point it will be easier since we have nothing left to lose."

"Good point." Sarra laughed. "Do you want me to go with you when you turn in your key?"

"If you want, but I'm not going until after two. The way I'm feeling right now, it's probably best I don't run into Marilyn."

Lynn giggled. "I'm heading down to the barn in a bit. Why don't you guys come down after and I'll introduce you to Liz. We could also drive by the Secret Ranch and take another look."

"Sounds like a plan." Sarra said.

I was contemplating ordering food to go with my alcohol when my phone rang. The caller was unknown, but since it was a local area code, I decided to answer.

"Hello?"

"Holly? A tentative voice responded. "It's Sharon...from the bookstore. Sorry for bothering you but the police are here and want to talk to someone in charge."

"I'm sorry Sharon, I can't help you. I was fired last night."

There was a sharp inhale of breath followed by a pause as she digested the news, so I continued.

"You'll need to call Roxy."

"I tried but there was no answer." She said.

"Sorry, then I guess you'll have to try Katrina."

Sharon sighed at that suggestion, but there wasn't much more I could do to help.

"The cops? Wonder what they want?" Lynn commented after I'd told them why Sharon had called.

"Guess we'll find out soon enough." Sarra said. "I'm going to have Sandwich Boy make me a BLT, how about you two?"

My growling stomach answered for me.

*   *   *

After lunch, Lynn left for the barn and Sarra rode with me over to the bookstore. We were just coming up to the turn for the shopping center when a familiar truck zipped out of the parking lot ahead of us, heading north on Front Street.

"Where the heck is she going?" I wondered out loud.

Parked in front of the store, both of us immediately noticed the hand-written closed sign taped to the door.

"Now what?" Sarra asked after I'd tried the handle and found it locked.

"Something's not right. I think we should go inside and check it out." I said, unlocking the door long enough for us to slip inside.

The overhead lights had been turned off but there was still plenty of daylight streaming through the front windows to see we were alone. Moving over to the desk, I noticed several empty plastic baggies scattered on top of the still-opened sales ledger.

"Why would they close so early?" Sarra whispered.

"Holly!" A voice called out, making us both jump. It was Sharon, followed closely by Mary, striding towards us down the main aisle.

"What's going on?" I asked them.

"Katrina told us to go home. In fact, you just missed her." Mary said. "We were just putting the cash into the safe."

Sharon let out an exasperated sigh. "I tell you, this whole thing stinks to high heaven. That woman went totally nuts when she found out what the cops wanted."

I was confused. "What do you mean?"

"They had a search warrant, not that we would have stopped them without one, and confiscated all the VHS." Sharon explained. "They even went through the back rooms looking for more."

Glancing over at the section, I could see every single shelf emptied of tapes.

"Why on earth would they want those old things?" Sarra asked.

"We have no idea," Mary answered, "they wouldn't tell us anything."

A banging sound drew all of our attention to the front. Someone was standing on the other side of the door, pounding their fists on the glass.

"Read the sign!" Sharon yelled, but the would-be customer either didn't hear or didn't care as they began to rattle the handle with significant force, obviously intent on gaining entry.

Moving closer, a tie-dye pattern came into focus.

"We're closed Kathy!" I called out.

"Why? What's going on?" She shrieked.

A couple who happened to be walking past physically cringed at the sound, so I quickly unlocked the door and opened it a few inches to talk face to face.

"I'm sorry, Kathy, but we had to close for the day." I told her.

"Did someone else die?" She gasped, putting a pudgy hand to her mouth.

"No," I chuckled. "that's not the reason."

"Can't I come in, sweetie? Please? I'm frazzled to pieces with what just happened. This beast of a truck was driving like a bat outta' hell and nearly sideswiped me on Acorn."

"I'm sorry to hear that but I can't let you in. Come back tomorrow, OK?"

I relocked the door before she had a chance to respond and quickly turned towards the others.

"Is she gone yet?" I asked, keeping my back to the door.

"No, not yet...Oh, wait - there she goes." Sharon laughed.

"Thank God. Come on, we need to get going."

After saying goodbye, Sarra and I hustled out to my car.

"Why the hurry?" She asked.

"I know where Katrina was headed."

ONE OF THOSE CREATIVE TYPES

(December 14, Wednesday afternoon)

D rugs? In the VHS?"

Sarra sounded more than a little skeptical as I explained my theory while driving us north on the interstate.

"Remember that exercise tape you wanted to throw away?" I said, attempting to keep my speed somewhat within range of the posted limit, "Well, someone actually bought it and returned the thing because of some sticky stuff inside. At the time I didn't think anything of it, but with the cops confiscating the rest I'm sure that substance had to be some sort of drug put there by someone on purpose."

"By someone you mean Katrina?"

"Exactly. Maybe she has a system where she hides drugs in certain tapes. That would explain why she got so pissed when you reorganized. Another customer must have found one and taken it to the police, why else would they have had a search warrant?"

"If that's true, why didn't the cops arrest her, especially since she's the one who shelves them?" Sarra countered.

"Sharon said she didn't get there until after they'd left and besides, she could have blamed it on a customer. It's not like we have any sort of security measures." I said, taking the exit for Acorn Drive. "Unless we catch her red-handed with some evidence, she might get away."

"But why do you think she went to OakLeaf?"

"It had to be her truck that nearly hit Kathy and also explains why she was heading north when we saw her. She could be using her Dad's unit as a place to store the drugs until she brings them to the bookstore."

"Holy cow, you've got this whole thing figured out. Shouldn't we call Sean and let him know what's going on?"

I gave her a quick sideways glance.

"You're right," she said, shaking her head, "what was I thinking. He'd probably just tell us to let the professionals handle it."

"If my theory's correct and we get proof, THEN we'll contact him."

"OK, but at least let me call Lynn and give her a heads up."

"Good idea, especially if Katrina goes down to the Secret Ranch after."

While Sarra pulled out her phone to contact Lynn, a mounting sense of trepidation began to wash over me. Although the prospect of solving this puzzle was exiting, I knew I was potentially putting us into grave danger.

"Don't you dare go up to the ranch! Wait by the gate and keep yourself safe." Sarra scolded Lynn as I pulled up alongside OakLeaf's entry keypad. When I typed in Gerald's code, nothing happened.

"They must have canceled it." I said, trying again for good measure.

"Should we see if Todd is there?" Sarra asked, having ended her conversation with Lynn.

"No, he wouldn't be able to help us anyway."

Staring at the buttons, I searched my brain for a possible code. How many possible combinations were there for a four letter password, 10,000 or so? Suddenly, an image of letters floating across a brightly colored background caused a certain word to pop into my head. When I typed the numbers 9867 into the keypad, the screen lit up with a *Welcome, Joseph.*

Sarra gasped when the gate began to open. "How the heck did you do that?"

"You know me, I'm one of those CREATIVE types." I chuckled, feeling somewhat redeemed for a certain uncomfortable moment back at the Big Buck Diner.

"Thank goodness karma's a woman." She laughed.

Since I already knew the location of unit 55, I drove into the neighboring row and parked where the lane ended.

"We have to be careful, we don't want her to see us." I told Sarra as we exited the car. Switching our phones to camera mode, we stealthily crept along the end unit to peer around the far corner.

Katrina's truck was parked three units down with the rear facing us and the driver's door ajar. I could hear crashing sounds coming from inside her Dad's opened unit but, from our current position, couldn't see a thing.

"Let's try over there." I whispered to Sarra, pointing to the opposite corner.

Hustling towards what I hoped would be a better vantage point, I soon realized the massive truck blocked any view from this angle. Katrina was inside, I could see her head bobbing up and down over the open bed, but beyond that I couldn't see much else within the shadowed interior.

"What is she doing?" Sarra asked, her breath tickling the nape of my neck.

"I need to get closer."

Indicating for her to stay put, I sprinted over to the truck and hunkered down next to the gigantic front tire. A part of me wanted to sneak a peek at the bumper for any signs of teal green paint, but decided this probably wasn't the appropriate time.

Rising up just enough to see over the hood, I finally had a clear view of the unit. It was the same size as Gerald's though nearly empty, containing only a 3-tier wire shelving unit set up against the back wall and a single plastic fold-up table to the side. The latter's surface was covered with piles of what looked like glossy black video tape, and a plastic fishing tackle box yawned open to reveal an assortment of tools.

Katrina had her back to me and was frantically pulling VHS tapes off the shelves and tossing them into cardboard boxes. Before I could take a photo, she suddenly turned and dashed towards the back of the truck, making my heart skip a beat as I hastily ducked out of sight. A few breathless seconds later, when it sounded like she had returned inside the unit, I slowly moved over to watch her through the passenger side window, but the tint was too dark for me to get a clear shot with my phone.

When the shelves were empty, Katrina closed the tackle box and threw it into the back of the truck, forcing me to return to my spot next to the tire. Loose gravel dug into the flesh of my hands and knees as I crouched even lower to watch beneath the chassis as her boots clicked back and forth across the unit's floor. When they seemed to pause for an extended period of time near the center, I slowly lifted myself back up to peek across the hood.

Katrina was wadding up some newspaper and throwing it into the boxes of tapes. When she dug into the pocket of her leather jacket and pulled out a shiny silver object, my heart froze.

Oh my god!

Quickly hightailing it back to Sarra, I told her what was about to happen.

"Should we call 911?" She asked, eyes wide.

"Yes!"

While she phoned, I could already make out thin whips of dark smoke streaming out of the unit, the tendrils rippling across the glossy surface of the truck's black roof like demonic fingers.

"I need to report a fire!" Sarra exhaled into her phone.

A door slammed shut and was quickly followed by the revving of an engine.

"She's taking off; we have to follow!" I yelled, already sprinting for my car. Behind me I could hear Sarra confirming the address with the emergency operator while attempting to keep up.

"They're on their way." She wheezed while clambering into the passenger seat.

The main gate was just swinging shut as we approached, and on the other side I could see Katrina's truck turning left onto Acorn Drive.

"She must be going to the Secret Ranch."

I reentered 'WUMP' into the keypad as fast as my fingers would allow.

"That's it, I'm calling Sean." Sarra said.

"OK, but call Lynn too, let her know we're on our way."

After waiting an eternity for the gate to reopen, I focused on catching up to Katrina while Sarra made her calls. I finally spotted the truck merging onto the interstate but quickly lost it again as it sped up, moving across lanes and weaving around slower moving vehicles. My little car didn't have a chance but, luckily, the highway's southern incline made the truck easy to spot even at a distance.

"Sean didn't answer so I left a message and Lynn says she'll meet us there." Sarra said, looking up from her phone at the exact moment Katrina's truck swerved towards the Front Street off-ramp.

"What the...?" I swore, barely avoiding clipping another car in order to follow. The maneuver caused Sarra to smash against the side of the door and yelp out in pain.

"Ow! Where the heck is she going?"

Following the truck across the overpass, the answer to her question suddenly became apparent.

"She's going back to the bookstore!" I exclaimed.

WWTHBD

(December 14, Wednesday afternoon)

Walking to the Sheriff's office had taken up most of the morning. Though he had eventually located the business card, his cell phone was still malfunctioning, necessitating hoofing across town on foot in order to speak with them in person.

Much to his surprise, the cop behind the front desk immediately took his clue seriously. She had jumped into action when he told her what the tape contained and had sped off to notify others. After speaking with several sheriffs, including the one whose card he possessed, he left feeling confident his detailed observations had been well received.

By the time he walked back to the shopping center, cops were already carrying boxes of what he assumed were more evidence out of the bookstore. Watching them drive away, he decided to reward his act of civic duty by buying a cappuccino at Rudy's. The nice lady working the counter gave him a day-old chocolate old-fashioned donut for free, and he savored the sweet treat along with his coffee while seated at an inside table.

Waving farewell to the barista, he began to head for home when a commotion by the bookstore drew his attention. Moving closer along the sidewalk, he observed the bulky hippie-esque woman who always hung around the place frantically waving her arms and banging on the door. Stealing behind one of the cement pillars protecting the bank's cash machine, he watched as she spoke with someone on the other side of the glass. A moment later, after she walked away, two people quickly exited the store and climbed into a familiar green car.

Why hadn't the police arrested her?

She had been parked in back the morning Stumpy had gone missing, acting suspicious. Later, upon finding his friend had been murdered and the library computer teacher also volunteered here, he began to connect the dots. When she showed up at the library looking for him, he knew he was on the right track and the drugs proved it; bad stuff was happening at the bookstore, things bad enough to kill for, and he was convinced this 'Holly Singer' was the mastermind.

Blundering cops. They obviously missed some major clues.

This was no different than what the brothers had to endure in all those stories, and why they always had to keep investigating on their own.

Just then, two other volunteers exited the bookstore. After locking up, they walked down the sidewalk to the far side of the building and turned the corner. He was confident he knew where they were going and, sure enough, within minutes they reappeared and climbed into their respective vehicles. Once they had driven away, he quickly retraced their path into the alley.

The lockbox had been cleverly hidden behind the water meter housing, but his keen observations had revealed its location. Since he didn't know the code he scoured the ground for a rock big enough to smack it open but, after a fruitless search, grabbed the unit and yanked on the clasp a couple of times out of sheer frustration. Much to his surprise, the box sprang open and the key went flying; his luck was holding as, in their haste to leave, the volunteers obviously hadn't clicked the cover properly into place.

After locating the prize, he scanned the back parking area for any signs of movement before making his way up the ramp.

CAT GOT YOUR TONGUE

(December 14, Wednesday, late afternoon)

Just as predicted, Katrina took a right-hand turn onto the dead-end street behind the bookstore. Following, I watched her swerve into the parking lot and come to a stop at the base of the ramp. Although the sun was making its earlier winter descent towards the horizon, I opted to remain somewhat hidden on the street. Slowing to a crawl, I inched past the dumpster wall until we had a clear view of the back door through the passenger side window.

"Why would she come here?" Sarra asked.

"No idea, especially since the cops took all the tapes." I said, turning off the engine.

"OK, Miss Nancy Drew, now what?"

"Try calling Sean again." I suggested.

While she redialed, only to leave another message, I kept my eyes on Katrina. She was still inside the truck's cab, though the combination of fading light and tinted windows made it impossible to see what she was doing.

Why WAS she here?

Assuming the tapes at OakLeaf were more evidence, it made sense her going there first to destroy them, and I could have kicked myself for not getting a photo of her in the act. But why come back to the bookstore – unless she had a good reason. All I could come up with was something important must be hidden within the locked cabinets in the office, and she was waiting for Roxy to show up to open them.

Sarra's phone suddenly blared with a trumpet ringtone, scaring me nearly half to death.

"It's Lynn." She said before answering.

I looked back outside to realize Katrina was half-way up the ramp. Tapping Sarra on the shoulder, I frantically pointed in that direction before opening my door. As the cool breeze hit my face, it suddenly occurred to me that following a proven pyromaniac and likely killer into an empty building wasn't such a great idea.

After opening Sarra's door, I leaned into the doorframe and waited for her to finish speaking with Lynn.

"Why don't you stay here," I told her after she'd hung up, "if I don't come out in a couple of minutes, call 911."

"No way, we're sticking together!" She snapped, "Roxy's at the ranch and Lynn says she'll make sure she doesn't go anywhere."

An absurd image of Lynn barricading the driveway with her body instantly popped into my mind.

"I hope she doesn't do anything crazy."

"You and me both, the last thing we need is more dead volunteers."

Sarra clambered out of her seat and we left the car, hustling around the dumpsters and skirting Katrina's truck.

"Good thing you still have your key." She whispered as we reached the top of the ramp.

I unlocked the door and opened it just wide enough for us to slip through before gently clicking it shut. Although the fluorescents were off, the late afternoon sun streaming through the front windows offered enough light to identify all the major obstacles and, motioning for Sarra to stay close, we slowly began to creep our way down the hall.

A piercing wail sliced through the quiet like a sharp blade.

"Yeowh!"

It was Teddy, his canny cat sense obviously picking up on our presence.

"Oh shut up!"

A muffled shout echoed from the end of the hallway. When a subsequent crash and thumping noise followed, I quickly pushed Sarra into the sorting room just as the door to the mystery room slammed open. From within the shadows of our hiding spot, we watched as Katrina strode around the corner and headed towards Teddy's enclosure.

"I told you to shut up, you stupid cat!" She screamed, whacking the front of his cage with what looked like a tightly twisted roll of newspaper.

The feline hissing that ensued was no doubt his concept of a response.

"You are SO dead!"

There was a familiar clicking sound and then a flame flickered near the paper. The intent obvious, I sprang into action and lunged for the shopping cart parked on the other side of the hallway. Grabbing the handle tight, I propelled it forward with all the force I could muster within the short distance of space.

Katrina didn't have time enough to react as the cart rammed her backside. Tumbling across the floor, she came to a crashing halt against one of Evelyn's knick-knack display cabinets, the impact causing a good portion of the items to fall off and shatter onto the floor in a breathtaking display of exploding porcelain. It also must have knocked her out as she was no longer moving.

"Way to go!" Sarra exclaimed.

"Watch her while I get something to tie her up with." I said before sprinting to the desk near the back door. Returning with a handful of zip ties, I was surprised to see her straddling Katrina's prone body while applying a rear wrist lock.

"She was starting to move. Hurry, give me those." She explained, grabbing a couple of ties and expertly securing them around both of Katrina's wrists and ankles.

"You look like you've done that before."

"Never underestimate a retired teacher." She chuckled as I helped her to her feet, "But now that we've got her, believe it or not, I have to go pee! Why don't you call Lynn and let her know what happened, and then call the cops?"

Katrina moaned but wasn't going anywhere, so I pulled out my phone to discover a text message. Reading it, the significance hit me like a brick as the muffled sound of a toilet flushing followed by subsequent footsteps told me Sarra had returned.

"You'll never guess what Emiko found out!" I said, "Now I know why Roxy is so protective of..."

"Holly!"

Turning, I saw a panicked expression on Sarra's face while behind her, a person in a bright pink tracksuit held a gun.

CURIOSITY KILLED THE CAT

(December 14, a few moments later)

What happened to Katrina?" Marilyn demanded.

"We tied her up." I said, stepping aside so she could see the body lying on the floor.

"Well, untie her, now!"

"I can't," I explained, "we used zip ties."

Marilyn jabbed the tip of the gun into the small of Sarra's back, forcing her to step forward, then waved the steel barrel in the air indicating she move next to me.

"There's a pair of scissors up in the desk, go get them." She barked, leveling the weapon at my head; the ease at which she brandished it pretty much destroying the last vestiges of her 'frail little old white-haired lady' routine.

I began to calculate how to discreetly dial 911 while running for the front when she abruptly squashed my plans with yet another command.

"Put your phones on the ground first and slide them over to me."

Damn it, I thought, she obviously had read some of the books she shelved.

Sarra and I reluctantly obliged and pushed our phones across the floor towards her feet. Instead of bending over, she began to violently stomp the devices with the thick treads of her pink running shoes, crushing them into little electronic bits.

"Seriously?" Sara asked.

In response, Marilyn moved her gun so it pointed directly at my friend's face.

"Hurry up, Holly, or I might just lose my patience!" She told me with a smile.

So much for stereotypes, I thought, sprinting for the front.

As I approached the desk, I glanced out beyond the empty sidewalk to a scene of fading daylight and glowing parking lot lights. For all the times I'd cringed, I would have given anything to see some tie-dye.

While I searched the drawers, I pondered the paradox of a gun-wielding Marilyn; gone was the frail and whiny volunteer I'd come to know. The pink tracksuit confirmed it had been her I'd seen jogging around the library a day after being in hospital and, at this point, I was pretty confident the entire health scare was an orchestrated ruse to throw me off the scent. With my mind racing a mile a minute, several of the various puzzle pieces I had yet to connect began to snap perfectly into place.

Scissors found, I hurried to the back and knelt beside Katrina to snip her free. As she struggled to her feet, she groaned and rubbed the side of her head where she'd smacked it against the cabinet. I have to admit the fact we'd caused her some physical pain gave me more than a little satisfaction.

"Give me those." She hissed, tearing the scissors away from me before slamming her palm hard against my solar plexus. The impact knocked the wind right out of me and I stumbled, falling backwards onto the floor.

Blinking back tears, I gasped for breath while Sarra helped me to my feet.

"There's no need for violence." She snapped at Katrina, her voice tinged with anger.

"A little late for that, don't you think." Marilyn laughed.

Her gun was still pointed directly at us and, when Katrina strode over next to her, it suddenly felt like the climax scene from some cheesy western movie. Somehow, I wasn't sure this one would have a life-saving cavalry on the way.

I gave them both a defiant look despite the throbbing in my chest.

"You killed Gerald."

My statement seemed to momentarily catch Marilyn off guard, but she quickly recovered.

"I told him to leave my books alone," she responded coolly, "but he wouldn't listen."

"And Pat? I know you killed her too, but how?" I asked, causing Sarra to gasp.

"We didn't." Katrina snickered. "She had a heart attack all on her own, right there in front of us after she followed us to OakLeaf."

"That's right." Marilyn said. "All we did was move her body back here. The disgusting homeless guy that showed up - him I had to kill, but no matter."

"His name was Francis and his life DID MATTER." Sarra said slowly, enunciating the last two words.

Her statement suddenly gave me an idea on how to keep these two talking and stall for more time.

"So, you're the one in charge of the financial transactions." I said looking directly at Marilyn.

"How did you figure it out?" She asked, raising one thin eyebrow above the thin platinum rim of her glasses.

"We saw the DigiCoin codes in the Evanoski books Gerald was hiding, and considering how fixated you are on them and your smart phone, it wasn't hard to put two and two together."

"I told you she's probably the one who told the cops." Katrina said.

"Shut up." Marilyn snapped back at her.

"So," I said, continuing to push as many buttons as possible, "I'm assuming Roxy runs this operation of yours and is making drugs down at the ranch?"

Marilyn and Katrina exchanged a quick glance before bursting into laughter.

"Roxy's an idiot and doesn't have a clue as to what's really going on. Besides, I only deal with designer product, not some homemade small-town garbage." Marilyn snorted in disgust.

"Yeah, plus she's addicted to pain meds and I'm helping keep her that way." Katrina snickered.

With the workings of their operation now becoming clearer in my mind, I turned back to Marilyn.

"So you're in charge."

"That's right," she responded, looking pleased with herself, "in fact, if it wasn't for me this ridiculous non-profit would have folded long ago."

"You mean the large donations to BARF?" Emiko's text message had explained a lot.

"Aren't you the clever one. You know, I tried warning Pat to back off but, like you, she just couldn't keep out of other people's business. Now you've gone and ruined everything."

"Shit!" Katrina suddenly cried out, looking at her phone. "I still gotta get my Dad!"

She rushed over to Teddy's cage and picked up her lighter.

"Get those too." Marilyn said, pointing to the unused zip ties scattered on the floor by my feet. When she waved the gun again and instructed us to get into the empty enclosure next to Teddy's, my heart sank.

"Guess curiosity really does kill the cat." Katrina sniggered as she fastened a single zip tie into the door's hasp.

"What do you mean?" I asked, but she ignored me and threaded more ties around the entire door frame, zipping them together at the front.

"I'm getting the rest of the codes, meet me in back." Marilyn said before leaving.

When Katrina disappeared from sight, I began to yank on the door as hard as I could, shaking the entire length of the enclosure with the effort. Teddy started to howl pitifully from his side of the divider, staring at us with saucer-sized eyes.

"Holly, look!" Sarra suddenly exclaimed, pointing towards the hallway.

Katrina had reappeared with a handful of twisted newspapers. Horrified, we watched as she walked up the main aisle and began to light the fire starters, laying each burning torch across the bottom of the bookshelves on either side.

"Stop Katrina! Don't do that!" I screamed, shaking the door handle with even more intensity.

She retraced her steps and threw the last flaming piece atop the romance sorting table directly in front of us.

"Say goodbye to your stupid bookstore!" She laughed, and seconds later we heard the back door slam shut.

Chapter
48

NUMBER ONE SUSPECT

(December 14, a few moments later)

The paperbacks on the table burst into flames. As gray smoke billowed towards the ceiling, I could see more fire flicking its way up the shelves where Katrina had thrown her torches, highlighting the severity of our situation.

"We have to get out of here!" I yelled, attacking the door with increased energy. The plastic didn't break and I wasn't surprised; I lived with a man who loved zip ties.

"We have to try something else!" Sarra cried out in frustration, her eyes filled with fear.

I knew she was right. If we didn't figure out a way to get out of this cage soon, we were toast. In desperation, I grabbed hold of the wire meshing and began to pull, the metal digging into the flesh of my fingers but only bending a few inches; whoever built this thing had made it impenetrable. What size cats were they expecting?

"Help, help!" Sarra screamed in hopes someone might hear as the air around us grew thick with smoke.

I could feel panic overtaking my senses as I frantically searched the enclosure for a potential tool.

"Here, help me with this!" I said, reaching for the carpeted cat tree in the corner. Sarra helped me drag the five-foot tower to the front of the cage and topple it onto the ground with a satisfying thud.

"Now what?" She asked, giving me an incredulous look.

"Let's ram the door."

Following my lead, she picked up the opposite side and we began to rock the tree back and forth in a coordinated motion while I counted upwards from one, hurling it forward like a battering ram at three. Although the tree's weight successfully bent the entire doorframe outward a few inches, the wire and plastic ties held, throwing us back onto the floor with force during the subsequent rebound.

"We have to try again!" I said, quickly clambering to my feet. When Sarra didn't move I realized a portion of the tower was pinning down her legs. As I began to pull it off, she suddenly succumbed to a painful sounding coughing fit, causing her to hunch over and lie in a fetal position against the cold cement floor. Not knowing what else to do, I knelt down and patted her on the back while apologizing for our current situation.

"Good grief," she said between gasps for air, "it's not your fault we've been volunteering with a bunch of drug dealers and murderers."

The smoke was getting thicker and I knew at this rate, we wouldn't last long. Over in the abandoned cat beds, I spotted the small flannel quilts a volunteer had sewn to keep our rescue kitties warm. Handing one to Sarra and indicating she use it as a mask, I placed the Hello Kitty patterned piece over my own nose and mouth.

"It smells like cat pee." She said in a muffled voice.

"Deal with it." I mumbled back, "It's better than nothing."

"Why isn't the fire alarm going off?"

Sarra was right; there were no bells ringing. Trying to hear anything over Teddy's continual yammering was next to impossible, but straining my ears I was pretty sure I couldn't hear any approaching sirens. I knew the store must have some sort of alarm system, especially for insurance purposes, meaning either it was malfunctioning or someone had purposely turned it off.

"We have to get out on our own!"

In desperation, I began to frantically kick at the cat tree with both feet, forcing it into the door jamb while trying to keep my face covered with the fabric to avoid inhaling any more smoke. I was starting to make headway, with the wood frame bending outward and looking ready to give, when I saw something move through the thick haze.

Somebody was approaching the front of the enclosure; was it Marilyn, returning to finish us off?

I scooted backwards across the floor in hopes of using my body as a shield to protect Sarra, but instead of a gun saw the flash of a knife blade cutting away at the zip ties. The door sprang open and a heavily bundled figure loomed above the cat tree.

"Come on!"

Helping Sarra to her feet, we stumbled out of our prison. Through the heavy smoke I could see the midsection of the store was engulfed in the growing inferno, with fire spreading across several rows of bookshelves; all seemed lost.

"Come on!" Our rescuer called out again as he shuffled towards the hall.

We followed, keeping our bodies as low to the ground as possible while avoiding the flames licking off the general fiction table. Sarra suddenly came to an abrupt halt and squeezed my arm.

"Teddy!" She cried out.

With all the excitement of our own escape, I had completely forgotten the poor cat and realized he had stopped crying some time ago.

"Stay here, I'll get him." I told her before rushing back to his cage. Opening it, I lurched around the limited visibility and finally found him huddled on the floor in the far corner. His green saucer eyes were open, much to my relief, and for once in his life he didn't make a sound as I swept him up and transported him into Sarra's open arms.

Katrina must have set more fires as waves of smoke were pouring out of the mystery room. Navigating our way through the dark hallway, we eventually met up with our waiting rescuer near the exit. When I pushed the door outward, the four of us stumbled onto the landing and gulped in a lungful of fresh air. Over my thumping heart I thought I heard wailing sirens, and when a welcome stream of red flashing lights flowed past on their way to the front of the store, I knew; the cavalry had arrived.

"Can't stay here." The mysterious savior said, motioning us to follow him down the ramp.

Trudging across the empty lot, we ended up at the back door of the Mexican restaurant with its brightly blazing security light. While Sarra plopped down onto the landing with Teddy still clutched firmly in her arms, I surveyed the man who had rescued us. As I echoed the smiling yellow logo emblazoned on his cap, he took it off and began twisting it in his hands.

"I sure messed up." He mumbled, "Guess I'm not as good as the brothers at picking out the right suspect."

Suddenly, it became clear why he'd been following me; he must have thought I had something to do with his friend's death, and maybe even Pat's.

"That old lady sure isn't anything like Aunt Gertrude, is she?" he continued.

"No she isn't!" I responded, instantly making the connection with the books he was referencing. "But, I know Fenton would be proud of you."

Chapter
49

BLOOD ORANGE CIDER

(December 20, Tuesday afternoon)

Blood orange cider never tasted so good.

Although it had been five days since the fire, my throat still felt dry and irritated from all the smoke I'd inhaled and the cold drink was proving a soothing remedy.

"I still can't believe Marilyn got away." Sarra said, savoring her own goblet of our favorite local brew.

"Well, at least they arrested Katrina." I responded.

"Yeah, thanks to you two." Lynn said, and she was right; once the police had shown up at the bookstore, we were able to tell them about Katrina saying she needed to get her Dad. They had quickly acted on the information and, according to local news outlets, successfully apprehended her while she was at his house.

Marilyn, on the other hand, had completely disappeared.

"How's Teddy?" I asked Sarra.

"He's doing great. Daphne said she'll handle all the adoption paperwork so there's no problem for me to keep him."

"That's awesome, he's a lucky guy."

"Looks like Sean is here." Lynn said, motioning towards the front door, and within minutes he had joined us at the front counter with a beer in hand.

"How are you two feeling?" He asked Sarra and me.

"Much better, thanks." I responded, the question reminding me just how lucky we had been to escape with only a mild case of smoke inhalation.

"The cider is helping." Sarra chuckled before diving right in with her own question. "Any good news?"

"Some... we were able to apprehend Katrina's four accomplices so have pretty much busted up that portion of the ring. Unfortunately, none of them gave us any useful information on where the drugs came from or where Marilyn might be located. We're in the process of checking with authorities in Marin County to see if we can get some leads. Thanks for giving us that tip, by the way." He said, nodding in my direction before taking a sip from his mug.

"What about the DigiCoins, is there any way to track her with those?" I asked.

Sean shook his head. "No, we looked at the photos you took but the numbers proved to be a dead end."

I wasn't surprised, but it was worth asking. Marilyn, it seemed, was both a master actor and a cunning criminal. From the subsequent news articles written since the fire, I had learned the apartment she rented near the library had been cleaned of any evidence. With most of the bookstore's mystery books burned, even obtaining her fingerprints had proven impossible.

"Dang it! So you mean she got away with murdering three people AND trying to kill two others?" Lynn snorted with disgust.

"Technically, she only murdered two." Sean said, sounding exactly like a stand-in for Nate.

Although Sean was right, I still blamed Marilyn for my friend's death. I was certain Pat had become suspicious of her well before learning about the large donations to BARF. Perhaps she had witnessed Marilyn jogging around the library while volunteering, smashing the 'little helpless old lady' facade, or maybe Gerald had shared something he'd seen while at Oakleaf. Regardless, the fact of the matter remained there had been enough concern for her to personally follow and confront Marilyn which triggered her heart attack.

Now, a murderer was on the loose, and I still had several unsolved puzzle pieces floating around to deal with.

"Well, thanks for keeping us in the loop." I told Sean, thankful for at least having some of my questions answered.

"Of course." He responded with a sheepish grin," I'm sorry I didn't take you ladies serious in the first place. You were spot on about the drug aspect, though not exactly accurate on where they were being kept."

"Who would have thought they would be at the bookstore, and in VHS tapes no less." Sarra retorted.

"At least we were right about them using the storage unit," Lynn chuckled, "but I still can't believe there wasn't anything illegal going on down at the Secret Ranch."

"Nope, just horses and dogs." Sean said.

"But Katrina told us she was keeping Roxy supplied with pain medications, and we saw them exchanging money." Sarra added, but he merely shrugged.

"I know, but the only drugs we found were ones Roxy had a prescription for, so if there was some sort of blackmail going on there's no way to prove it, especially since she's refusing to make a statement."

"Darn! She probably flushed them down the toilet when she heard me banging on the door." Lynn said with disappointment.

"You really are a trouble maker." Sean told her, prompting a signature giggle.

I wasn't surprised to learn Lynn had bypassed waiting at the gate to go directly up to the house; fortunately, for both their sakes, Roxy hadn't answered the door.

"This whole thing is unbelievable," Sarra said, "I don't see how Roxy can possibly be allowed to remain in charge of BARF, especially after all of this."

I couldn't agree more. With all the tough talk and outward bravado, Roxy had folded like an umbrella when questioned by the authorities, blaming an extreme allergic reaction from a recent cat bite as reason for her erratic behavior and memory loss. This did help explain the mystery over why she no longer rescued felines since, apparently, even being near Teddy caused her heart to race. After claiming Pat had given her the pills I had found to help with anxiety, she had quickly checked into a long-term rehabilitation center to prevent further fallout, abandoning the bookstore and all the volunteers in the process.

"Speaking of which, sorry about what happened to the bookstore." Sean said, looking over at me. "I know it meant a lot to you."

"Yeah, it did."

I thought about the charred mess we'd inspected earlier that morning; it had been a heart-wrenching sight, to say the least. Over half the books had been destroyed by the fire, and I had no doubt more would eventually have to be tossed due to smoke and water damage.

"What are the plans for the future?" He asked.

"Hard to tell." I said. "The board had an emergency meeting last night and it sounds like all but one resigned. At this point I'm not sure what will happen to either the store or BARF."

The remaining board member had been kind enough to inform all the volunteers, via email, that with Roxy in rehab and its primary source of income gone, the very future of the non-profit was in question; apparently, there was barely enough money left in the bank account to feed the animals at the ranch. Since then, I'd been getting scores of messages from former co-workers asking what could be done to save the bookstore, but since I was still technically fired, I hadn't been able to offer much in the way of hope.

"Oh, that reminds me." Sarra interjected. "Evelyn told me Zina is petitioning to get onto the new board. She's apparently some sort of financial guru and has all these ideas on how to reorganize."

"Really," I said, not knowing what to make of this bit of news, "that would be great, but even if BARF does survive, it will be months before the bookstore can reopen. The building is seriously damaged."

"Maybe you could move to another location." Sean suggested.

Sarra nodded in agreement. "I heard the real estate office a couple doors down is closing. It's a smaller space, but could definitely work."

"Oh, and Liz and her crew offered to help." Lynn added. "She said we could store books or anything else we need down at the barn."

Although their optimism was infectious and a part of me wanted to join in, I also felt worn out and ready to think of something other than the bookstore for a while. Sarra must have noticed my shift in mood and quickly changed the subject.

"When's Nate getting in?" She asked.

"Tonight at six. Philip offered to go down and pick him up."

"Fantastic." Lynn said.

It was going to be wonderful to finally have Nate back home, even though he had been more than a little frustrated upon hearing the news of our near escape. There was no way I could have kept it from him, especially with 'Drug operation in Used Bookstore' making the national news, and it had taken some major convincing to get him to agree to stay put the last couple of days to finish the job before rushing home.

"You 'cider girls' ready for another round?" The bartender called out from behind the bar, and within minutes we each had a refill. Quietly sitting and enjoying our drinks, I gazed out the front window and noticed the trailing wisps of people's breath as they walked past; the temperature must have dropped significantly since we entered the pub.

"Looks like it wants to snow." Sarra said, motioning toward the darkening sky.

"Oh, wouldn't a white Christmas be wonderful!" Lynn exclaimed. "I haven't had one of those in ages."

I began to picture my family snugly gathered by a roaring fire as a Sierra snow storm raged outside. The scene abruptly shattered, however, when an image of a particular person surviving the elements on their own popped into my head.

"What did you find out about Mr. Smiley?" I asked Sean, hoping to hear some news about our rescuer. He had promptly disappeared into the night as soon as the firefighters and police had arrived, and I hadn't seen or heard from him since.

"His real name is Joe Dixon." Sean explained. "In fact, he's the one responsible for bringing in the VHS tape with the drugs in the first place. You were right about Francis Smith being his missing friend, according to him they were like brothers."

"I wish there was something we could do to thank him." Sarra said.

"Didn't you say he liked Hardy Boy mysteries?" Lynn asked. "I could see about getting some copies from Liz."

"What a great idea," I said, recalling how excited he had been at seeing the copy in Evelyn's hands.

"Say, why don't we all pitch in and make him a package for the holidays. Once we put it together, could you be sure he gets it?" Sarra asked Sean, and he nodded in agreement.

"Well, Ladies, it's been a real pleasure but I need to get going." He stood and flashed a smile, "Hope you have a great Christmas."

Before we let him go we each gave him a hug which made his cheeks flush pink.

"I should probably get going too, I've still got some shopping to do." Lynn said after he'd left.

Sarra sighed and reached for her bag. "Me too. I need to go to the pet store and get more food for Teddy. Who knew cats could eat so much."

As the two of them put on their coats, I went up to the bar to pay my tab.

"You ladies sure you want to take off?" The bartender asked. "They just delivered that seasonal cranberry cider you've been wanting to try."

Reluctantly declining, I handed him my credit card. When he handed me my receipt, I noticed he'd only charged me for one drink. Pointing out the error, he responded with a wide grin.

"No worries, Holly, the second was on the house."

"Why?"

"I have a good feeling you're going to save our bookstore."

His statement caught me off guard; I hadn't realized he might know about the bookstore, let alone be savvy to everything else going on.

"Thanks, but I'm not so sure about that." I told him.

Saying goodbye, I was about to leave when a flicker of determination concerning a certain nagging mystery made me return.

"You have me at a disadvantage," I told the man behind the bar, "You seem to know all the details about our lives yet we don't even know your name. What is it?"

A tremendous crash from the back of the kitchen interrupted my inquiry. Colorful language ensued, quickly followed by Sandwich Boy appearing in the doorway with a panicked expression on his face and an entire torso drenched in red.

This can't be good.

AUTHORS NOTE

MUCH THANKS FOR READING MY FIRST mystery book! I've always wanted to be the author of one of those volumes classified with a 'Mystery' sticker at the public library, especially the ones with the little red skulls....

Hopefully, you have enjoyed my cast of characters and the used bookstore they inhabit and adore - and if you are as anxious as I am in finding out if it can be saved, please stay tuned: the next Used Bookstore Mystery ("Murder Isn't New") is coming soon!

My book is dedicated, in no small part, to that often silent individual: the volunteer, who gives freely of their time and efforts to a variety of causes or endeavors in the hopes it will make a positive difference.

In the course of my life, I've been fortunate in meeting some of these special people, and they never cease to amaze and inspire me.

Some of them have even decided to be my friends.

Hearing your feedback would be most appreciated, and if you enjoyed the book, please consider reviewing it on Amazon.

For more trivial information on me as well as updates on any upcoming projects, please visit http://www.heidibuck.com

- Heidi

CAST OF CHARACTERS

THE USED BOOKSTORE IN THIS STORY has a relatively small set of volunteers and visitors, but, this guide is provided in case the reader is confused and would like to have an assist as to who is who.

The Bartender: at The Belgium Public House & Reading Room, knows everyone, and yet no one seems to know his name.

Cheryl Helm: Volunteer in charge of paperback mysteries.

Evelyn: In charge of the boutique section at the bookstore, also helps sort books.

Daphne: Another volunteer, who has a penchant for stickers and shelves the Classics.

Emiko: Autumn Public Library volunteer who knows Pat.

Francis Smith (aka Stumpy): A homeless man who loves Westerns and lives in the woods behind Rudy's grocery store.

Gerald: A bookstore volunteer with an annoying habit of piling books while sorting.

Holly Singer: An ex-art teacher and volunteer at the BARF Used Bookstore who especially enjoys sorting and also shelves Horror and Cookbooks.

Joe Dixon (aka Mr. Smiley): A homeless man who frequents the Dollar Store and who greatly enjoys reading Hardy Boys Mysteries.

Kathy (aka Cookbook Kathy): A bookstore customer who has a distinctive fashion style and purchases vast amounts of cookbooks.

Katrina Bale: Volunteer in charge of scheduling bookstore cashiers, helps pick up large monthly donations and also shelves the VHS tapes.

Lynn Mason: New bookstore volunteer who helps with the sorting and especially appreciates the Belgian's Firehouse Special.

Marilyn Stokes: Volunteer in charge of the hardcover mysteries at the bookstore.

Nate Singer: Holly's husband, an engineer, who comes in after bookstore hours to shelve Science Fiction and Fantasy.

Pat Mulderry: Lead volunteer at the BARF used bookstore and technology volunteer at the Autumn Public Library.

Peg: Oldest bookstore volunteer, likes to wear white.

Philip Singer: Holly and Nate's son, who is away at college.

Roxanne Rossen: (aka Roxy) Founder, President and acting animal rescue officer of the non-profit BARF (Benevolent Animal Rescue Foundation).

Sarra Anderson: Holly's friend who decides to volunteer at the bookstore to help sort books.

Sean Stratton: County Sheriff who reminds Holly of her son, Philip.

Sharon: A bookstore volunteer who only works at the front desk.

Teddy: A gray tabby cat with weight issues.

Zina: A bookstore volunteer who handles the Politics and Business sections

Made in the USA
Middletown, DE
28 July 2018